SCI-FI MOVIE FREAK

by ROBERT C. RING

Published by

Krause Publications, a division of F+W Media, Inc.
700 East State Street • Iola, WI 54990-0001
715-445-2214 • 888-457-2873
www.krausebooks.com

To order books or other products call toll-free 1-800-258-0929
or visit us online at www.krausebooks.com or www.Shop.Collect.com

ISBN-13: 978-1-4402-2862-9
ISBN-10: 1-4402-2862-0

Cover Design by Shawn Williams and Jana Tappa
Designed by Shawn Williams
Edited by Kristine Manty

Printed in USA

Front cover movie stills and posters: main photo: *Terminator 2: Judgment Day*-Carolco/The Kobal Collection; bottom photos from left: *Metropolis*-UFA/Heritage Auctions; *Godzilla*-Toho/The Kobal Collection; *E.T.: The Extra Terrestrial*-Universal Pictures/Amblin Entertainment/The Kobal Collection; Darth Vader publicity shot-Lucasfilm/20th Century Fox//Heritage Auctions; *Blade Runner*-Warner Bros./The Kobal Collection; *Forbidden Planet*-Metro-Goldwyn-Mayer/Heritage Auctions. **Back cover:** *2001: A Space Odyssey*-Metro-Goldwyn-Mayer/The Kobal Collection. **Contents page**: *Star Wars*-Lucasfilm/20th Century Fox/The Kobal Collection.

Dedication

To Lindsey and Kathryn

Acknowledgments

Thanks to Dr. Jim McKelly of Auburn University for fueling my love for cinema and my understanding of the art. Thanks also to Nate Yapp of Classic-Horror.com, without which my own website, The Sci-Fi Block, likely never would have existed, and to Sci-Fi Block writers John Dubrawa and Eric Miller, who also played vital roles in the growth of the site. If it weren't for all of you, I probably would never have written this book.

A very special thank you to my wife Lindsey and to the most fun baby in the world, Kathryn, for putting up with my long nights of writing and movie-watching.

Thanks to Kris Manty and Paul Kennedy at Krause Publications, for placing their bets on me.

Also thanks to Heritage Auctions (www.ha.com) and The Picture Desk (www.picture-desk.com), the online home of The Kobal Collection, for the photos used in this book.

About the Author

Robert Ring has been a science fiction fan ever since his exposure to *Star Wars* at an age that predates his awareness of his own age. His heightened appreciation of cinema in general started in college, during which time he accidentally enrolled in a film studies course and never looked back. Since then, Robert has enjoyed an insatiable love for movies of all types, though science fiction has remained his unrivaled favorite genre. Robert started the website The Sci-Fi Block in 2008 in order to celebrate the genre through measured, analytical film reviews, and he hopes that *Sci-Fi Movie Freak* will help to reinforce others' love for science fiction as well as, with a little luck, create some new genre fans. During his off-hours, Robert consumes literature of practically every medium imaginable, from poetry to comics to yet more movies; plays video games a little too much; introduces his daughter to new movies; and occasionally stumbles upon topics and hobbies which he, against his own better judgment, attempts to add to his areas of full-blown enthusiasm. If you're into the whole Twitter thing, you can follow Robert at www.twitter.com/Robert_Ring. Just try not to stalk him. He's a dashing gentleman.

CONTENTS

INTRODUCTION

In its attempts to broaden our appreciation of ourselves and the world around us, science fiction is a genre that removes the boundaries of the conventional. In doing so, it creates an allure that is two-fold: On the one hand, it allows itself to create surface-level dynamics, mostly in the form of visuals, that only the horror and fantasy genres are prepared to approach. On the other hand, by reaching beyond the realm of modern possibility, science fiction is able to raise questions that non-genre works are rarely able to consider. When either one of these explorative abilities is used properly, the result is a work that is fun or intriguing. In the cases in which both of these attributes, the superficial and the substantial, are present, the genre reaches art's highest calling in ways that, though at times surpassed, are always unique.

Looking at cinema specifically, the 1950s will no doubt go down as the heyday of science fiction. However, the genre seems to have experienced a renewed public perception throughout roughly the latter half of the past decade. This is revealed through, along with a general feeling of heightened preference for science fiction within the pop culture community, a cursory analysis of factors such as record attendee numbers at sci-fi-heavy conventions like San Diego Comic Con, greater recent acceptance by the Academy of Motion Picture Arts and Sciences, and, for better or worse, the increased number of blockbuster films that are being made within the genre. Regardless of the reasons behind this revitalization, it indeed seems that recent years have seen a growing public interest in science fiction.

During what is hopefully still the beginning of this revitalization of the genre, *Sci-Fi Movie Freak* is here for two types of reader. For newcomers to science fiction, it is meant to serve as an introduction to sci-fi cinema's many high points (as well as a few of its lowest) and to briefly identify some of the reasons these works are so great or otherwise important. For the established science fiction fan, the book's goal is to add to the discourse of why we love these movies so much. The films included in this book are not all necessarily science fiction's best; rather, they are a mixture of the genre's best, most important, most influential, and, in a brief final chapter, endearingly worst. *Sci-Fi Movie Freak*'s goal can be summed up thusly: to celebrate science fiction cinema.

The movies in the book are divided into five chapters: Best of the Best, Vital Viewing, Further Essentials, Lesser-Known Gems, and The Failures. Within each chapter, movies are listed chronologically. Some movies also have icons related to the author's Top 10 lists starting on P. 222 and which denote the following:

 Movies with a red star are included in the author's Top 10.

 Movies with a gold star are included in the American Film Institute's Top 10 science-fiction films.

 Movies with a dollar sign are Box-Office blockbusters that earned at least $200 million.

 A camera denotes a movie directed by one of the author's Top 10 directors.

 A female silhouette denotes a movie with one of the author's Top 10 female characters.

 A robot head denotes a movie with one of the author's Top 10 robots.

 A Darth Vader mask denotes a movie with one of the author's Top 10 villains.

WHAT IS
SCIENCE FICTION?

Attempting to define any genre in absolute terms is a dangerous, if not futile, pursuit, as there always seem to be works that fall outside of definition yet *feel* perfectly fitting for a given categorization. Then there are fringe works that fall into subjective areas of the definition, leaving them straddling the line. The criteria for determining what films could be included in this book, therefore, are not definitive; rather, they serve only as guidelines.

With this approach to "defining" science fiction, the criteria are relatively simple and slightly fluid. For our purposes, in order for a film to be considered science fiction, it must utilize, in a way that significantly affects the film's style or substance and with respect to the time the film was made, at least one of the following elements:

• A technology that mankind is not currently capable of creating

• A scientific process that mankind is not currently capable of carrying out

• A scientific phenomenon that mankind has never witnessed, encountered, or experienced

• A scientific finding that mankind has not discovered

• The setting of a future society that is significantly different from our own

Broadly speaking, though there is some room for subjectivity here (particularly with the use of the term "significantly," as well as what exactly constitutes a "phenomenon"), at least one of these criteria should apply to each film included in *Sci-Fi Movie Freak*. (Note that, according to this definition, "science fiction" is not synonymous with "fantasy.")

Two opposite examples of films that fall near the border of these guidelines are *Sunshine* and *Ghostbusters*. Though *Sunshine* involves a crew of astronauts coming into unprecedentedly close proximity with the sun, Dr. Brian Cox, consulting physicist for the film's writing team, has stated that we are actually currently capable of constructing a vessel that could come quite close to the sun without burning up, should we ever need to build such a thing. Still, it is not something we have ever attempted, and the phenomenon that spurs the action of the film (the sun dying) is one that we have not experienced, thus it is included in *Sci-Fi Movie Freak*. *Ghostbusters* is an example of a borderline movie that does not quite fit our classification. With its many ghost entrapment and ghost elimination devices, there is a fair dose of science infused with some of the film's elements, but these items ultimately serve as mere plot devices for dealing with the exclusively supernatural and fantastical threats faced by the characters. Thus, any of these elements that could be considered sci-fi-esque in themselves have no *significant* bearing on the story and thus do not necessitate a sci-fi classification.

Finally, there is a frequently held sentiment, for whatever reason, that the science fiction and horror genres (as well as, presumably, others, such as comedy) are mutually exclusive – that for a film to be one means it cannot also be the other. There is no reason this should be considered the case. The terms "horror" and "science fiction" are merely means of identifying the types of content contained within the film (or whatever literary medium is being discussed). If a film contains elements of both, therefore, it simply falls within both genres. There's no reason that *Alien*, for instance, should be considered only horror, with its deep-space setting, alien life form, and themes of extra-terrestrial life and artificial intelligence. Likewise, it should never be considered purely science fiction when it is phenomenally effective at scaring its audiences. In this book, such films as these are generally termed "sci-fi/horror" films. This term is not used to say that the movie being discussed could be considered either science fiction or horror but to denote that it should be considered both simultaneously, with no crisis of identity.

Alien, with its setting in deep space and alien monster, falls within both the science fiction and horror genres. See more on P. 38.

In this promotional shot from the 1933 classic *King Kong*, Kong is depicted against the New York skyline and holding Fay Wray.
RKO Radio Pictures/Heritage Auctions

CHAPTER 1

BEST OF THE BEST

We start with the best of the best. These are the films that stand out not just as great but as borderline perfect. Each special in its own way, these "Best of the Best" are masterworks that were written, filmed, and polished so carefully that the filmmakers seemed to be channeling some pure understanding of the art.

It is difficult to break down the areas in which these particular films excel. Some of them do one thing unimaginably well. In other cases, it seems like every element of the film contributes to its mastery. If there is a commonality among these movies, it is the profuse care that went into their making. These are unmistakable works of love.

Movies like *2001: A Space Odyssey* and *Blade Runner* combine provocative storytelling with unmatched visuals and music. *Frankenstein* and *Bride of Frankenstein* inject a rendition of a classic story with great acting, stunning sets and makeup, and an expressionism that constantly fuels the emotions at play. *Alien* is like *The Birds* of science fiction, instilling fear through a combination of measured pacing, claustrophobic atmosphere, and startling images. Then there are movies like *Metropolis* (1927) and *E.T.: The Extra-Terrestrial*, which focus on one element. *Metropolis* contains such strong visuals that it could almost exist without a story at all. *E.T.* is a simple story about love and friendship, but it's told in such an earnest and endearing manner that it can move viewers to tears.

Though not nearly all technical wonders can be considered masterpieces, this chapter does contain a handful of such films, elevated beyond the status of "groundbreaking" by not only pushing filmmaking technology but by combining advancements in that technology with superb storytelling. *Star Wars* is the chief example here, as it ushered in technology that made various special effects possible for the first time ever and at the same time enhanced the kinetics of perhaps the most exciting coming-of-age tale of modern time. *King Kong*, though surpassed by *Star Wars* in both its story and effects breakthroughs, achieves masterwork status by utilizing special effects techniques that were new and shockingly realistic (not to mention painstakingly labor-intensive), in order to create a story that essentially becomes a fable of capitalism.

These are the movies we feel compelled to revisit even if we can't initially pinpoint their allure. Upon one's first viewing, *2001* and *Blade Runner* can remain enigmatic and obscure. Others, like *Star Wars*, are so viscerally entertaining that the attraction is obvious. But they are all alike in that they demand to be watched repeatedly, either because of layers of meaning that are revealed upon subsequent viewings or because of a sheer beauty that we can't ignore (and sometimes both). These are the movies that make us proud to be fans of the genre.

Han Solo (Harrison Ford), with his co-pilot Wookiee Chewbacca (Peter Mayhew), becomes a reluctant hero in *Star Wars*. *LucasFilm/20th Century Fox/Heritage Auctions*

Metropolis

YEAR 1927
COUNTRY Germany
RUNTIME 2 hrs. 33 min.
RATED Not Rated; mild adult content
DIRECTED BY Fritz Lang
WRITTEN BY Thea von Harbou
STARRING Gustav Fröhlich, Brigitte Helm, Rudolf Klein-Rogge, Alfred Abel
SIMILAR SCI-FI *Blade Runner*, *Metropolis* (2001), *Woman in the Moon*

Metropolis autocrat Joh Frederson (Alfred Abel), right, consults with his former friend and now rival C.A. Rotwang (Rudolph Klein-Rogge), a brilliant but mad inventor, about some mysterious papers found. At left is Rotwang's greatest achievement, the Machine-Man. *UFA/Heritage Auctions*

Metropolis is best approached as you would a painting. Don't follow it for an engaging plot. View it as a particular artist's vision of the world. In a somewhat generic story of class repression, director Fritz Lang's visuals convey such a sense of urgency and desperation that the work cannot be ignored. The world's first sci-fi epic, and at the time the most expensive film ever made, *Metropolis* stands as a monument of imagistic filmmaking.

In a future city called Metropolis, the rich live in obscenely tall skyscrapers and spend their days playing and conducting business while the poor live in a destitute underground society, laboring ten hours a day over the machines that keep the upper class rich. The plot centers on a Metropolis autocrat's son, Freder (Gustav Fröhlich), who experiences a spiritual awakening and sets out to become the savior of the working class. Unfortunately, his father and a mad scientist are equally determined to see that Freder fails, and they have a robot disguised as a religious leader to help them achieve their goal. It may sound like a high-school-caliber plot, but the film's merits far outweigh its shortcomings.

Metropolis has some of the most unforgettable images of any movie, and they work to convey Lang's fears of classist society. One of the film's earliest shots is of a shift-change, in which we see groups of workers entering and leaving a factory in unison, with a pace and demeanor with which you would expect one to walk to his death. Soon after, we see the inside of one

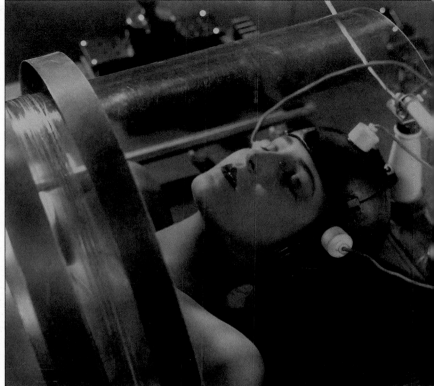

Maria (Brigitte Helm) is the pure-hearted religious leader who gets a machine-made double. *UFA/Heritage Auctions*

of these factories, in which the laborers' motions are so timed and inhuman that the individuals seem to have become gears themselves. When Freder visits and witnesses a horrible accident, he has a vision of the machinery turning into Moloch and devouring those who work the dials and levers. From there, the imagery rarely lets up as we are treated to such elements as a mad scientist's robot, hypnotic erotic dances, and architecture that seems to be challenging God. As malignant as are the elements of society represented by these visuals, they always retain an undeniable beauty.

Lang was a master of silent cinema. With *Metropolis*, he created a film so visually salient that its plot almost does not matter. For modern viewers largely accustomed to movies based on the unfolding of events, this can be off-putting. If approached with the right mindset, however, *Metropolis* emerges as an obvious work of genius.

"BETWEEN THE MIND THAT PLANS AND THE HANDS THAT BUILD THERE MUST BE A MEDIATOR, AND THIS MUST BE THE HEART." -MARIA

Frankenstein

YEAR 1931
COUNTRY United States
RUNTIME 1 hr. 11 min.
RATED Not Rated; has mild monster violence
DIRECTED BY James Whale
WRITTEN BY Mary Shelley (source novel), Peggy Webling (source play), John L. Balderston, Garrett Fort, Francis Edward Faragoh
STARRING Boris Karloff, Colin Clive, Mae Clark, John Boles, Edward Van Sloan
SIMILAR SCI-FI *Bride of Frankenstein*, *Dr. Jekyll and Mr. Hyde* (1931), *The Invisible Man*, *King Kong* (1933), *Re-Animator*, *Son of Frankenstein*, *Young Frankenstein*

Frankenstein is one of the first sci-fi/horror films ever, and it remains one of the best. In this movie, director James Whale succeeds not only in adapting what is arguably the first ever work of science fiction but in forever influencing our culture's understanding of that work. With its poignant story and ghastly visuals, this movie is equally moving and haunting.

Dr. Henry Frankenstein (it's Victor in the novel) dares to defy God and the natural order of things by assembling dead body parts and infusing them with life, the scientific secret of

"IT'S ALIVE. IT'S ALIVE! IT'S ALIVE! IT'S ALIVE! IT'S ALIVE!" - HENRY FRANKENSTEIN

Dr. Frankenstein (Colin Clive) comes face to face with the creature he created (Boris Karloff). In the photo below, Dr. Frankenstein conducts an experiment in his lab.
Universal Pictures/Heritage Auctions

Frankenstein's assistant, Fritz (Dwight Frye), taunts the monster. *Universal Pictures/Heritage Auctions*

which he has discovered. Though he succeeds, Frankenstein soon realizes he does not know how to care for such a being, so he neglects the so-called monster, leaving it to the torment of his assistant. Before long, the enraged creature escapes his cell, and the town takes to arms to rid themselves of the abject but innocent thing. The film, like the novel, is about taking responsibility for that which you create, but it is also about the consequences inherent in attempting to wield power beyond one's control.

Though the story is strong alone, the acting and visuals are what make *Frankenstein* one of the greatest science fiction films of all time. The dynamic, almost logic-defying design of Frankenstein's laboratory remains unmatched today, with its combination of stone architecture, arcing electricity, and larger-than-life devices. Colin Clive plays Dr. Frankenstein with a feverish madness as he shuns his loved ones, works tirelessly over dead body parts, and succumbs to outbursts of hubris, all with an intensity assisted by dramatic camera angles.

The monster steals the show, though, played by one of the greatest actors of all time, Mr. Boris Karloff. Karloff manages to make the creature both pathetic and frightening with his primal moans, angry fits, and deathly stiffness. The design of the creature, with its trademark flat head, neck bolts, and large stature, also accounts for its impact. Whale's version of the monster is so influential that it would establish the template for our visual understanding of the creature forever.

Thanks to its acting, imagery, and story, *Frankenstein* is beyond great. It is legendary. This is a film of such power that it burns itself into your memory.

King Kong

YEAR 1933
COUNTRY United States
RUNTIME 1 hr. 44 min.
RATED Not Rated; some mild monster violence
DIRECTED BY Merian C. Cooper, Ernest B. Schoedsack
WRITTEN BY James Creelman, Ruth Rose
STARRING Robert Armstrong, Fay Wray, Bruce Cabot, Frank Reicher
SIMILAR SCI-FI *20 Million Miles to Earth*, *Cloverfield*, *Creature from the Black Lagoon*, *Godzilla* (1954), *King Kong* (2005), *The Lost World*, *Jurassic Park*

The beauty of Ann Darrow (Fay Wray) captivates King Kong.
RKO Radio Pictures/Heritage Auctions

King Kong the monster is referred to as the eighth wonder of the world. *King Kong* the film should be considered so as well. Imbued with technical expertise and ambition far ahead of its time, it remains a fun, believable, and at times intense experience even after decades of special effects advancement. Beyond that, though, it is built on a strong foundation: a classic "beauty and the beast" tale. Whether you want drama, action, or plain visual fun, this film has it all.

"THEY'LL HAVE TO THINK UP A LOT OF NEW ADJECTIVES WHEN I COME BACK." -CARL DENHAM

Filmmaker Carl Denham (Robert Armstrong) sets out with his crew and a naïve actress, Ann Darrow (Fay Wray), to find Skull Island, home to some colossal, fabled terror. His goal is to use the location as the setting for the world's next great film. Soon after Denham arrives, a giant ape called Kong takes Darrow for himself, and the crew is forced to track her and the beast down. In a world where dinosaurs and giant lizards exist, though, you can bet not all of them will make it back alive, and that's not to mention the mayhem that ensues after Kong is freighted to New York City.

King Kong's standout quality is without a doubt its animatronic special effects, the product of Willis O'Brien. O'Brien pioneered the animatronic stop-motion technique starting with his previous work on *The Lost World* in 1925, and in *King Kong* the technique was perfected. The monsters themselves are detailed and proportional, and their movements, despite being stop-motion-rendered, are astonishingly natural. Kong's fight against the T-Rex, a fight including all manner of athletic moves, remains one of cinema's great achievements in special effects.

The "beauty and the beast" theme on which the story is based may not be original, but the visuals add a sort of primordial symbolism to it. Not only does the giant ape, representing both immense destructive power and the prehistoric ancestry of man, serve as a perfect symbol of the id, but the scenes of him chasing Darrow around New York and later climbing the Empire State Building with her in hand can also be viewed as a metaphor for capitalist society. We all want to ascend the social ladder and carry a damsel along for the ride. Most of us just don't put New York in a state of emergency while we do so.

For those who haven't seen it, it's easy to think of *King Kong* as a mid-grade sci-fi/adventure film with a monster made popular by superb special effects. It is so much more, though. This is the story of a creature so in love that he will literally fight off dinosaurs to make sure his woman stays with him. The ape may be misguided in his endeavors, but even capitalists struggle to show that much devotion.

In an iconic scene, a squadron of military planes goes on the attack after King Kong climbs the Empire State Building. *RKO Radio Pictures/Heritage Auctions*

Bride of Frankenstein

YEAR 1935
COUNTRY United States
RUNTIME 1 hr. 15 min.
RATED Not Rated; adult content, mild violence
DIRECTED BY James Whale
WRITTEN BY William Hurlbut, John Balderston
STARRING Boris Karloff, Elsa Lanchester, Colin Clive, Ernest Thesiger, Valerie Hobson
SIMILAR SCI-FI *Frankenstein* (1931), *The Invisible Man*, *Re-Animator*, *Son of Frankenstein*, *Young Frankenstein*

The *Bride of Frankenstein* monster appears for only a few minutes but makes a lasting impression. *Universal Pictures/Heritage Auctions*

Bride of Frankenstein may have a campy title, but any corresponding preconceptions are slowly crushed as the film plays out. This sequel to *Frankenstein* manages to uphold the original's sense of urgency and seriousness even as it expands into wilder territory. James Whale had a lot to live up to in this follow-up to his sci-fi/horror masterpiece, but he handled the task with confidence and proficiency.

The monster (Boris Karloff) and Dr. Frankenstein (Colin Clive) are back. Still reviled by humanity, the creature finds himself roaming the countryside in this film, and Dr. Frankenstein is visited by a scientist whose madness surpasses his own. This scientist, Dr. Pretorius (Ernest Thesiger), has likewise created life, though in a far different form, and proposes a partnership to create "a new world, of gods and monsters." Before long the monster finds Pretorius and Frankenstein, at which case Pretorius, thirsting for godlike power, promises the creature a mate. Using Frankenstein's kidnapped fiancée as leverage, Pretorius will rope the doctor into once again bringing life to a dead body.

In taking on this task, Frankenstein and Pretorius learn the dangers of unchecked hubris. Specifically by creating their own forms of life, the doctors are meddling with powers not meant for man. Frankenstein, despite being forced into the matter against his will, eventually takes on his role as creator with the same fervor he exhibited when reanimating dead tissue for the first time. Both characters' goals are demolished, though, as their new creation, a bride for the monster, comes to life with a will contrary to that which they imagined.

The Bride (Elsa Lanchester) meets her intended groom (Boris Karloff).
Universal Pictures/Heritage Auctions

"ALONE: BAD. FRIEND: GOOD!"
-THE MONSTER

Karloff once again delivers a magnificent performance as the monster. In one famous scene, the monster comes across a blind hermit's hut in the woods. Transcending barriers of sight and intellect, the two characters immediately form an intimate friendship. In this scene, the creature learns what it means to have a friend and, even more surprisingly, begins to learn language. On paper this sounds absurd, but Karloff's infantile utterances of statements like, "Alone: bad. Friend: good!" are completely convincing. Even scenes in which the creature drinks wine and smokes cigars come across as heartwarming instead of comical.

Bride of Frankenstein takes such risks that you would never expect it to remain cohesive. However, it manages to uphold the same expertise demonstrated in *Frankenstein*. This ranks easily as one of the greatest movie sequels of all time.

The Day the Earth Stood Still

YEAR 1951
COUNTRY United States
RUNTIME 1 hr. 32 min.
RATED Not Rated; some gunplay, some things and people dissolved by ray beams
DIRECTED BY Robert Wise
WRITTEN BY Edmund H. North, Harry Bates
STARRING Michael Rennie, Billy Gray, Patricia Neal, Sam Jaffe
SIMILAR SCI-FI *The Box*, *The Brother from Another Planet*, *The Day the Earth Stood Still* (2008), *Things to Come*

The Day the Earth Stood Still is a moral against nuclear weaponry and war in general. It is also a well-written, well-acted film. Its success lies not in its message alone but in the delivery of its message. This is the classic anti-war sci-fi film.

In Washington, D.C., a human-looking alien named Klaatu (Michael Rennie) has arrived. He has come with a message of peace, but his message is also a warning. Since humankind has developed both rockets and nuclear weaponry, we have now put other planets at risk. So, the message is this: Stop your childish fighting, or the forces of other planets will destroy you in preemptive self-defense. The problem Klaatu faces is that the world's leaders will not gather to listen to him. But he's got a few tricks up his sleeve to get their attention.

Helen Benson (Patricia Neal) cowers from Gort, but later joins forces with him. *20th Century Fox/The Kobal Collection*

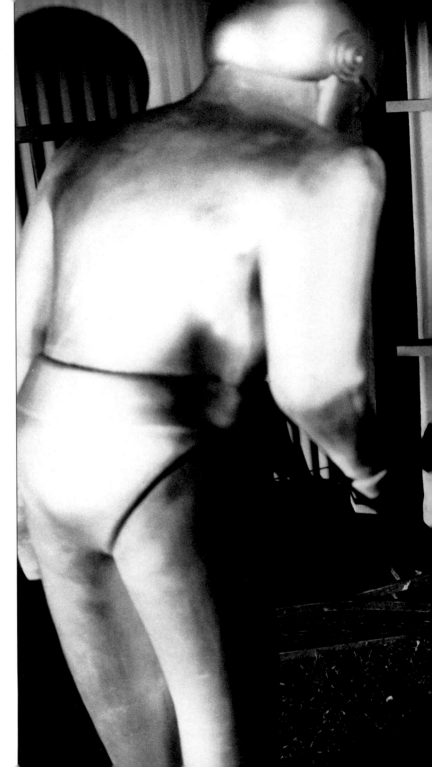

The poster depicts the 8-foot Gort's ability to shoot a laser beam from his visor. *20th Century Fox/Heritage Auctions*

From the moment Klaatu arrives, Earth is depicted as a violently leery and even ridiculous place. When Klaatu presents a gift for delivery to the president, he is immediately shot by an overanxious soldier. When the visitor requests an audience of the world's leaders, he is told simply that relations are so awkward between nations that the leaders of the world would never agree to meet, even for an occasion such as this.

Klaatu, by assuming the name "Carpenter" and performing one particular act near the film's end, becomes an obvious Christ symbol, but he is also an intriguing character at face value. He demonstrates affection for the childlike human race, but he is stern in his conditions for our peace, at one point suggesting the possibility of destroying New York to get our attention. During all of his communications with us, he is simultaneously kind and straightforward, conveying a politeness even as he openly refers to our society's stupidity. The character warrants analysis free of its symbolism.

In the end, *The Day the Earth Stood Still* is more than a warning of our destructive nature. It is an illustration of our senselessness. Not only are we prone to killing each other with horrible devices of war, we are so immature as to be unwilling to work together in the face of extreme adversity. This is a message that never grows stale.

Godzilla

YEAR 1954
COUNTRY Japan
RUNTIME 1 hr. 38 min.
RATED Not Rated; monster destruction
DIRECTED BY Ishirô Honda
WRITTEN BY Ishirô Honda, Shigeru Kayama, Takeo Murata
STARRING Akira Takarada, Akihiko Hirata, Momoko Kôchi, Takashi Shimura
SIMILAR SCI-FI *The Beast from 20,000 Fathoms*, *Cloverfield*, *Godzilla* (1984), *Godzilla Raids Again*, *The Host*

Godzilla leaves a burning city behind him. *Toho*

"I CAN'T BELIEVE THAT GODZILLA WAS THE ONLY SURVIVING MEMBER OF ITS SPECIES. BUT IF WE KEEP ON CONDUCTING NUCLEAR TESTS, IT'S POSSIBLE THAT ANOTHER GODZILLA MIGHT APPEAR, SOMEWHERE IN THE WORLD, AGAIN." -KYOHEI YAMANE-HAKASE

There are two classic giant monster movies that stand above the rest: *King Kong* (1933) and *Godzilla* (1954, a.k.a. *Gojira*). The former is fun, frequently humorous, and occasionally frightening. The latter is an exercise in terror. As outdated as its visual effects may be, *Godzilla* remains one of the best and most austere giant monster films of all time.

Set in Japan, *Godzilla* was released not quite ten years after the bombings of Hiroshima and Nagasaki, and it plays into those fears unabashedly. The story follows Japan's coping with the emergence of a giant monster, the product of nearby hydrogen bomb tests. This monster, which towers over buildings, has begun attacking villages, boats, and cities at will, destroying everything it comes across. If anything can save Japan from Godzilla, it will have to be a weapon as terrifying as the monster itself.

There are so many things that make *Godzilla* work, including the pacing, the score, the acting, the subplots, and even the lighting. This movie does not revel in its monster attacks; rather, it fears them. It builds tension for prolonged periods of time by showing intermittent scenes of devastation caused by the creature and thereafter pondering the nature of the beast. Throughout the film a doomsday score, melancholy acting, and dark lighting keep the mood consistently depressed. In the end, when we witness a full-on monster attack on Tokyo, it is not exciting but horrifying. How many other monster movies have you seen that contain a woman huddling with her children in the street, telling them, "We'll be with Daddy soon?"

Beneath all of this you can find subtexts not only concerning atomic warfare but about the destructive nature of the subconscious—a place

from which this monster almost seems to have materialized. Whether you watch the film for its visceral value or its meaning, though, there will be plenty to draw you in. No giant monster film has yet matched it in the thoroughness with which it evokes dismay.

A note to *Godzilla* newcomers: Two versions of the 1954 *Godzilla* exist: the original Japanese version, as titled above, and the Americanized version, called *Godzilla: King of the Monsters!* It is the original you must view in order to experience the creators' intended emotional effect. The American-edited version, featuring inserted scenes of an American reporter in Japan, is little more than a simple mystery that leads to the spectacle of a giant monster.

Born from nuclear fallout, Godzilla seems unstoppable. *Toho/The Kobal Collection*

Forbidden Planet

YEAR 1956
COUNTRY United States
RUNTIME 1 hr. 38 min.
RATED G; some mild adult content
DIRECTED BY Fred McLeod Wilcox
WRITTEN BY Irving Block, Allen Adler, Cyril Hume
STARRING Leslie Nielsen, Walter Pidgeon, Warren Stevens, Anne Francis, Robby the Robot
SIMILAR SCI-FI *Dark City*, *The Day the Earth Stood Still* (1951), *Solaris* (1972)

"MY EVIL SELF IS AT THAT DOOR, AND I HAVE NO POWER TO STOP IT!" **-DR. EDWARD MORBIUS**

On the surface, *Forbidden Planet* is the epitome of 1950s sci-fi. It has a faster-than-light UFO, an analog robot, and a mysterious monster, all on a distant planet with a landscape both desolate and peculiar. However, as the film progresses and its story digs deeper into the setup, it reveals a center with more imagination than almost any genre film of that decade. This is a movie about the inextinguishable evil at the heart of man and the dangers of wielding absolute power, and it's wrapped in a package visually representative of the finest classic science fiction.

A crew of military space travelers (think *Star Trek* more than *Starship Troopers*) is sent sixteen light years away to investigate the fate of a lost ship on the planet Altair IV. Upon arriving they find a scientist, his daughter, and a robot that would become one of science fiction's most famous: Robby. The scientist, Dr. Morbius (Walter Pidgeon), explains that the other members of his ship's crew were killed by a monster, and he refuses to return to Earth for questioning. Needless to say, the investigating crew (led by a shockingly straight-faced Leslie Nielsen) immediately becomes suspicious of Morbius, even

though the man treats them with only the most generous hospitality.

Eventually, however, the protagonists realize that Morbius is telling the truth, and this truth is worse than what they expected. The monster that killed the original crew is, in a sense, the same force responsible for the extinction of the entire civilization that once ruled Altair IV. Even more amazingly, this civilization had achieved the highest possible level of technology: the ability to alter reality through mere will. Would you believe that this technology and the monster's existence are inherently tied together?

Whereas so many films of this era of science fiction are focused on presenting established ideas in new ways, *Forbidden Planet* demonstrates original thought, pondering the implications of achieving complete scientific knowledge and power. When the true nature of the monster is

Forbidden Planet is the first science fiction movie to be set in deep space.
Metro-Goldwyn-Mayer/Heritage Auctions

Robby the Robot was one of the first movie robots to have a distinct personality. *Metro-Goldwyn-Mayer/Heritage Auctions*

discovered, we fear not only for the characters' lives but for humanity itself. If technological progression means the increased speed and effectiveness of fulfilling our desires, what happens when our tech gets so good that our desires are fulfilled before they even leave the subconscious?

The great thing about *Forbidden Planet* is that along with its imagination it also offers plenty of casual fun. There's a compelling mystery, there are great visuals, and the drama near the end of the film becomes far more intense than you'd expect from a work with a character called "Robby the Robot." This is one of the genre's best entries of one of its best decades—in every way, a classic.

Invasion of the Body Snatchers

YEAR 1956
COUNTRY United States
RUNTIME 1 hr. 20 min.
RATED Not Rated; has some mildly frightening scenes
DIRECTED BY Don Siegel
WRITTEN BY Jack Finney (source novel); Daniel Mainwaring
STARRING Kevin McCarthy, Dana Wynter, Larry Gates, King Donovan
SIMILAR SCI-FI *Body Snatchers* (1993), *Invaders from Mars*, *The Invasion* (2007), *Invasion of the Body Snatchers* (1978), *It Came from Outer Space*

Dr. Miles Bennell (Kevin McCarthy) makes an unpleasant discovery.
Allied Artists/Heritage Auctions

If you're looking for the ultimate paranoia film, look no further. The original *Invasion of the Body Snatchers* is a paragon of "aliens among us" tales. Infusing a thrilling story into a masterful production, this film, more effectively than perhaps any other, evokes the fear of being trapped in a world where anyone can be the enemy.

When Dr. Miles Bennell (Kevin McCarthy) returns to his small-town home from vacation, he arrives to patients complaining that their loved ones are acting strange. They're not doing anything bizarre, though. In fact, the problem is that they're acting too normal. Soon Bennell, his girlfriend Becky (Dana Wynter), and a couple of friends discover that the town has been silently overtaken by sentient alien plants (a.k.a. "pod people") that exist as physically exact copies of the town's residents, who are individually killed in the process. The pod people's goal: to do the same to

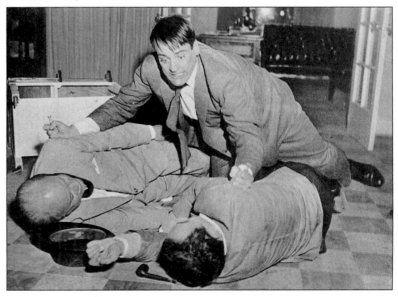

Dr. Bennell doesn't know who he can trust, so he's not taking any chances.
Allied Artists/Heritage Auctions

everyone on Earth, with the sole purpose of propagating their species.

The driving force of the film is Bennell's attempt to escape a world in which he doesn't know who can be trusted, for anyone can be one of these aliens. The cinematography and set design intensify the horror of the situation. While attempting to flee the invaders, Bennell and Becky find themselves in tight spaces that highlight the claustrophobia that stems from such paranoia. When they reach open areas, they are not liberated but are exposed instead to a more agoraphobic horror, with elements such as windowpane shadows showing them to be dangerously visible to anyone. Whether he runs or hides, Bennell cannot find solace.

Throughout the years, countless critics have noted the similarities between Bennell's situation

Becky (Dana Wynter) and Dr. Bennell (Kevin McCarthy) realize something's not right with the townspeople.
Allied Artists/Heritage Auctions

and the Red Scare of the McCarthy era, which was in its heyday when the film was released. This is a valid observation, but the film also works as a catharsis of any sort of paranoia. How do we know our neighbors are who they say they are? And what can we do when we don't know who to trust?

The Incredible Shrinking Man

YEAR 1957
COUNTRY United States
RUNTIME 1 hr. 21 min.
RATED Not Rated; some mildly frightening scenes, especially for those with arachnophobia
DIRECTED BY Jack Arnold
WRITTEN BY Richard Matheson
STARRING Grant Williams, Randy Stuart, Raymond Bailey, April Kent
SIMILAR SCI-FI *The Fly* (1958), *The Invisible Man, The Monolith Monsters, Tarantula*

The Incredible Shrinking Man is an anomaly. In an age when science fiction was fixated on killer monsters, invading aliens, and romantic subplots, this film came out as a rare example of science fiction that is both humanist and transcendental. Directed by sci-fi master Jack Arnold, it somehow never acquired the long-lasting popularity of his other genre works like *It Came from Outer Space* and *Creature from the Black Lagoon*, but *The Incredible Shrinking Man* is daring and uplifting, placing a

A FASCINATING ADVENTURE INTO THE UNKNOWN!

THE INCREDIBLE SHRINKING MAN

A Universal International Picture starring
GRANT WILLIAMS · RANDY STUART
with APRIL KENT · PAUL LANGTON · RAYMOND BAILEY
JACK ARNOLD · RICHARD MATHESON · ALBERT ZUGSMITH

modern man in an increasingly primal existence in order to discover fundamental truths of life.

A man named Scott Carey (Grant Williams) is relaxing on a boat with his wife when a glittering mist drifts by and passes immediately around his body. After several days of weight loss, height loss, and clothes fitting too loosely, Carey is forced to face the unbelievable reality that he is shrinking. That mist, it turns out, was radioactive.

The film has two distinct halves. The first half follows Carey as he struggles with his continual emasculation. As Carey shrinks, he becomes more and more dejected, and his defensive temper soon leads to a marred relationship with his wife. He seeks companionship with others facing similar difficulties (e.g. human circus attractions), and before long his marriage is all but broken. Carey's sense of masculinity hits rock bottom when his condition demands that he live in a dollhouse.

One night, all hope for a return to normalcy is lost when the family cat chases Carey out of his dollhouse and into his (real) house's basement, where he has no chance of being discovered. It is here where

One of the dangers Scott Carey faces as a shrinking man is his pet cat, played by animal actor "Orangey," who had a prolific career in movies and television.
Universal Studios/Heritage Auctions

"ALL THIS VAST MAJESTY OF CREATION, IT HAD TO MEAN SOMETHING. AND THEN I MEANT SOMETHING, TOO. YES, SMALLER THAN THE SMALLEST, I MEANT SOMETHING, TOO. TO GOD, THERE IS NO ZERO. I STILL EXIST." -SCOTT CAREY

Trapped in the basement, Scott Carey (Grant Williams) has to battle a hungry spider. *Universal Studios/Heritage Auctions*

Carey spends the second half of the film. Shrunken below an inch in height, the character finds himself in a world that offers an old piece of cake as the only source of nourishment and a relatively monstrous spider as a threat he must defeat in order to reach that nourishment. This is a land Carey must conquer in order to survive, and he suddenly finds himself committing acts of bravery unthinkable in modern society. In the end, he finds himself both empowered and enlightened. "To God," the ever-shrinking man concludes, "there is no zero."

This is a film that dares to search dark corners for truth because it realizes that it is only through hardship that enlightenment can be found. It is a story of a man's success in glimpsing the infinite, even while approaching the infinitesimal.

2001: A Space Odyssey

YEAR 1968
COUNTRY United States
RUNTIME 2 hrs. 21 min.
RATED G; mild language, intense imagery
DIRECTED BY Stanley Kubrick
WRITTEN BY Arthur C. Clarke, Stanley Kubrick
STARRING Keir Dullea, Gary Lockwood, William Sylvester, Douglas Rain
SIMILAR SCI-FI *2010*, *Solaris* (1972), *Sunshine*

It is impossible to communicate the full greatness of *2001: A Space Odyssey*. This is a film directed so confidently that it is often content to rest on images that hardly progress the plot. It is a film of such imagination that it relies more on what we don't understand than what we do. It is a masterpiece, and it is arguably the greatest science fiction film ever made.

The plot of *2001* is not at all weak, but it is about as thin as a competent plot can be. The film begins with a void, progresses to mankind's evolution from non-reasoning apes, continues to a future world of space exploration, and ends somewhere you could never expect. There is something peculiar about this movie's history of man, though. Throughout the story of our evolution and technological advancement, our race encounters exactly four black, solid, rectangular monoliths, placed by who knows who for who knows what reason. The first of these randomly appears before a group of our ape-like ancestors one day, inciting both amazement and fear. A second is found millions of years later on

Cunning and determination help Dr. Dave Bowman (Keir Dullea) outwit HAL 9000.
Metro-Goldwyn-Mayer/The Kobal Collection

An epic drama of adventure and exploration

Space Station One, your first step in an Odyssey that will take you to the Moon, the planets and the distant stars.

2001: a space odyssey

STANLEY KUBRICK'S

STARRING KEIR DULLEA · GARY LOCKWOOD · SCREENPLAY BY STANLEY KUBRICK AND ARTHUR C. CLARKE
PRODUCED AND DIRECTED BY STANLEY KUBRICK · IN SUPER PANAVISION* · METROCOLOR
G GENERAL AUDIENCES · MGM · Limited Artists

Despite mixed reviews when it was first released, *2001* today is recognized by critics as one of the greatest films ever made. *Metro-Goldwyn-Mayer/Heritage Auctions*

"I'M AFRAID. I'M AFRAID, DAVE. DAVE, MY MIND IS GOING. I CAN FEEL IT. I CAN FEEL IT. MY MIND IS GOING. THERE IS NO QUESTION ABOUT IT. I CAN FEEL IT. I CAN FEEL IT. I CAN FEEL IT..." -HAL 9000

the moon, emitting a radio signal to Jupiter. The plot is concerned with the discovery of the moon monolith and an exploration mission to the point of its signal.

Instead of expounding upon its story, *2001* is devoted to exploring the beauty inherent within the story's bare elements, such as man, his technology, and his place in the universe. Much of the film is spent marveling at our technological prowess. The wonder of our ability to travel to other celestial bodies is highlighted by an early low, vertical shot of the first monolith pointing to the moon from the ground, as if it were placed to tell the nearby pseudo-humans, "One day you will go there." Later, we spend minutes on end watching space stations floating in orbit, spacecraft flying over the moon and through space, and future astronauts carrying out ordinary tasks in zero gravity. The images, enhanced by a camera that always seems too enthralled to move, are stunning on their own, and the delicacy of our technology is emphasized by the classical soundtrack, consisting of pieces such as *Also Sprach Zarathustra* and *The Blue Danube*.

Regardless of its proclivity to appreciate things for face value, *2001* is at times able to build tension that rivals and occasionally surpasses that of movies that exist solely to provide tension, thanks largely to HAL 9000, a computer that becomes a character itself. In a way, these moments are further expressions of awe at the things of which man is capable. Not only do we have the capability of interplanetary travel; we are also able to create artificial intelligence so advanced as to surpass, at times, our own ingenuity.

The film's final act consists of twenty-five of the most breathtaking and confounding minutes in all of cinema. It is a sequence that would be spoiled if discussed in any concrete terms, but in seeking the purpose of the monoliths, it approaches staggering levels of thought. It is an act that can be dissected and analyzed endlessly, and those who do so may yield beautiful ideas, but no fully comprehendible, objective discovery of its meaning can ever be reached. Sometimes things are more exciting when we don't fully understand them. That is how the world works, and that, in the end, is how *2001* works.

2001 is an expression of amazement at humankind and our possible distant future. There are those who criticize the movie for its sterility and slowly paced plot. Those who do so overlook its pervading surface beauty. When you step back and appreciate its elements for what they are, *2001* becomes a sublime experience.

A Clockwork Orange

YEAR 1971

COUNTRY United Kingdom, United States

RUNTIME 2 hrs. 16 min.

RATED X; disturbing and intense violence including rape, graphic nudity, sexual content, profanity, some drug use

DIRECTED BY Stanley Kubrick

WRITTEN BY Stanley Kubrick, Anthony Burgess (source novel)

STARRING Malcolm McDowell, Michael Bates, Patrick Magee, Carl Duering

NO SIGNIFICANTLY SIMILAR SCI-FI

Mrs. Alexander (Adrienne Corri) is a victim of Alex's ultra-violence.
Warner Bros./Heritage Auctions

Unlike most antiheros, there is nothing redeemable about Alex (Malcolm McDowell), the main character of *A Clockwork Orange*. This character has three pleasures: beating, raping, and Beethoven. Even when he is wronged, his sadness stems from the fact that he is being disallowed from committing heinous acts. Frighteningly, despite his persistently and egregiously evil nature, Alex maintains a certain allure.

A Clockwork Orange, adapted from the novel by Anthony Burgess, tells the story of Alex's exploits, his clinical reformation, and the outcome of his being forced to become a law-abiding member of society. After being jailed for murdering a woman, Alex, distressed over his new inability to inflict harm upon others, requests to be placed in a program that rehabilitates pathological wrongdoers in a matter of weeks and thereafter frees them from whatever penal debts they owe. When he begins his new conditioning, however, he learns that this process of reformation is nearly torturous, as is life after being cured.

At the most basic level, this is a story about the freedom of action and will. Alex's actions, until he is cured, are perfectly uninhibited. Later, in a disturbing way, the film effectually demonstrates the merits of the ability to carry out evil acts. Even if we are rendered physically unable to do such things, immoral thoughts can still be had, as we see with Alex. At least we were initially able to see visual evidence of what makes such desires so evil. There is no scientific cure for evil, we learn; the most we can do is suppress it. By the end of the film, the thought of Alex regaining the ability to commit such crimes feels almost refreshing.

The film's classical/synthetic soundtrack, along with director Stanley Kubrick's tendency to portray the main character as more normal than those around him, suggests a sort of beauty to Alex's actions. This seeming admiration for the character is a controversial aspect of the film and has indeed been reproved by critics as renowned as Pauline Kael and Roger Ebert. However, like the music he so loves, Alex's beauty stems from his defiance and willpower. Perhaps it is this quality specifically that Kubrick admires—the character's willingness to act so freely. Indeed, the music of Beethoven eventually becomes a repulsive force, a weapon even, against

Alex after his reformation. Thematically, it is as if this music, as beautiful and free as it is, is a reminder of the individual's former freedom to do whatever he pleased.

Even for those who find *A Clockwork Orange* to be offensive, it can still be enthralling. Its motives are difficult to pinpoint, but its frequent beauty counterbalances its more disturbing elements into an experience that is, if not enjoyable, provocative. And at the least, it is proof of how difficult it can be to see into the mind of Stanley Kubrick.

"AND IT WAS LIKE FOR A MOMENT, O MY BROTHERS, SOME GREAT BIRD HAD FLOWN INTO THE MILKBAR AND I FELT ALL THE MALENKY LITTLE HAIRS ON MY PLOTT STANDING ENDWISE AND THE SHIVERS CRAWLING UP LIKE SLOW MALENKY LIZARDS AND THEN DOWN AGAIN. BECAUSE I KNEW WHAT SHE SANG. IT WAS A BIT FROM THE GLORIOUS NINTH, BY LUDWIG VAN." -ALEX

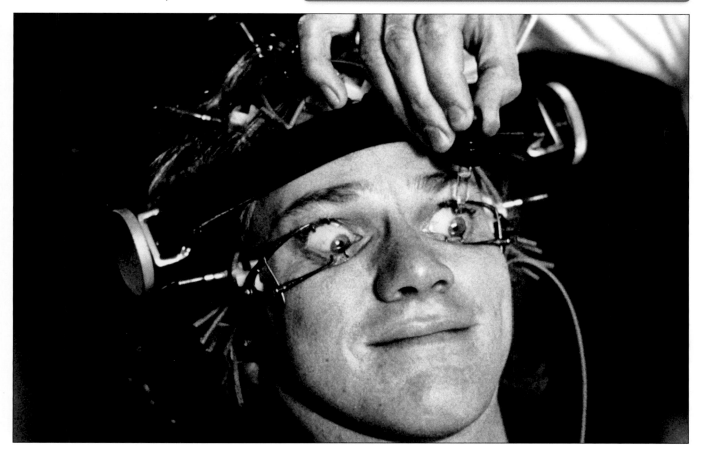

Strapped into Ludovico technique apparatus, Alex undergoes aversion therapy. *Warner Bros./The Kobal Collection*

Solaris

YEAR 1972
COUNTRY Soviet Union
RUNTIME 2 hr. 45 min.
RATED PG; complex adult themes
DIRECTED BY Andrei Tarkovsky
WRITTEN BY Stanislaw Lem (source novel), Andrei Tarkovsky, Fridikh Gorenshtein
STARRING Donatas Banionis, Natalya Bondarchuk, Jüri Järvet, Vladislav Dvorzhetsky
SIMILAR SCI-FI *2001: A Space Odyssey*, *Solaris* (2002), *Stalker*

Solaris is one of the best science fiction movies of all time. It is also one of the slowest. Similar to *2001: A Space Odyssey*, this is a film that is driven more by contemplation than by plot. Its ideas are provocative and at times upsetting, but the film itself is thoroughly beautiful. It is an experience that can change your fundamental notions of life.

Psychologist Kris Kelvin (Donatas Banionis) is sent to a space station orbiting the possibly sentient oceanic planet Solaris to assess the mental health of the scientists stationed there, following fantastical but unfounded reports by others who have visited. When he arrives, he discovers that one of the scientists has died. After speaking with the others, glimpsing one or two unexplainable things, and taking a short nap to recoup, Kelvin wakes to a situation that is either a paradise or a nightmare—he can't decide. Solaris has materialized Kelvin's long-deceased wife, Hari (Natalya Bondarchuk), in perfect health.

Kelvin's simultaneous rapture and horror at having a perfect construct—not hallucination—of his wife to once again be with supplies the film's existential dilemma. Kelvin and the viewer are left to ponder whether this fully living and feeling Hari, whose only difference from the original is that she is made up of neutrinos, can be said to be real. Along with this pondering comes the question of love. What is it Kelvin loved about his wife? Even if he does determine that the new Hari is not "real," can he avoid loving her? That's the kind of stuff you're getting into in *Solaris*.

Running nearly three hours in length, *Solaris* contains long stretches of silence in which the plot simply ceases to progress. Furthermore, Kelvin does not even go into space until the forty-five-minute mark, and one infamous scene consists of nothing more than a car driving on a highway for five minutes of screen time. Naturally, this is a barrier to more casual film fans. However, for those willing to give it a chance, the ideas and emotion contained in *Solaris* trump any slowness. Indeed, even the so-called boring moments become filled with thought concerning the reality of Hari and the nature of love.

I prescribe a test for assessing your ability to enjoy *Solaris*. Watch the first scene of the film, which consists of Kelvin gazing at reeds. If you don't find beauty in it, move on to a different movie. If you do, sit tight for science fiction's premier existential masterpiece.

Psychologist Kris Kelvin (Donatas Banionis) finds himself becoming attached to an alternate reality. *Mosfilm Studios/The Kobal Collection*

"IN HIS ENDLESS SEARCH FOR TRUTH, MAN IS CONDEMNED TO KNOWLEDGE." -SARTORIUS

Kris Kelvin's dead wife Hari (Natalya Bondarchuk) reappears aboard the space station. *Mosfilm Studios/The Kobal Collection*

Young Frankenstein

YEAR 1974
COUNTRY United States
RUNTIME 1 hr. 46 min.
RATED PG; some mild sexual humor, mild slapstick violence
DIRECTED BY Mel Brooks
WRITTEN BY Gene Wilder, Mel Brooks
STARRING Gene Wilder, Peter Boyle, Marty Feldman, Cloris Leachman, Madeline Kahn, Teri Garr
SIMILAR SCI-FI *Bride of Frankenstein, Frankenstein, Son of Frankenstein, Spaceballs, Weird Science*

Mel Brooks is the king of cinematic parody, and *Young Frankenstein* is arguably his best work. In this film, he juggles humor, respect for the source material, and even a moving story, all without the slightest hint of uncertainty. *Young Frankenstein* is not only a great parody of Universal's *Frankenstein* franchise, it could stand beside them as part of the mythology.

Young Frankenstein picks up down the lineage of the doctors Frankenstein, this time with Victor Frankenstein's grandson, Frederick, as the main character. Frederick leads a life as a respected doctor and professor, distancing himself as far as possible from his unsavory lineage to the point that he becomes incensed when students press him on the topic of reanimating of dead tissue. The legacy of the Frankenstein family runs too thickly in his veins, though, and he almost accidentally finds himself performing reanimations in his grandfather's castle laboratory in Transylvania. It's

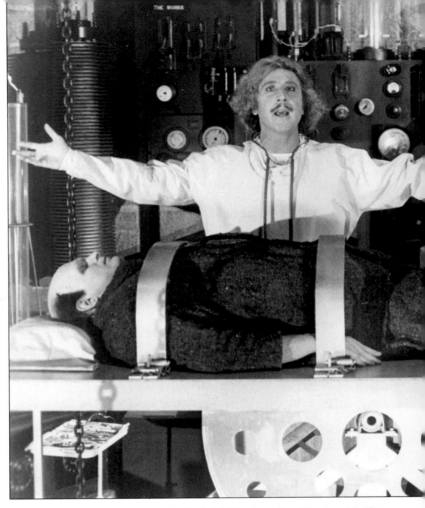

At first scornful of his family legacy, Dr. Frederick "Fronk-en-steen" Frankenstein (Gene Wilder) eventually creates his own monster (Peter Boyle). *20th Century Fox/Heritage Auctions*

"TONIGHT, WE SHALL HURL THE GAUNTLET OF SCIENCE INTO THE FRIGHTFUL FACE OF DEATH ITSELF. TONIGHT, WE SHALL ASCEND INTO THE HEAVENS. WE SHALL MOCK THE EARTHQUAKE. WE SHALL COMMAND THE THUNDERS, AND PENETRATE INTO THE VERY WOMB OF IMPERVIOUS NATURE HERSELF." -DR. FRANKENSTEIN

as if he cannot escape his destiny.

First and foremost, *Young Frankenstein* is hilarious, thanks to a combination of Brooks' wit and the actors' comedic timing. Gene Wilder as Frederick "Fronk-en-steen" Frankenstein, Peter Boyle as the monster, and Marty Feldman as Igor (pronounced, so fittingly, "eye-gore") devote themselves to their roles with an enthusiasm that is rarely equaled. Wilder's outbursts are as amusing as they are heaven-defying, Feldman's continual glances at the camera with his bulbous eyeballs are priceless, and Boyle plays the monster so believably that it is not difficult to imagine him taking the role in one of the original films. When these actors' sensibilities are applied to Brooks' humor, the result is comedy gold. We get unending, random, and self-deprecating quips from Feldman; a slapstick recreation of *Bride of Frankenstein*'s famous monster/hermit scene; and, possibly *Young Frankenstein*'s most famous sequence, Dr. Frankenstein and his monster performing "Puttin' on the Ritz." You just can't top stuff like this.

Brooks does an immaculate job of recreating the visual style and feel of the original *Frankenstein* films, not only shooting *Young Frankenstein* in black and white but also using some of the same camera techniques. Furthermore, he famously reused props from Universal's original *Frankenstein* for his laboratory scenes. The result is a completely authentic-looking Frankenstein film and an obvious work of love.

Young Frankenstein must be one of the greatest parodies of all time. You would be hard-pressed to find any such film so true to its source and so consistently funny. It stands as undeniable proof that Brooks is not only a funny director, he is a great one.

It's reported that the cast and Mel Brooks had so much fun making the movie that Brooks added more scenes so they could continue shooting.
20th Century Fox/Heritage Auctions

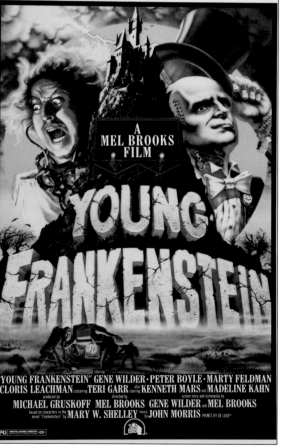

Star Wars

YEAR 1977
COUNTRY United States
RUNTIME 2 hrs. 5 min.
RATED PG; sci-fi violence, brief mild language
DIRECTED BY George Lucas
WRITTEN BY George Lucas
STARRING Mark Hamill, Harrison Ford, Sir Alec Guinness, Carrie Fisher
SIMILAR SCI-FI *Star Wars: Episode V – The Empire Strikes Back*, *Star Wars: Episode VI – Return of the Jedi*

What praise needs to be lavished on *Star Wars* these days? A breakthrough in its time, it has since retained every bit of its potency, amassed legions upon legions of fans, and spawned an empire of marketing. *Star Wars* was a phenomenon and is arguably the single most important contribution to modern sci-fi cinema.

In *Star Wars*, director George Lucas, a fan of classic sci-fi serials like *Buck Rogers*, weaves a story that seems to follow every tradition of pulp science fiction. In a galaxy filled with hundreds of inhabitable star systems and thousands of sentient species of creatures, a young moisture farmer gets pulled into a galactic civil war between the ruling, oppressive Empire and a Rebel Alliance. To fight this Empire, he will have to learn the ways of a mystic, all-powerful entity called the Force. Along the way he will form friendships, experience loss, mature in the ways of the Force, and possibly help save the galaxy.

On paper, *Star Wars* is hardly original. It is a classic sci-fi adventure story injected with a coming-of-age theme of mythological descent. Its aesthetics, though, elevate *Star Wars* beyond all sci-fi/adventure films preceding it. The problem with so many of the film's predecessors, Lucas realized, was that they feel sterile. Characters wear matching (and often ridiculous) clothing, every object looks like it is deep-cleaned by the hour, and weapons lack any sort of kinetics or pop. This is true even for famous (and great) works like *Forbidden Planet* and *Star Trek*. *Star Wars*, on the other hand, is filled with the grit and energy necessary to create a sense of realism and familiarity.

Contained in this film is a universe that has been used, a place in which things get dirty or fail to work properly. It is a place where blasters emit actual blasts, not quiet streams of light. One of the film's major contributions to science fiction lies in the special effects' departure from the genre's naval warfare-style spacecraft battles. The space battles in this movie are not simply exchanges of firepower but are full-on dogfights between quickly moving spacecraft, modeled directly after World War II footage. This design philosophy lends urgency and physicality to the events portrayed. The old *Buck Rogers* and *Flash Gordon* serials are fun, but they play out like flights of fancy. *Star Wars* is something you believe could plausibly exist in some far, far away corner of the universe.

These aesthetics give a boost to the film's surface elements, which combine to make it one of the most fun and exciting movies of all time. It takes all the best elements of the samurai, western, war, and fantasy genres and wraps them in a sci-fi-themed package. There are lightsaber duels, blaster shootouts, and the aforementioned dogfights and mystical powers, all in an environment filled with robots, aliens, and spaceships. Likewise, the world of *Star Wars* is populated with characters of all types—from smugglers and bounty hunters to wizards and royalty—without any of the cheesy clichés that usually come attached to such characters. It is a fully living universe.

With most other films, even great and complex ones, you can explain their allure to an adequate extent. *Star Wars*, however, has to be watched firsthand in order to understand its greatness to any significant degree. It is an astounding cinematic feat and is probably the most universally enjoyable sci-fi film ever made.

Princess Leia (Carrie Fisher) and Luke Skywalker (Mark Hamill) are two of the main protagonists. The third is Han Solo (Harrison Ford). *Lucasfilm/20th Century Fox/Heritage Auctions*

"THE FORCE WILL BE WITH YOU, ALWAYS."
-OBI-WAN

World War II footage influenced the dogfights between spacecraft. *Lucasfilm/20th Century Fox/Heritage Auctions*

Star Wars introduced the world to one of the greatest movie villains: Darth Vader (David Prowse and James Earl Jones). *Lucasfilm/20th Century Fox/The Kobal Collection*

Alien

YEAR 1979
COUNTRY United States
RUNTIME 1 hr. 57 min.
RATED R; sci-fi violence, gore, language
DIRECTED BY Ridley Scott
WRITTEN BY Dan O'Bannon, Ronald Shusett
STARRING Sigourney Weaver, Tom Skerritt, Ian Holm, John Hurt
SIMILAR SCI-FI *Aliens*, *Alien 3*, *Alien: Resurrection*, *Predator*, *The Thing*, *The Thing from Another World*

Things will not end well for engineer Brett (Harry Dean Stanton).
20th Century Fox/The Kobal Collection

Alien is not only possibly the best sci-fi/horror film, it is one of the best sci-fi films, period. With it, director Ridley Scott and his crew created an experience that haunts at first, then outright scares you, and finally erupts into a horrifying game of cat and mouse. The film's realistic feel and measured pacing combine to create a harrowing experience that in less talented hands could have been a simple bloodbath.

In the deep of space, the crew of a spaceship towing an ore refinery receives a transmission from an unexplored planet, LV-426. Following company orders, they set down to investigate, and, through one of the most disturbing means imaginable, a bloodthirsty life form finds its way aboard their ship. Though the crew at first thinks they have relative control over the situation, this alien soon escapes their observation and sets out to hunt them one at a time. It's seven space truckers versus one born killing machine. Those aren't good odds.

The film transcends sci-fi/horror convention by refusing to rely on the creature alone for scares. Practically every element of *Alien* is

"I ADMIRE ITS PURITY. A SURVIVOR ... UNCLOUDED BY CONSCIENCE, REMORSE, OR DELUSIONS OF MORALITY." -ASH

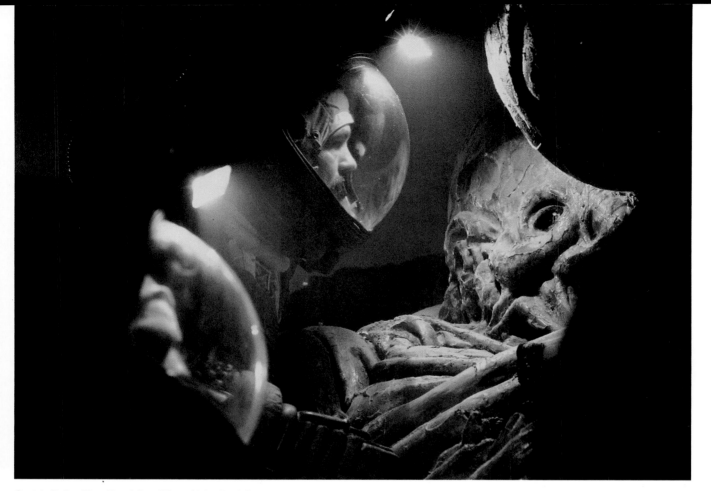

Captain Dallas (Tom Skerritt) and Kane (John Hurt) find the remains of a large alien creature. *20th Century Fox/Heritage Auctions*

used to maximize its terror. The blackness and desolation of LV-426, the mystery of the things they discover on the planet, the tension among the crew members, and the stealthy violence of the alien create an unease that never stops building. On top of that, the characters are everyday people, more concerned with things like food and paychecks than with technical space jabber. Because of this, we relate to them all the more. They are not distant heroes trying to eliminate a threat. They could be us.

That is not to downplay the merits of the alien itself, though, which is the film's single greatest asset. In the alien's appearance, behavior, and method of reproduction (if you somehow don't already know about it, you're really missing out), it is endowed with a combination of bloodlust and sexuality that evokes a fear not only of whether it's going to get you but of what it's going to do to you if you're caught.

Alien has some of cinema's most creative visceral horrors. Their effectiveness is multiplied, though, by the ways in which the filmmakers establish the movie's pervasive darkness, grit, and uncertainty. Because of those aspects of the film, there is no happy nook in which we can seek solace when the mayhem begins.

Star Wars: Episode V - The Empire Strikes Back

YEAR 1980

COUNTRY United States

RUNTIME 2 hrs. 7 min

RATED PG; sci-fi action and violence

DIRECTED BY Irvin Kershner

WRITTEN BY George Lucas, Leigh Brackett, Lawrence Kasdan

STARRING Mark Hamill, Harrison Ford, Carrie Fisher, Billy Dee Williams, David Prowse

SIMILAR SCI-FI *Star Wars*, *Star Wars: Episode III – Revenge of the Sith*, *Star Wars: Episode VI – Return of the Jedi*

After learning the way of the Jedi, Luke Skywalker (Mark Hamill) duels with the Dark Lord Darth Vader (David Prowse). *Lucasfilm/20th Century Fox/Heritage Auctions*

When *Star Wars* was released, it was a smash hit and a game-changer, so George Lucas was naturally eager to continue telling the story of the *Star Wars* universe. However, he did not feel up to the task of directing another film at the time, so he offered the job to one of his film school instructors, Irvin Kershner. Kershner was intimidated by the task, however, knowing that the sequel would be directly compared to the first film, one of the best sci-fi movies of all time. After some assurance that he would have full directorial control, though, Kershner accepted. It is good that he did, for he succeeded in accomplishing the unthinkable: Kershner made a film that, in many respects, surpasses the greatness of its predecessor.

In this installment, we're back with the characters from the first film as they continue their journeys of maturation and their fight against the Empire. This time, things don't go so smoothly. After suffering a military defeat at the beginning of the film, the core characters split into two paths. Luke (Mark Hamill) and R2-D2 (Kenny Baker) head off to find a Jedi Master to train Luke while Han (Harrison Ford), Leia (Carrie Fisher), Chewie (Peter Mayhew), and C-3PO (Anthony Daniels) find themselves pursued by both the Empire and bounty hunters. The latter group encounters constant peril even when they think they are safe, and by the end of the film, Luke is tested in a way he could hardly have imagined.

Whereas *Star Wars* is a film about adventure and victory, *The Empire Strikes Back* is about the pain and difficulty encountered when one's strengths are tested. Luke's training reveals that his largest obstacle is his own ambition, and, not heeding the lesson, he comes out both physically and emotionally traumatized by the end of the film. The other characters undergo similar

"IF YOU END YOUR TRAINING NOW, IF YOU CHOOSE THE QUICK AND EASY PATH AS VADER DID, YOU WILL BECOME AN AGENT OF EVIL." -YODA

The *Star Wars* universe features many fantastical creatures, such as this tauntaun. *Lucasfilm/20th Century Fox/Heritage Auctions*

challenges as their confidence in their ability to escape virtually any danger is cracked throughout the entire plot, resulting in events potentially more tragic than those Luke experiences. In *Star Wars*, the world seemed designed for the triumph of the characters. In this film, they are hammered by obstacle after obstacle.

The Empire Strikes Back also contains some of cinema's most famous characters, lines, and images. This is the movie that gave the world the ever-wise and masterfully created Yoda (Frank Oz), the mysterious fan-favorite Boba Fett (Jeremy Bulloch), and Darth Vader's famous revelation of the true fate of Luke's father, occurring via a line of dialogue recognizable even by those with no interest in the genre. The movie is simply packed with great elements.

More so even than films like *Terminator 2* and *Aliens*, *The Empire Strikes Back* stands as one of the greatest sequels ever made. It is about the pain you must endure on the path to triumph. We've seen that these characters have great potential to succeed in the things they set out to do. Now we watch them struggle, and at times fail, to reach that potential.

The renowned and powerful Jedi Master Yoda. *Lucasfilm/20th Century Fox/Heritage Auctions*

Blade Runner

YEAR 1982

COUNTRY United States

RUNTIME 1 hr. 57 min.

RATED R; violence and brief nudity (Definitive Cut)

DIRECTED BY Ridley Scott

WRITTEN BY Hampton Fancher, David Webb Peoples, Philip K. Dick (source novel)

STARRING Harrison Ford, Rutger Hauer, Sean Young, William Sanderson

SIMILAR SCI-FI *A.I.: Artificial Intelligence, Battlestar Galactica: The Plan, Metropolis* (2001)*, Natural City*

"Basic pleasure model" Pris (Daryl Hannah) is the girlfriend of fellow replicant Roy Batty. *Warner Bros./The Kobal Collection*

One could devote an entire book to discussing the themes and ideas at play in *Blade Runner*. What they all seem to come down to, though, is an examination of the destructive and creative cycle of technology. This film is Ridley Scott's masterpiece, and though its greatness is topped by Stanley Kubrick's *2001: A Space Odyssey*, no sci-fi film may be as tightly packed with meaning and detail as this one.

In the early 2000s, a type of android called "Replicants," built for off-world labor purposes, have been outlawed on Earth after developing emotion and engaging in a revolt. Men known as Blade Runners are trained to hunt and kill any such androids that return to our planet. When four of these Replicants make their way to Earth for a reason that is not immediately clear, former Blade Runner Rick Deckard (Harrison Ford) gets roped into one last job, with orders to destroy them. During his search for the Replicants, though, something will happen that will change the way he views such beings—and himself.

From the sweeping opening shots of future Los Angeles, to beautifully designed scenes such as a Replicant crashing through layers of glass, to quick details like a cloud of blood in a shot glass, *Blade Runner* is thoroughly devoted to providing beautiful imagery. Beyond this, though, is a focus on specific, recurring images—including such objects as eyes, ostriches, and unicorns—and strongly hued lighting techniques that show up throughout the film. All of these visual elements beg to be analyzed, but never do they distract from the core story.

One common denominator among many of the film's themes is the inextricable nature of destruction and progress. At the same time that society seems to have found bliss on other planets, the Earth has begun to decay. Yet, even while Earth has become an increasingly decadent place, it has become an orchestra of neon lights, often in the form of commercial advertisements. The creation of the Replicants themselves was meant to create an easier life for humanity, but it has at the same time resulted in loss of life. One character lives alone in a decrepit apartment building yet within those conditions wields the power essentially to create life. As for the story itself, at the same time that it destroys notions of what it means to be human, it creates a new understanding of the nature of humanity.

The chief contributing element to this theme is the lead Replicant, Roy Batty (Rutger Hauer). Batty is simultaneously symbolic of Christ and

Opposite page: Rick Decker (Harrison Ford) on the hunt. *Warner Bros./The Kobal Collection*

the final moments of the film, imagistic Christ parallels are drawn with the character at the same time that he expresses contempt at those who fated him to his existence.

In the end, *Blade Runner* does not posit an answer for the paradoxes it presents. Instead, it accepts them as unanswerable. For Deckard, who is essentially a detective, to accept non-truth as an indisputable truth is to adopt an entirely new worldview. For the viewer, the same result may potentially occur. *Blade Runner* is not here to shock us into epiphany, though. It is here to depict the world as a place where truth is not black and white and where beauty not only coexists with but thrives on destruction. Indeed, by the time we reach the end, the feeling is not one of confusion or dismay but of a contentment that had not arisen throughout the entire story. And the more we return to it, the more intimately we may understand that contentment.

Note: Over the years, *Blade Runner* has been edited into a number of different cuts. The cut most generally regarded as the definitive vision of Ridley Scott is the most recent, known as the "Final Cut." It is interesting to view each version to watch for added scenes and deleted elements (the most prominent of which is Deckard's voiceover, present originally but later removed, to most everyone's delight), but the Final Cut is indeed the best.

the Devil, descending from the sky as a beautiful and powerful being, fully robot and fully man, disrupting the daily goings-on of society, seeking both to free his own kind from their mortality and to punish his maker for the same cause. Even up to

E.T.: The Extra-Terrestrial

YEAR 1982
COUNTRY United States
RUNTIME 2 hrs.
RATED PG; language, mild thematic elements
DIRECTED BY Steven Spielberg
WRITTEN BY Melissa Mathison
STARRING Henry Thomas, Robert MacNaughton, Dee Wallace, Drew Barrymore
SIMILAR SCI-FI *CJ7, Close Encounters of the Third Kind, The Iron Giant, WALL-E*

"I'LL BELIEVE IN YOU ALL MY LIFE." -ELLIOT

The premise of *E.T.: The Extra-Terrestrial* is so simple: a harmless alien gets left behind on Earth and befriends a boy who tries to keep him hidden from the authorities. Yet, with non-sensationalist storytelling, Steven Spielberg takes the premise beyond simple sentimentality and makes a movie about unconditional childlike love and acceptance.

Elliot (Henry Thomas) forms a close bond with the alien he befriends.
Universal Pictures/Amblin Entertainment

In doing so, he creates one of the most heartwarming sci-fi films ever made.

When this young alien gets left behind on our planet, he is found by a boy named Elliot (Henry Thomas). Elliot knows to keep his new friend a secret, and as he does so, the two form a bond as close as any two humans. Eventually, however, the government learns of the alien's arrival and sets out to find him. It is at this point that Elliot and E.T. have to evade the authorities in order to somehow get the latter back to his home.

Even though *E.T.* is sci-fi plot-wise, it is fantastical in its tone. It is concerned not with the idea of the alien itself but with the friendship Elliot establishes with it. It follows the events not with a sense of excitement but with a feeling of whimsy. Because of this, the film presents the alien not as a scientific phenomenon but as a source of wonder. In fact, when science (always depicted as a cold, faceless entity) does step in to examine E.T., the consequences are disastrous. Ultimately, the film is about the virtue of childlike awe, about marveling at the world for what it is. There are times to dissect things and figure them out, but when we grow up, we don't leave ourselves enough time for unadulterated amazement.

E.T. is one of the few alien arrival movies not concerned with excitement, horror, action, or the pondering of extraterrestrial life. It uses its title alien only to tell a story about love. The world, as it moves forth, seems to become a progressively analytical place. This is a plea for us to slow down.

Elliot's sister Gertie (Drew Barrymore) teaches E.T. how to talk. *Universal Pictures/Amblin Entertainment*

This scene of Elliot and E.T. flying away on Elliot's bike is one of the most iconic in movies. *Universal Pictures/Amblin Entertainment/The Kobal Collection*

Videodrome

YEAR 1983
COUNTRY United States
RUNTIME 1 hr. 27 min.
RATED R; stong graphic images, violence, sexual content and language
DIRECTED BY David Cronenberg
WRITTEN BY David Cronenberg
STARRING James Woods, Deborah Harry, Jack Creley, Leslie Carlson
SIMILAR SCI-FI *Altered States*, *eXistenZ*, *The Fly* (1986)

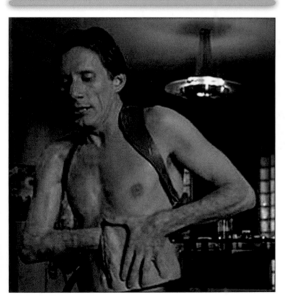

Max goes through several body-altering experiences.
Universal Pictures

Max Renn (James Woods) watches his girlfriend Nicki (Debbie Harry) become part of *Videodrome.* *Universal Pictures/The Kobal Collection*

The interaction between technology and the flesh is a classic theme of David Cronenberg's work, and *Videodrome* is perhaps his quintessential achievement in this sense. This film takes the idea of TV violence as a cathartic experience to its absolute extreme. In *Videodrome*, technology doesn't so much feed reality as it supersedes it. The result is some sort of bizarre and gruesome masterpiece.

Max Renn (James Woods), the president of a TV station, is looking for the next bold, sleazy show for his network's lineup when an engineer intercepts signals of an underground show called *Videodrome*. The broadcast scrambles itself whenever an unintended receiver picks it up, but from what Renn is able to see, it has no plot, takes place in a single room, and consists solely of realistic, sadomasochistic torture sessions. When Renn searches for

Andy Warhol reportedly called this "A *Clockwork Orange* of the '80s." *Universal Pictures/ Heritage Auctions*

television is reality, and reality is less than television." As Renn progresses through his body-altering experiences, this idea plays out literally. The viewing of extreme violence does more than sate perverse, and perhaps subconscious, desires. In the case of *Videodrome*, it creates a hallucination, a new reality, in which those desires and experiences are a core part of our being, even to the extent that they control our actions. But here's the thing: If such an incident as that which Renn experiences were to become widespread so that violence is an inherent part of life, where we are all hallucinating the same thing, would violence still be considered a social evil?

By the end of the film, reality has indeed been replaced by hallucination. When this happens, the vicarious experience of violence is no longer cathartic. It is real. The result is a new existence and a new flesh. Cronenberg tells this story as if he is beyond condoning or renouncing such a progression of society. He seems to be convinced (and probably frightened) that, in some metaphoric way, it is an inevitability.

the source of this broadcast, hoping to buy the rights to it for his station, his body begins undergoing transformations as the result of simply watching the show. After he grows a gaping slit in his abdomen (which promptly heals itself after he hides a gun in it), he sets out to find answers.

Videodrome is filled with philosophies concerning television, film, and those mediums' effect on reality. One character, who has resolved to communicate only through pre-recorded videotape sessions, at one point argues, "Whatever appears on the television screen emerges as raw experience for those who watch it. Therefore,

"THE BATTLE FOR THE MIND OF NORTH AMERICA WILL BE FOUGHT IN THE VIDEO ARENA – THE VIDEODROME. THE TELEVISION SCREEN IS THE RETINA OF THE MIND'S EYE. THEREFORE THE TELEVISION SCREEN IS PART OF THE PHYSICAL STRUCTURE OF THE BRAIN. THEREFORE WHATEVER APPEARS ON THE TELEVISION SCREEN EMERGES AS RAW EXPERIENCE FOR THOSE WHO WATCH IT. THEREFORE TELEVISION IS REALITY, AND REALITY IS LESS THAN TELEVISION." -PROF. BRIAN O'BLIVION

The Fly

YEAR 1986
COUNTRY United States
RUNTIME 1 hr. 35 min.
RATED R; strong sexuality, gory images, graphic violence, language
DIRECTED BY David Cronenberg
WRITTEN BY George Langelaan (source story), Charles Edward Pogue, David Cronenberg
STARRING Jeff Goldblum, Geena Davis, John Getz, Leslie Carlson
SIMILAR SCI-FI *Alien: Resurrection*, *The Fly* (1958), *The Fly II*, *RoboCop*, *Videodrome*

With his gory remake of the 1958 film *The Fly*, David Cronenberg takes a classic moral of the dangers of losing control of science and goes metaphysical with it. The original film was somewhat daring for its time, especially with its bleak ending. The remake dares to dig into deeper territory, however, questioning fundamental assumptions about humanity. Just what is it that makes us who we are?

Seth Brundle (Jeff Goldblum) is a sort of genius hack scientist. He doesn't understand any particular aspect of technology, and he doesn't know exactly *how* any of his purchased, hi-tech devices work, but he does know how to combine them into amazing new things. His latest pseudo-creation: a teleportation device. Once he works out the kinks, he tries it on himself, not knowing that a simple fly has flown into the teleportation pod with him. When he comes out the other end, all seems well at first, but soon enough Brundle learns that his body is slowly morphing into that of a human-fly hybrid.

Visually, *The Fly* is brilliantly disgusting. As Brundle's body undergoes its metamorphosis, he

"MOST PEOPLE WOULD GIVE ANYTHING TO BE TURNED INTO SOMETHING ELSE." -SETH BRUNDLE

becomes increasingly fleshy, slimy, and disfigured to the point that he is not even recognizable as his former self. This is an important aspect of the film. As Brundle's use of technology so drastically alters his flesh, it also seems to affect his core being. In modern society, we typically view any individual's "inner" self as independent from their physical makeup. In *The Fly*, however, Brundle's physical transformations directly alter his identity. The question is not, "Is this still Brundle?" The entity is clearly something new. Instead the question is, "Is there any part of Brundle left in this new being?"

As in Cronenberg's *Videodrome* (P. 46), *The Fly* is also a clear allegory for technology's effect on the flesh. Brundle's body and his work are not separate. Just as technology is ultimately aimed at serving the body, it also challenges our understanding of it—and at times contorts it. This idea is taken a step beyond the character's fly metamorphosis in the film's final scene, in which he completes the process of melding with technology. The results, as you might guess, are less than pretty.

In the original version of *The Fly*, the man-fly metamorphosis consisted of a simple swapping (and re-sizing) of heads, and it served as a metaphor for meddling with powers beyond one's control. In Cronenberg's version, the concerns are more philosophical and fundamental. As difficult as it can be to watch, it is equally rewarding.

A teleportation experiment goes deeply wrong for scientist Seth Brundle (Jeff Goldblum). *20th Century Fox/Heritage Auctions*

Seth slowly begins to deteriorate and become less human.
20th Century Fox/Heritage Auctions

An Imperial Star Destroyer approaches the new Death Star in *Star Wars Episode VI - Return of the Jedi.* *LucasFilm/20th Century Fox/Heritage Auctions*

VITAL VIEWING

The films designated "Vital Viewing" are great films that lack the laser-precision of the "Best of the Best" but that are of a far higher level of aesthetic excellence than most filmmakers can reasonably expect to achieve in any given effort. Much like the masterpieces of chapter 1, the films of chapter 2 can be made special by a number of factors, including directorial skill, technical superiority, or visionary conception. These are the films that are executed not quite immaculately, but they nevertheless accomplish their various goals with a thoroughness and impact that is rarely matched.

Most every great film contains at least a competent story along with whatever other merits it has. *Terminator 2* was revolutionary in its special effects, but it also has an action-fueled plot that never seems to let up. *The Thing from Another World* is a fun and frightening monster flick (one of the first ever), but it also tells a tale about the ways mankind responds to unprecedented phenomena. *District 9* is viewed by many as a political allegory, yet its focus on a man's metamorphosis results in a story that is one of science fiction's most heart-rending ever.

The films in this chapter also vary by popularity and recognition. *Moon* had a rather small theatrical release in the United States, but even in a year in which it was up against science fiction behemoths like *Avatar* and *District 9*, it was without a doubt one of the best. *Planet of the Apes*, on the other hand, is a universally acknowledged classic, familiar even to those who haven't seen it. Each of them, however, deserves to be

A startling discovery is made after Riff Raff (Richard O'Brien), left, and Magenta (Patricia Quinn), the domestic help of Dr. Frank-N-Furter (Tim Curry), prepare a meal for guests in *The Rocky Horror Picture Show*. 20th Century Fox/Heritage Auctions

recognized by all lovers of cinema.

Some of these films were directed with an adroit hand (*Dr. Jekyll and Mr. Hyde*, 1931), some are paragons of drama and characterization (*Star Trek II: The Wrath of Khan*), and others are simply a blast to watch (*The Rocky Horror Picture Show*). Many of the "Best of the Best" are so far beyond what most filmmakers can plausibly create that they cannot even be used as benchmarks. Chapter 2's "Vital Viewing" are those movies that filmmakers strive to emulate. Even though they will rarely hit such a high mark, if they come anywhere close they will have a good film.

Dr. Jekyll and Mr. Hyde

YEAR 1931
COUNTRY United States
RUNTIME 1 hr. 38 min.
RATED Not Rated; some mild violence
DIRECTED BY Rouben Mamoulian
WRITTEN BY Samuel Hoffenstein, Percy Heath, Robert Louis Stevenson (source novel)
STARRING Fredric March, Miriam Hopkins, Rose Hobart, Holmes Herbert
SIMILAR SCI-FI *Dr. Jekyll and Mr. Hyde* (1920), *Dr. Jekyll and Mr. Hyde* (1941), *Frankenstein* (1931), *The Invisible Man* (1933)

Brilliant scientist Dr. Jekyll, right, unleashes his dark side as Mr. Hyde. Fredric March plays the dual role. *Paramount Pictures/Heritage Auctions*

Featuring some of science fiction's most playful cinematography as well as one of its creepiest villains, Rouben Mamoulian's take on *Dr. Jekyll and Mr. Hyde* stands as the best adaptation of the Robert Louis Stevenson novel of the same name. This is a story not only of the evil of which man is capable, but of the remorse of a man who sought out science at the cost of love and life.

Dr. Jekyll, a brilliant and inquiring scientist, develops a drug that separates the good half of man from the bad. This way, he argues, the good can excel without its opposing forces holding it down. He fails to consider the consequences of man's evil gaining complete freedom, though, and upon taking the drug is temporarily overcome by his base desires and hideously mutated. Unfortunately, Jekyll also happens to be sexually repressed, so when his id lets loose, there's pretty much only one thing he's after.

The stars of the show are actor Fredric March (who plays both Jekyll and Hyde) and the makeup

department. When the character transforms into Hyde, he takes on an appearance that implies not just depravity but evolutionary regression, and his actions follow suit. This is a man to whom morality is irrelevant, and he seems to relish the unrest he causes as he seeks to fulfill his desires regardless of consequence.

Mr. Hyde is far from the film's only asset, however. The progression of this character whose actions cause him to lose everything provides a dramatic arc to the events, as we genuinely feel sorry for Jekyll each time he wakes up and realizes his life is a little more ruined. Beyond that, the camera work and editing enhance choice moments of the film through cleverly placed foreground objects, symbolic fadeout contrasts, and angular split screens. If we show up to see the main character, we stay because the film as a whole pulls us in.

This adaptation of *Dr. Jekyll and Mr. Hyde* is one of the more carefully made films of its time, even when stacked against powerhouses like the *Frankenstein* films and *The Invisible Man*. It is also relevant because, to a certain degree, these things could happen to us. A moment or two of weakness is all it takes to ruin your life.

The brutish Mr. Hyde advances upon Ivy (Miriam Hopkins). *Paramount Pictures/Heritage Auctions*

"PERHAPS YOU PREFER A GENTLEMAN. ONE OF THOSE FINE-MANNERED AND HONORABLE GENTLEMEN. THOSE PANTING HYPOCRITES WHO LIKE YOUR LEGS BUT TALK ABOUT YOUR GARTERS."
-MR. HYDE

"OH, GOD. THIS I DID NOT INTEND. I SAW A LIGHT BUT DID NOT KNOW WHERE IT WAS HEADED. I HAVE TRESPASSED ON YOUR DOMAIN. I'VE GONE FURTHER THAN MAN SHOULD GO. FORGIVE ME. HELP ME!"
-DR. JEKYLL

The Invisible Man

YEAR 1933
COUNTRY United States
RUNTIME 1 hr. 11 min.
RATED Not Rated; some mild violence
DIRECTED BY James Whale
WRITTEN BY R.C. Sherriff , H.G. Wells (source novel)
STARRING Claude Rains, William Harrigan, Gloria Stuart, Henry Travers
SIMILAR SCI-FI *Bride of Frankenstein*, *Frankenstein*, *The Invisible Man Returns*, *King Kong* (1933)

There are so many things to like about *The Invisible Man*. It has a classic story, a great villain, a pervading humor, and the best special effects of its day. The result is a film that is undeniably fun.

The Invisible Man is a mad scientist film with less emphasis on the science and more on the mad. Dr. Jack Griffin has created a substance that renders its users invisible, and the first person he tests it out on is himself. Unfortunately but not unpredictably, his invisibility has also come with a zealous abandon for the power he now commands as the world's only invisible human. From the moment the movie begins (opening with him already invisible), he is terrorizing the town with the goal of bringing the world under his rule through fear. Lofty aims, perhaps, but you can't blame a guy for dreamin'.

Griffin, played by Claude Rains, might be the most purely evil main character in 1930s science fiction. This is a guy who doesn't hesitate at the thought of shoving an innkeeper down stairs or rolling a man's car off a cliff (with the man in it). Though you don't actually get to *see* much of Rains, his rolling voice dramatizes the evil of his

Dr. Jack Griffin (Claude Rains) reveals his secret to fiancee Flora (Gloria Stuart).
Universal Pictures/Heritage Auctions

Scientist Dr. Jack Griffin discovers how to render himself invisible, at the cost of his sanity. *Paramount Pictures/Heritage Auctions*

dialogue better than anyone else could have done. And with this evil also comes a bit of mischievous humor. It's difficult to do anything but laugh when we see his pants chasing a woman down the road while he happily sings, "Here we go gathering nuts in May!" You can hardly ask for a more entertaining villain.

The most laudable aspect of *The Invisible Man*, however, is its special effects. Though the film was released in 1933, its invisibility effects stand up even against those of modern cinema. Whether you're watching the invisible man unwrap gauze from his head or run around in nothing but a shirt, the effects, for the vast majority of the film, are seamless. There are times when visual tricks are given away by things like wires, but for the most part they are pulled off masterfully.

The Invisible Man is one of the boldest sci-fi films of its era. With this movie, director James Whale dared to give us a nearly irredeemable main character, and he dared to push the bounds of visual effects. He succeeded.

"*I MEDDLED IN THINGS THAT MAN MUST LEAVE ALONE.*"
-THE INVISIBLE MAN

"WATCH THE SKIES!"
-NED "SCOTTY" SCOTT

The Thing from Another World

YEAR 1951
COUNTRY United States
RUNTIME 1 hr. 27 min.
RATED Not Rated; some violence
DIRECTED BY Christian Nyby
WRITTEN BY John W. Campbell, Jr. ("Who Goes There?" source story), Charles Lederer
STARRING Kenneth Tobey, Robert Cornthwaite, Douglas Spencer, James Arness
SIMILAR SCI-FI *20 Million Miles to Earth*, *Alien*, *Creature from the Black Lagoon*, *The Thing*

An Air Force crew and scientists at a remote Arctic research outpost fight the malevolent alien being. *RKO Radio Pictures/Heritage Auctions*

One of the films that kicked off the sci-fi/horror monster craze of the 1950s, *The Thing from Another World* is surprisingly un-reliant upon its monster. This movie offers something more rewarding: a well-paced plot with fully rounded characters. The result is a film not about an unprecedented physical threat but about the ways we respond to such things.

A UFO has crash-landed in the ice near an Antarctic outpost. When the personnel stationed there bring the visitor's ice-encased body back to the facility, one of them accidentally thaws it out by tossing an electric blanket over it (oops). Now an angry plant-creature is loose and is literally hungry for the blood of any animal it comes across, including humans.

The Thing from Another World survives on its script. Its story centers on three characters—a soldier, a reporter, and a scientist—and their

Preceding page: The Thing (James Arness) gets his comeuppance. *RKO Radio Pictures/The Kobal Collection*

differing reactions to this threat (or story, or discovery, depending on the character you're talking about). Indeed the conflicts among these characters comprise more screen time than their conflict with the monster. The military captain's view may be unbalanced as the most reasonable by far, but the core idea is still sound: people bring their own preconceptions and needs to any conflict.

This era of science fiction is known for being hit-or-miss with its monster designs, but even the misses tend to at least be amusing. Such is the case with *The Thing from Another World*. Looking like a human pachyderm that somehow descended from the Frankenstein monster, this creature is one that the filmmakers did well to keep off the screen as much as possible. The fact that it is a plant lends it originality, but it otherwise just looks silly.

The setup of *The Thing from Another World* is similar to that of *Alien*: everyday people confronted with a single, deadly, otherworldly monster. However, whereas *Alien* focuses on the horror of being hunted by something so vicious, *The Thing from Another World*'s primary draw is the character interaction spurred by the monster's presence. It's always refreshing to see a monster film in which the monster is of secondary importance to the characters.

The War of the Worlds

YEAR 1953

COUNTRY United States

RUNTIME 1 hr. 25 min.

RATED G; Martian invasion scenes contain violence

DIRECTED BY Byron Haskin

WRITTEN BY H.G. Wells (source novel); Barré Lyndon

STARRING Gene Barry, Ann Robinson, Les Tremayne, Bob Cornthwaite

SIMILAR SCI-FI *Earth vs. the Flying Saucers*, *The Mysterians*, *War of the Worlds* (2005)

In *The War of the Worlds*, humanity is faced with an attacking alien force that doesn't take the time to hunt us down one-by-one or convert us into mindless automatons. This enemy simply progresses through the civilized world, destroying everything it encounters. By presenting us with this terror, the film is able to achieve a heightened appreciation of life and love.

An alien spacecraft arrives in California, and there is hardly a chance to assess the situation before more of them arrive and begin an all-out invasion of Earth. We follow main character Dr. Clayton Forrester (Gene Barry) while he attempts to evade the aliens and try to find a way to fight them off. However, the situation becomes progressively hopeless. Eventually, even Forrester must give up his fight and simply search for his recently met love, Sylvia Van Buren (Ann Robinson), to spend their final moments together.

Largely through expert use of silence, director Byron Haskin is able to uphold a bleak tension throughout the film. We watch the alien forces float

At left: Dr. Clayton Forrester (Gene Barry) gets caught up in the invasion and fights to find a biological weakness in the aliens. Above: An alien spacecraft doesn't waste time destroying a city. *Paramount Pictures/Heritage Auctions*

through the state of California, emotionlessly demolishing everything in their path, and when the characters find themselves in the way, all they can do is hide, remain quiet, and hope their location doesn't become a target. All attempts to fight back prove futile. Throughout these events, the aliens make no commands, no communication of any sort. They are simply here to destroy us. We don't know why.

The movie's climax is masterful, featuring Forrester running through a Los Angeles overcome with looters and its own rubble, searching for Sylvia not because he thinks he can save her but because he simply wants to be with her for a few more minutes before they die. It is the kind of sequence that will evoke sympathy from even the most hardened viewers.

In a final analysis, it is arguable whether *The War of the Worlds* is an optimistic or pessimistic film. However, it is certain that the bulk of it is downbeat. It puts us through a possibly hopeless scenario so that we can see the overlooked beauty of our world.

"ALL RADIO IS DEAD, WHICH MEANS THAT THESE TAPE RECORDINGS I'M MAKING ARE FOR THE SAKE OF FUTURE HISTORY - IF ANY." *-RADIO ANNOUNCER*

The Gill-man (Ben Chapman) becomes enchanted by beauty Kay Lawrence (Julia Adams) in *Creature from the Black Lagoon.*
Universal Pictures/Heritage Auctions

Creature from the Black Lagoon

YEAR 1954
COUNTRY United States
RUNTIME 1 hr. 19 min.
RATED Not Rated; contains some mild violence
DIRECTED BY Jack Arnold
WRITTEN BY Harry Essex, Arthur A. Ross, Maurice Zimm
STARRING Ricou Browning (uncredited), Richard Carlson, Julia Adams, Richard Denning
SIMILAR SCI-FI *The Creature Walks Among Us*, *Frankenstein* (1931), *King Kong* (1933), *Revenge of the Creature*, *The Thing from Another World*

The Gill-man doesn't enjoy his territory being invaded. *Universal Pictures/Heritage Auctions*

Creature from the Black Lagoon is one of the most classically charming films from science fiction's golden age. It is an adequate "beauty and the beast" tale elevated by its monster, which is one of cinema's greatest creatures to date. Yet, underneath, it is also a story about humanity's apathy toward understanding others.

Following the discovery of a unique fossil, ichthyologists David Reed (Richard Carlson) and Kay Lawrence (Julia Adams), along with their boss, venture deep into the Amazon in search of a creature they determine must be stuck halfway between the evolution of fish to man. The good news is they find it. The bad news is that their aggression toward this "Gill-man" provokes a reaction that will threaten their lives.

We have to ignore an early kill as manufactured mostly for thrills, but once the plot gets rolling, the Gill-man emerges not as bloodthirsty but as misunderstood. This thing is enraptured by the beauty of Kay, but when confronted with hostility on the part of the researchers, he has no choice but to fight them. What ensues is a *King Kong*-esque series of events. This is fitting. Both are innocent creatures lashing out after provocation.

The best thing about this movie is not its story, though. It is the monster. With its scaly body, expanding head gills, and blank eyes, the Gill-man remains one of the best-designed monsters ever. Furthermore, the man inside the suit for the underwater scenes (a bafflingly un-credited Ricou Browning) plays him with a seeming ease that is nothing short of phenomenal. Despite wearing a waterlogged foam rubber suit, Browning moves as gracefully as a Gill-man probably would. Never do we sense that a human is just beneath the skin of the creature.

Though *Creature from the Black Lagoon* will not thrill or frighten modern audiences like it did in its day, it remains a thoroughly entertaining classic and the best swamp monster movie to date. This is the kind of film that is archetypal in its appeal.

"BY STUDYING THESE AND OTHER SPECIES, WE ADD TO OUR KNOWLEDGE OF HOW LIFE EVOLVED, HOW IT ADAPTED ITSELF TO THIS WORLD. WITH THAT KNOWLEDGE, PERHAPS WE CAN TEACH MEN HOW TO ADAPT THEMSELVES TO SOME NEW WORLD OF THE FUTURE." *-LUCAS*

The Curse of Frankenstein

YEAR 1957

COUNTRY United Kingdom

RUNTIME 1 hr. 22 min.

RATED Not Rated; some violence/gore

DIRECTED BY Terence Fisher

WRITTEN BY Jimmy Sangster

STARRING Peter Cushing, Christopher Lee, Robert Urquhart, Hazel Court

SIMILAR SCI-FI *The Evil of Frankenstein*, *Frankenstein* (1931), *Frankenstein and the Monster from Hell*, *Frankenstein Created Woman*, *Frankenstein Must Be Destroyed*, *The Horror of Frankenstein*, *The Revenge of Frankenstein*

Universal's Frankenstein films of the 1930s may always be the best and most famous, but in 1957 the British studio Hammer Film Productions started its own spin on the Frankenstein story with great aesthetic success. Whereas Universal relied heavily on the monster and other visuals to achieve horror, the Hammer films take a more subdued approach. The first of these, *The Curse of Frankenstein*, focuses almost exclusively on Dr. Frankenstein himself and his dedication to achieving his goals through even the most evil of means.

"WE'VE ONLY JUST STARTED. WE'VE JUST OPENED THE DOOR. BUT NOW'S THE TIME TO GO THROUGH THAT DOOR, FIND WHAT LIES BEYOND IT." -BARON FRANKENSTEIN

This movie helped revive gothic horror. *Hammer Film Productions/Heritage Auctions*

The basic Frankenstein story is intact here. Victor Frankenstein, a genius by any standard, has dared to seek out the scientific basis of life. Eventually, he is able to apply that knowledge to a corpse and create a living

Baron Victor Frankenstein (Peter Cushing) puts his scientific powers to use to create his own creature (Christopher Lee). *Hammer Film Productions/Heritage Auctions*

being out of it. However, in order to perfect this creation, he is going to have to commit some, shall we say, unsavory acts, and he won't be immune to a few problems afterward.

Peter Cushing, in the role of Baron Frankenstein, perfectly portrays a man who is simultaneously refined and willing to get his hands dirty. He is so refined, in fact, and so dedicated to his work that his character retains a certain appeal even after he begins doing things like murdering innocents in his quest to perfect his newfound scientific powers. Though we condemn his actions,

we still admire this man who is willing to do anything to achieve greatness. That's the trick of *The Curse of Frankenstein*; it demonstrates our readiness to forgive the most heinous acts if they are committed by an alluring and magnetic individual on the path to perfection. It is not until the film nears its end that we begin to view the character as, though intelligent, an unhinged madman.

The Curse of Frankenstein illustrates the ease with which noble mannerisms can draw our attention away from immorality and is bookended with a depiction of the depravity that can hide beneath a cultivated façade. Here's the catch, though: it's not uncommon to find yourself retaining a hint of admiration for Baron Frankenstein even after the credits roll. That might be the scariest thing about the film.

Village of the Damned

YEAR 1960
COUNTRY United Kingdom
RUNTIME 1 hr. 17 min.
RATED Not Rated; creepy kids may spook parents
DIRECTED BY Wolf Rilla
WRITTEN BY Wolf Rilla, Stirling Silliphant
STARRING George Sanders, Barbara Shelley, Martin Stephens, Laurence Naismith
SIMILAR SCI-FI *Children of the Damned*, *These Are the Damned*

"PEOPLE, ESPECIALLY CHILDREN, AREN'T MEASURED BY THEIR IQ. WHAT'S IMPORTANT ABOUT THEM IS WHETHER THEY'RE GOOD OR BAD, AND THESE CHILDREN ARE BAD."
-ALAN BERNARD

Mysterious tow-headed children share a spooky connection and sinister plan.
Metro-Goldwyn-Mayer/The Kobal Collection

It's the sci-fi lover's *Lord of the Flies*. *Village of the Damned* tells the story of a group of children who, through mysterious cosmic circumstances, acquire great powers of the mind. With their young age affording them such little restraint, they begin to present quite a threat to those around them, and as their powers grow and grow, there is less and less the adults of the town can do to control the children.

For no discernible reason, everyone in the village of Midwich, England, suddenly falls unconscious one day. When they wake up, all the women of childbearing age are pregnant; however, these immaculate conceptions turn out to be anything but divine. When the children are born, the first thing everyone notices is that they are incredibly healthy and intelligent. The second thing is that these kids have the ability to read minds and make people do horrible things. Unfortunately, they are also quick to hold a grudge. Before long, the entire town is at the mercy of a handful of grade-schoolers. Can you imagine a worse scenario?

Children wore padded wigs to give the impression of larger heads. *Metro-Goldwyn-Mayer/Heritage Auctions*

Village of the Damned contains fears that may be more socially relevant than we would like to think, focusing on the horror of children. While the children in this movie are hyper-intelligent and at least somewhat sadistic, they also share some fundamental similarities with your everyday child: they are soft-spoken with occasional outbursts, have little understanding of morality, and are, above all, unpredictable. You want to believe that they are purely innocent beings, as do some of the film's adult characters, but when they glare at you after you do something to upset them (and I'm not even talking about the glowing eyes), you have to assume the thoughts they harbor are sinister. When they do begin lashing out, you can't help but wonder how truly innocent any given child may be.

Ever the eerie film, *Village of the Damned* opts for an ending that is haunting rather than uplifting. It is not here to frighten us momentarily but to plant a single seed of fear that causes us to question the assumptions we want to hold dear. It discovers a well of horror in a place we rarely think to look.

Planet of the Apes

YEAR 1968
COUNTRY United States
RUNTIME 1 hr. 52 min.
RATED Not Rated; some violence, mild language
DIRECTED BY Franklin J. Schaffner
WRITTEN BY Pierre Boulle (source novel), Michael Wilson, Rod Serling
STARRING Charlton Heston, Roddy McDowall, Kim Hunter, Maurice Evans
SIMILAR SCI-FI *Beneath the Planet of the Apes*, *Escape from the Planet of the Apes*, *Forbidden Planet*, *Planet of the Apes* (2001), *Star Trek IV: The Voyage Home*

Planet of the Apes is famous for two things: its final twist and its imagining of a world in which monkeys rule society and keep humans as animals. Nowadays, it can likewise be easy to view the film as a simplistic "Think about *that*" story. More broadly, however, *Planet of the Apes* is about the relativity of truth—even those truths we deem sacred.

The title says it all. A small crew of space explorers finds themselves on a planet run by intellectually evolved apes. The planet's humans, on the other hand, are of animal-like intelligence and live in the wild. When these apes discover Taylor (Charlton Heston), a human who can speak (!), they deem him a freak of nature and refuse to grant him the rights afforded the planet's intelligent species. When Taylor goes to trial to prove his intelligence, the upstanding members of society are ready to pull out their skewed notions of science, religion, and logic to demonstrate otherwise.

Animal psychologist Zira (Kim Hunter), right, and her fiance Cornelius (Roddy McDowell) take an interest in astronaut George Taylor (Charlton Heston) after he crash lands on their planet. *20th Century Fox/The Kobal Collection*

Specifically, *Planet of the Apes* is concerned with the difficulty of accepting truths that contradict established beliefs, even when those truths arrive with indisputable proof. This concept comes into play even before the apes appear, when a fellow crew member expresses doubt concerning the notion that the passage of time is altered when one approaches the speed of light. The truth-rejection idea then comes to the forefront when Taylor is placed in captivity, only to be treated like an animal, laughed at when he attempts to communicate, and eventually ruled unintelligent and ordered lobotomized. If the apes were to give in to the notion that Taylor is an intelligent being, everything they believe would be wrong.

We tend to overlook the other side of the story, though. Similar to the apes' rejection of Taylor, Taylor can hardly bring himself to believe that the apes are evolutionarily advanced beings. When he refers to one of his captors as a "damn dirty ape," for instance, it seems he does so more out of disdain for their dominion than for their mistreatment of humans. Just as the apes cannot accept the idea of an intelligent human, Taylor cannot accept the idea of apes controlling the world.

Some consider *Planet of the Apes* to be camp. Actually, it only looks like camp. In its examination of the vigor with which we fight to hold off truths that upset society, this film also highlights the absurdity of believing that the truths of any given society are absolute.

"IT'S A MAD HOUSE! A MAD HOUSE!"
-GEORGE TAYLOR

Tim Curry gives a tour-de-force performance as the magnetic Dr. Frank-N-Furter in *The Rocky Horror Picture Show*. *20th Century Fox/Heritage Auctions*

"HOT PATOOTIE, BLESS MY SOUL, I REALLY LOVE THAT ROCK-AND-ROLL!" -EDDIE

The Rocky Horror Picture Show

YEAR 1975
COUNTRY United Kingdom; United States
RUNTIME 1 hr. 40 min.
RATED R; adult situations, adult language, mild violence, brief nudity
DIRECTED BY Jim Sharman
WRITTEN BY Richard O'Brien, Jim Sharman
STARRING Tim Curry, Susan Sarandon, Barry Bostwick, Richard O'Brien, Peter Hinwood
SIMILAR SCI-FI *The American Astronaut, Ed Wood, The Hitchhiker's Guide to the Galaxy, Young Frankenstein*

Janet (Susan Sarandon), Brad (Barry Bostwick), Rocky (Peter Hinwood) and Dr. Scott (Jonathan Adams) lose some of their inhibitions. *20th Century Fox/Heritage Auctions*

The Rocky Horror Picture Show is so caught up in simply having a great time that it's easy to think of it as something other than a science fiction film. When we return to this rock-and-roll musical, though, the opening theme song, directly referencing movies from *The Invisible Man* to *Forbidden Planet*, quickly reminds us of the genre in which it lies. This is a movie that sci-fi fans are lucky to be able to claim as at least partially theirs, because few other films allow us to experience such gleeful abandon.

An engaged couple, Brad and Janet (Barry Bostwick and Susan Sarandon), find themselves at the door of a mansion in the woods after their car breaks down in the rain. When they enter said mansion, they enter a world secluded from the rules and morals of civilization. It is a place where visitors revel in decadent pursuits of all types. It's the home of a mad scientist, Dr. Frank-N-Furter, who some would consider evil but who is actually just perfectly uninhibited—and who also happens to be the most charismatic transvestite ever to hit the screen.

It's the combination of the Frank-N-Furter character and the music that makes *Rocky Horror* the cult classic that it is. Tim Curry plays Frank-N-Furter with such magnetism that he transcends the character's own transgressive nature, becoming one who isn't so much breaking rules as he is existing beyond them. As he commits these acts that would otherwise be considered deviant, those actions are accompanied by musical numbers that, along with being some of the catchiest in all of cinema, evoke an inexorable feeling of rapture, as if this yielding to decadence results in a glee that could never be matched.

Unsurprisingly, however, this decadence cannot be sustained. In the end, Frank-N-Furter's abandon is put to a stop, at which point the film nearly crashes to its conclusion. We don't learn precisely what becomes of the main characters because there is no moral to be found here. Just like Brad and Janet, the viewer is simply allowed to revel in a momentary loss of inhibition. And some appropriately rockin' music is there to accompany the experience.

Close Encounters of the Third Kind

YEAR 1977

COUNTRY United States

RUNTIME 2 hrs. 12 min.

RATED PG; has some mildly frightening moments

DIRECTED BY Steven Spielberg

WRITTEN BY Steven Spielberg

STARRING Richard Dreyfuss, François Truffant, Bob Balaban, Melinda Dillon

SIMILAR SCI-FI *2001: A Space Odyssey, CJ7, Cocoon, The Day the Earth Stood Still* (1951), *E.T.: The Extra-Terrestrial, Super 8*

While investigating a power outage, Roy Neary's (Richard Dreyfuss) truck stalls and he's bathed in a bright light from above. Soon after, he starts having strange visions.
Columbia/Heritage Auctions

Generally speaking, Steven Spielberg favors the idea of affable aliens over maleficent ones. This is true with *E.T.: The Extra-Terrestrial*, and it was true five years earlier with *Close Encounters of the Third Kind*. In this earlier film, his first directorial effort in the sci-fi genre, Spielberg imagines aliens as amicable beings who want to take something of a parental role toward our race.

All over the world, strange things are happening. Ships and World War II planes are showing up in the desert. Pilots are spotting unexplained vessels in the sky. Main character Roy Neary (Richard Dreyfuss) outright sees a handful of UFOs racing along Indiana roads. After he and a few others begin experiencing visions of a strange mountain, they eventually head to the place where they have discovered that the aliens plan to land, but first they have to get through the government's cover-up operation.

The payoff of *Close Encounters of the Third Kind* lies primarily in its final act, when we meet the alien visitors. The majestically designed UFOs and the score that suggests a great, unprecedented experience convey a sense of awe that must be similar to what you would feel in such a situation. Amazingly, Spielberg manages to sustain this awe for roughly twenty minutes of screen time.

Throughout the film, the human race is depicted as an infantile one, not so much in a condescending or critical way as in a loving way. When the aliens arrive, they communicate to us via musical tones and colored lights, which the human reception party (i.e. the government) repeats to them via synthesizer and light board. As the aliens produce various musical phrases, our reiteration of them is like a child repeating words spoken by parents. We don't quite know what we're saying back; we're just happy to be communicating. The government's attempted cover-up of the aliens' arrival can be viewed in the same way. Just like children, they are wary of letting

Aliens make contact. Rather than treating the aliens as warmongering monsters, the movie presents them as peaceful beings. *Columbia/The Kobal Collection*

others be involved in their fun.

Close Encounters of the Third Kind can be slow at times, as it is primarily geared toward setting up its finale, but there is fun and tension to be had in the meantime (such as one home invasion by the aliens), and the payoff is well worth it. Spielberg's first sci-fi film remains one of the genre's greats.

Star Trek II: The Wrath of Khan

YEAR 1982

COUNTRY United States

RUNTIME 1 hr. 56 min.

RATED PG; violence and language

DIRECTED BY Nicholas Meyer

WRITTEN BY Harve Bennet, Jack B. Sowards

STARRING William Shatner, Ricardo Montalban, Leonard Nimoy, DeForest Kelley

SIMILAR SCI-FI *Star Trek III: The Search for Spock*, *Star Trek IV: The Voyage Home*, *Star Wars: Episode V – The Empire Strikes Back*

A scene in which William Shatner yells "Khaaaaaaaaaan!" has become a running in-joke with fans. *Paramount*

Following a lackluster first cinematic installment, the writers of *Star Trek II: The Wrath of Khan* turned to one of the best villains of *Star Trek's* original series, Khan Noonien Singh, to fuel the second *Trek* movie. What resulted is arguably still the best entry in a film franchise that now has over ten parts.

Set years after the adventures of the original *Star Trek* series, *The Wrath of Khan* returns once again to the classic characters of the show's first run—namely, James T. Kirk (William Shatner), Spock (Leonard Nimoy), and Dr. Leonard McCoy (DeForest Kelley)—and presents them with a demon from the past. Khan (Ricardo Montalban), who Kirk once left stranded on a deserted planet after the former tried to take over the *USS Enterprise*, is back and ready for revenge. Considering he is one of the few men alive who is able to rival Kirk's leadership and ingenuity, that's a big deal.

Khan's presence, along with an unrelated familial revelation concerning Kirk, represents our inability to escape the past. Kirk had long forgotten about Khan, one of the most dangerous threats he ever faced, but the enemy is back and once again poses an immediate threat. His resurfacing also accomplishes something more interesting than its symbolic implications, though. At this point in the main characters' lives, they are in higher roles of leadership, but those roles do not seem to fit their core personalities. They've accepted the roles because they are promotions, not because they allow them to do what they do best. When Khan arrives, he presents such a threat that he seems to knock them back into place, as, in their response, they effactually assume the positions for which they were once so famous. It is as if Khan is so dangerous that his presence forces them to return to their true selves to have any chance of defeating him.

The character dynamic between the bold Kirk, the logic-ruled Spock, and the sardonic McCoy has always been a staple of the original series, and it is as present here as ever. In one scene, a character's convictions are tested in a way that leads to one of the most dramatic moments in *Star Trek* history and that accounts for much of the reason that this film is so loved. This makes the movie rewarding not only for its overarching themes, but for its ongoing effect on the characters.

Naturally, *The Wrath of Khan* will be best appreciated by *Trek* fans, but it supplies all the background information needed—without becoming overtly expository—for anyone to follow its story and grasp its importance. This is a story that could be told in any franchise. With the *Star Trek* mythology, though, it finds the characters that maximize its payoff.

"THE NEEDS OF THE MANY OUTWEIGH THE NEEDS OF THE FEW." -SPOCK

Khan (Ricardo Montalban) doesn't play nice with Mr. Chekov (Walter Koenig), Capt. Clark Terrell (Paul Winfield), and the rest of the *USS Enterprise* crew.
Paramount/The Kobal Collection

Star Wars: Episode VI - Return of the Jedi

YEAR 1983
COUNTRY United States
RUNTIME 2 hrs. 15 min.
RATED PG; sci-fi action and violence
DIRECTED BY Richard Marquand
WRITTEN BY George Lucas, Lawrence Kasdan
STARRING Mark Hamill, Harrison Ford, Carrie Fisher, James Earl Jones
SIMILAR SCI-FI *Star Wars, Star Wars: Episode V – The Empire Strikes Back*

Thematic arcs of the Star Wars story, including the eternal battle between good - Luke Skywalker (Mark Hamill) - and bad - Darth Vader (David Prowse) - reach a conclusion in *Return of the Jedi*.
Lucasfilm/20th Century Fox/Heritage Auctions

The final entry of the original *Star Wars* trilogy (episodes IV-VI), *Star Wars: Episode VI - Return of the Jedi*, is frequently thought of as the weakest of the three, if not downright bad. However, most complaints are leveled at one or two aspects of the film. Aside from these missteps, *Return of the Jedi* stays true to the *Star Wars* franchise, and its overall story arcs to the most appropriate conclusion George Lucas could have brought to the saga. This is a tale of redemption played out in the most dynamic mythology of our time.

After suffering blow after blow by Darth Vader and the Galactic Empire in *The Empire Strikes Back*, Luke Skywalker (Mark Hamill) and the other characters have regrouped and are ready to once again take on the evil that controls the galaxy. This is going to be a difficult task, considering Han Solo (Harrison Ford) needs to be rescued from carbonite freezing, and the Empire is building a new Death Star. Luckily, Luke has become a Jedi knight, and

The strike team's command crew aboard the stolen Imperial shuttle Tydirium. *Lucasfilm/20th Century Fox/Heritage Auctions*

the Rebels are more organized than ever.

Return of the Jedi wraps up every thematic arc of the *Star Wars* story, namely those of redemption, maturation, and the eternal battle between good and evil. As it does so, it also provides much more straight-up action than *Empire Strikes Back*, which was a more dramatic work. Beginning with a great show of heroism from Luke, the movie continues with a thirst for adventure until it culminates in one of the series' best space battles and an emotional final duel between Luke and Vader, who Luke is not so much trying to defeat as he is trying to save from the Dark Side. The stakes are not only galactic. They are familial.

The common complaint against *Jedi* is its inclusion of a race of creature that Han, Leia (Carrie Fisher), and a Rebel ground force meet while trying to destroy the Death Star's shield generator on a nearby forest moon—the Ewoks. These cute, furry, teddy bear-like creatures really don't belong in *Star Wars* and tend to detract from the installment's otherwise serious tone, especially when they begin taking down fully armed Imperial forces with primitive bows and arrows. However, despite the Ewoks' implausibility, their presence as an unlikely but necessary ally does coincide with one of *Star Wars*' major themes. There's no denying that they could have been replaced with a race of creature that fit the theme without producing a tonal speed bump, but they aren't the movie-killer that many deem them to be.

If *Return of the Jedi* is in any way disappointing, it is only by comparison to its predecessors. It is a continually kinetic sci-fi action/adventure film filled with the charm that made *Star Wars* so popular. It has its imperfections, but they are merely blemishes on an otherwise exciting and emotional experience.

NEVER. I'LL NEVER TURN TO THE DARK SIDE. YOU HAVE FAILED, YOUR HIGHNESS. I AM A JEDI. LIKE MY FATHER BEFORE ME. -LUKE SKYWALKER

The Terminator

YEAR 1984
COUNTRY United States
RUNTIME 1 hr. 48 min.
RATED R; violence, language, some sexuality
DIRECTED BY James Cameron
WRITTEN BY James Cameron, Gale Anne Hurd, William Wisher Jr.
STARRING Arnold Schwarzenegger, Linda Hamilton, Michael Biehn, Paul Winfield
SIMILAR SCI-FI *Aliens, RoboCop, Terminator 2: Judgment Day, Terminator 3: Rise of the Machines, Terminator Salvation*

Often considered James Cameron's warm-up effort for his smash hit *Terminator 2: Judgment Day*, *The Terminator* is actually a great sci-fi action film in its own right and in some ways is superior to its successor. It is filled with action, but it also presents a story that is mythological in scope. This is a film about the interruption of everyday life by godlike forces.

Sarah Connor (Linda Hamilton) is an everywoman. She grinds a thankless job, copes with equally thankless male interests, and otherwise just tries to get through life in as non-tedious a way as she can. That all changes drastically when she is suddenly hunted by an android called a Terminator (Arnold Schwarzenegger), which has traveled back through time with the sole purpose of killing her. But another soldier from the future, Kyle Reese (Michael Biehn), has come to protect her, and the two of them discover that Sarah is much more resilient than anyone would have thought.

The Terminator is different from many sci-fi action movies in that the focus is not on the action

Beneath the Terminator's seemingly human exterior lies a metal skeleton. This special effect wowed audiences at the time. *Orion/The Kobal Collection*

itself but on a story that happens to require heavy use of action sequences. When we watch Kyle battle the Terminator throughout Los Angeles, we don't see amazing physical stunts so much as we see two inexorable forces fighting amidst a city that has essentially become their playground. The film becomes a metaphor for the uncontrollable forces of the world and for what those forces can reveal about us.

The film's visual effects are nothing special by modern standards but for their day were simply awesome. Never before had we seen an evil metal skeleton peeking from beneath human flesh. And the naked metal robot itself was as realistic and ominous as any such cinematic creation could be. Schwarzenegger is certainly partially to thank for the greatness of the android, but the special effects team and Stan Winston's legendary design skills are what lend the killer robot its terrifying verisimilitude.

The Terminator tells the story of an ordinary woman who is ripped from the everyday concerns of modern life and plunged into a battle of dueling gods. It foregoes complexity in favor of confident simplicity. This is a classic among sci-fi action films, and, though its sequel was bigger and flashier, the original retains a fundamental, almost primordial appeal.

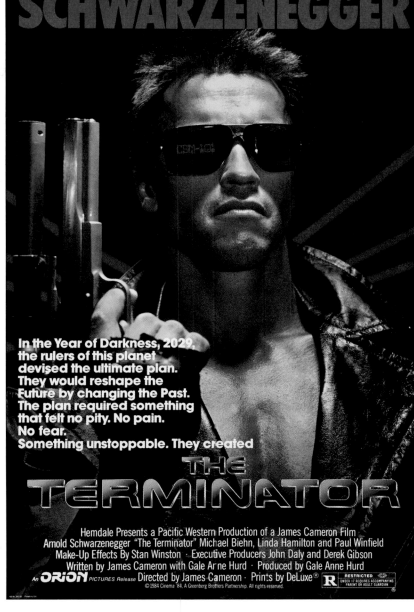

Though not expected to be, the movie was a commercial and critical success and launched the careers of James Cameron and Arnold Schwarzenegger.
Orion/Heritage Auctions

Aliens

YEAR 1986
COUNTRY United States
RUNTIME 2 hrs. 17 min.
RATED R; strong creature violence, gore, terror, language
DIRECTED BY James Cameron
WRITTEN BY James Cameron, David Giler, Walter Hill
STARRING Sigourney Weaver, Carrie Henn, Michael Biehn, Paul Reiser
SIMILAR SCI-FI *28 Weeks Later*, *Alien*, *Alien 3*, *Alien: Resurrection*, *Predator*, *The Thing*

Ridley Scott's *Alien* relied on the mystery of its extraterrestrial monster to instill horror, but James Cameron took a different approach in his sequel, *Aliens*. Instead of hiding a monster in ducts and corridors for it to sneak around and pick off people one-by-one, Cameron goes all-out, bombarding his characters with waves of the things. The resulting film is not so much sci-fi/horror as it is sci-fi/thriller with select horrifying moments, and it remains one of the most breathtaking experiences in science fiction cinema.

At the end of *Alien*, Ripley (Sigourney Weaver) secures herself in a cryogenic escape pod to escape the alien threat. Fast forward fifty-seven years, and her pod, in which she has been safely preserved, is finally discovered by a deep-space salvage team. It is not long after her discovery and reawakening that the company for which she works loses contact with a colony they have established. Here's the kicker: that colony is on the very planet on which the alien was originally discovered. After some coercion involving her job security, Ripley agrees to accompany a team of marines back to LV-426 to

Ripley faces down the alien queen. *20th Century Fox/The Kobal Collection*

find out what happened. Any guesses?

Cameron wisely begins the action on LV-426 by showing us what happens to those who are caught by the creatures. When we see a woman wrapped in a slimy, sinuous cocoon whispering, "Kill me," we gain an immediate desperation for the main characters' survival. From there, the film breaks into episode after episode of mayhem, including several sequences in which aliens launch all-out assaults, a scene in which Ripley and a young girl are stuck in a room with a facehugger, and a showdown between Ripley and a queen alien. The film is relentless in its onslaught of bloody (and highly acidic) alien action.

Sigourney Weaver's Academy Award nomination for Best Actress was considered a milestone for the science fiction genre. *20th Century Fox/ Heritage Auctions*

"THAT'S IT! GAME OVER, MAN! GAME OVER! WHAT THE F**K ARE WE GONNA DO NOW? WHAT ARE WE GONNA DO?" -PRIVATE HUDSON

Though it's not the masterpiece that its predecessor is (Cameron demonstrates a weakness for military clichés that never lets up throughout the film), *Aliens* is extremely effective in what it sets out to do. This head-on approach to the threat first imagined by the creators of *Alien* results in a work so intense that when the credits hit, all you can do is sit back in your seat and collect yourself.

Terminator 2: Judgment Day

YEAR 1991
COUNTRY United States
RUNTIME 2 hrs. 17 min.
RATED R; strong sci-fi action/violence, language
DIRECTED BY James Cameron
WRITTEN BY James Cameron, William Wisher Jr.
STARRING Arnold Schwarzenegger, Linda Hamilton, Edward Furlong, Robert Patrick
SIMILAR SCI-FI *Aliens, The Terminator, Terminator 3: Rise of the Machines, Terminator Salvation, Transformers*

The first *Terminator* was an action film made great by its combination of originality and structure. In this first sequel, the most famous entry in the franchise, writer/director James Cameron opts to improve upon what he's already demonstrated works so well. Instead of taking a different approach with *Terminator 2: Judgment Day*, Cameron simply multiplies the original formula exponentially. The result is a kick-ass sci-fi action film.

John Connor (Edward Furlong), the future leader of the military resistance, has been born and is in his teenage years, and the T-800 robot from the original film (Arnold Schwarzenegger) is back. The good news is that this time the T-800 is a good guy, reprogrammed by the resistance to protect Connor. The bad news is that there's a better and badder Terminator, too, and that's the bad guy. Macho stuff ensues.

The film doesn't stand out so much today for its special effects, but, in typical Cameron fashion, it was a special effects breakthrough for its time. This is mostly because of the new Terminator, the T-1000 (Robert Patrick), which is made of liquid

"THE UNKNOWN FUTURE ROLLS TOWARD US. I FACE IT FOR THE FIRST TIME WITH A SENSE OF HOPE, BECAUSE IF A MACHINE, A TERMINATOR, CAN LEARN THE VALUE OF HUMAN LIFE ... MAYBE WE CAN TOO." -SARAH CONNOR

In the future, the machines have their day. *Carolco/The Kobal Collection*

metal. As such, its physical shape is alterable, and it recovers from virtually any type of wound by simply reforming. One particularly impressive moment involves the T-1000 being shattered to pieces…which then melt into liquid, join together, and reform as the whole robot.

What makes *T2* so good, though, is not the special effects themselves but the way they are used. Shotgun blasts to the T-1000's face result in a split head and torso, waving semi-limply before regaining human form. For weapons, this new machine can freely alter its limbs into whatever it wants (it seems to have a penchant for giant blades). Schwarzenegger as

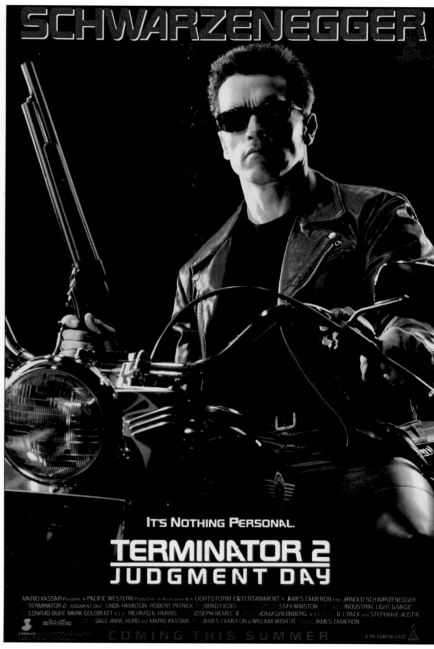

the T-800 gets plenty of spotlight, too. One memorable scene has him removing the skin on his arm with a knife in order to reveal his robot self beneath. Of course, he also gets to shoot a lot of people while taking bullets to the face and torso.

Don't expect a deep character study when you watch *T2*. The story here is a sound one, but it exists almost exclusively to support the action. When the action's as good as this, though, that is just fine.

Terminator 2 has been influential in the genres of action and science fiction, and has had an impact on pop culture. *Carolco/Heritage Auctions*

Dark City

YEAR 1998
COUNTRY Australia, United States
RUNTIME 1 hr. 51 min.
RATED R; violent images, some sexuality
DIRECTED BY Alex Proyas
WRITTEN BY Alex Proyas, Lem Dobbs, David S. Goyer
STARRING Rufus Sewell, Kiefer Sutherland, Jennifer Connelly, William Hurt, Richard O'Brien
SIMILAR SCI-FI *Blade Runner*, *Forbidden Planet*, *Knowing*, *The Matrix*, *Solaris* (1972)

Dark City takes a postmodern idea and treats it with classic film-noir style. It presents to us a world in which nothing is certain, and even typically concrete truths are nebulous. This is an exploration of the possibility that everything we know is false.

This move tells the story of a man named John Murdoch (Rufus Sewell), who wakes up in a hotel bathtub with a murdered woman in his room and no memory of who he is, save for some brief flashes of personal history that flame up in his mind. As he searches for his own identity and attempts to find out what happened to him, he gradually discovers something horrible: he, everyone else in the city, and the physical city itself are under the control of a race of aliens that appear as pale, floating humans called Strangers.

The best thing about *Dark City* is its way of chipping away at reality until we come to learn the fragility of every truth we take for granted. Murdoch discovers that the aliens, unbeknownst to those in the city, regularly alter reality in even the most implausible ways in order to find a point of constancy in the human psyche. He then, desperate to find an iota of

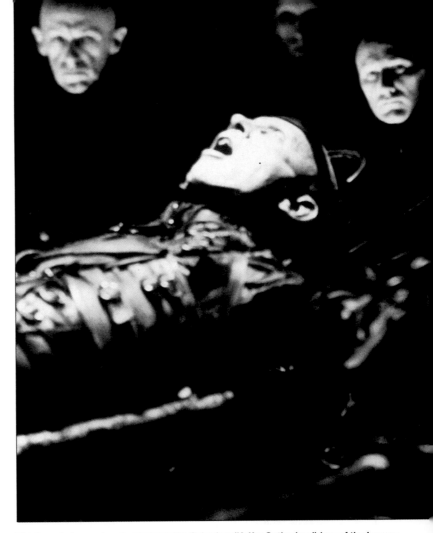

The knowledge and understanding Dr. Schreber (Keifer Sutherland) has of the human mind is valuable to the Strangers. *New Line Cinema/The Kobal Collection/Jasin Boland*

truth in his life, his past, or his sense of self, sets out to discover who he really, at one point, was. From this beginning as a search for one's own identity, the film turns into a search for any kind of absolute truth.

There is one recurring image in *Dark City*, and it sums up the film as a whole: a spiral. It circles in and in on itself until it stops at a pinpoint. Such is the nature of Murdoch's investigation. In a subtle development at the very end of the film, he discovers that there is but one tiny reality to be found at the core of everything. But that would be a spoiler to tell.

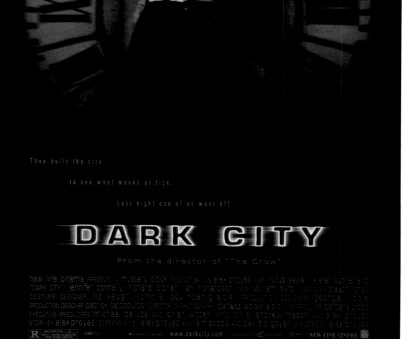

*"THE ONLY PLACE HOME
EXISTS IS IN YOUR HEAD."*
-DR. DANIEL SCHREBER

In the years since its release, *Dark City* has become a cult classic.
New Line Cinema/Heritage Auctions

28 Days Later

YEAR 2002
COUNTRY United Kingdom
RUNTIME 1 hr. 53 min.
RATED R; strong violence/gore, nudity, language
DIRECTED BY Danny Boyle
WRITTEN BY Alex Garland
STARRING Cillian Murphy, Naomie Harris, Brendan Gleeson, Megan Burns
SIMILAR SCI-FI *28 Weeks Later*, *The Crazies* (1973), *The Crazies* (2010), *Day of the Dead*

Generally speaking, the fast and furious zombies of today's cinema are the result of the mislead belief that since *fast* is more intense than *slow*, *fast* is also scarier or otherwise better than *slow*. Those with the slightest familiarity with the George Romero-era of the zombie genre know otherwise. However, in *28 Days Later*, director Danny Boyle manages to imbue his zombies with speed in an effective way. Boyle's zombies are sprinters because they are not so much undead as they are overcome with a pure lust for violence, designed so by the director and his writer in order to create one of the most perilous scenarios imaginable.

Researchers in London have identified the gene that causes us to commit acts of violence and, for

"YOU WERE THINKING THAT YOU'LL NEVER HEAR ANOTHER PIECE OF ORIGINAL MUSIC EVER AGAIN. YOU'LL NEVER READ A BOOK THAT HASN'T ALREADY BEEN WRITTEN OR SEE A FILM THAT HASN'T ALREADY BEEN SHOT." -SELENA

Jim (Cillian Murphy), left, and other survivors are lured to what they think is safety by Major Henry West (Christopher Eccleston). *DNA/Figment/Fox*

testing purposes, have isolated it in a virus called "Rage." On the cusp of the scientists' discovery of a way to block this gene, however, a group of animal rights extremists breaks into their lab, releases their Rhesus monkeys, and thus releases the Rage virus upon the world. Those who become infected turn into mindlessly furious and bloodthirsty zombies (think rabies multiplied by a million). The film follows a group of survivors as they search for a haven unaffected by the plague.

As the characters traverse this world overrun with beings whose sole intent is to kill every living thing they see, *28 Days Later* makes a surprising discovery: the world is a fundamentally beautiful place. We see this at near-regular intervals. Practically every time the characters are able to rest from fleeing the infected, their interaction becomes caring, happy, and even playful. The film's frequent shots of various aspects of the practically empty world contribute to this philosophical discovery. It seems that everything, from wind turbines to fields of horses, has a distinct beauty.

The second half of the movie examines the antithesis to viewing the world as an end in itself rather than a place simply to perpetuate life. At this point the characters find themselves at the mercy of an isolated society based purely on survivalism, and their existence becomes miserable. This reinforces the film's conclusion that the Earth is meant to be appreciated for what it is, not for how we can exploit it and its inhabitants. To view it in such a way is to confine ourselves to a hell.

28 Days Later is consistently frightening, but it is consistently optimistic as well. It just so happens that its search for beauty requires a confrontation of the ugly. Horrible things can happen to the world, but the world always remains a good place.

Jim runs for his life from one of the infected. *DNA/Figment/Fox/The Kobal Collection/ Peter Mountain*

Eternal Sunshine of the Spotless Mind

YEAR 2004

COUNTRY United States

RUNTIME 1 hr. 48 min.

RATED R; language, sexual content

DIRECTED BY Michel Gondry

WRITTEN BY Charlie Kaufman, Michel Gondry, Pierre Bismuth

STARRING Jim Carrey, Kate Winslet, Mark Ruffalo, Tom Wilkinson

SIMILAR SCI-FI *Dark City*, *Solaris* (1972), *Source Code*

"ARE WE THOSE BORED COUPLES YOU FEEL SORRY FOR IN RESTAURANTS? ARE WE THE DINING DEAD?" -JOEL BARISH

Surreal in execution and sci-fi in concept, *Eternal Sunshine of the Spotless Mind* is one of those movies that you can't help but to love. In fact, that is part of what *Eternal Sunshine* is about—our helplessness when it comes to trying to escape our strongest feelings. Despite a whimsical premise and style, this movie is grounded in emotion, making it accessible for anyone regardless of whether their proclivities lie in the fantastic or the ordinary.

When the introverted and socially awkward Joel Barish (Jim Carrey) meets a blue-haired woman, Clementine (Kate Winslet), he finds a happiness he has seldom known. One day during an argument, however, he says some hurtful things, and from that point on, Clementine acts as if she literally does not recognize who he is. Joel soon learns that she had her memories of him erased through a doctor that specializes in such procedures, Dr. Mierzwiak (Tom Wilkinson). Joel in turn goes in for the same procedure, but while the process is underway he changes his mind. Unconscious but dreaming while the doctors remove memories from his brain, Joel tries to find a way to hide Clementine among his other memories. Even if the procedure is successful, though, might they fall back in love if they were to meet again?

It's not the love story or the pseudo-surrealism of Joel's journey through his memories that makes *Eternal Sunshine* special; it's the combination of the two. A peculiar sense of urgency arises when, for instance, we see Joel explaining his past actions to his memory of Clementine while the house around them falls apart, being deleted by the scientists performing the procedure. When Joel reveals his darkest memories to dream-Clementine so that she can hide in them, the combination of humor (Joel reliving his childhood memories as an adult) and humiliation (at revealing such secrets even to a dream entity) evokes a feeling of intimacy so strong that the deepest insecurities can be accepted. Perhaps it is through a reliving of memories that love can be best illustrated.

Though it presents a plot twist or two even while it attempts to mold the dream world into a semi-cohesive plain of reality, *Eternal Sunshine* is almost always coherent. That alone is an achievement. When the plot does stray into obscure territory, the film's focus on love keeps the core story relatable and moving. This film is not nearly as difficult to follow as it could have been, but that is just an additional benefit. Its dedication to emotion is its reason for existing, and it exhibits that dedication all the way through.

As his memories of Clementine (Kate Winslet) start to unravel, Joel (Jim Carrey) does everything he can to try and save them. *Focus Features/The Kobal Collection/David Lee*

Children of Men

YEAR 2006
COUNTRY United Kingdom, United States, Japan
RUNTIME 1 hr. 49 min.
RATED R; strong violence, language, brief nudity
DIRECTED BY Alfonso Cuarón
WRITTEN BY P.D. James (source novel), Alfonso Cuarón, Timothy J. Sexton, David Arata, Mark Fergus, Hawk Ostby
STARRING Clive Owen, Julianne Moore, Clare-Hope Ashitey, Michael Caine
SIMILAR SCI-FI *28 Days Later, 28 Weeks Later, A Clockwork Orange, Fahrenheit 451*

A British bureaucrat (Clive Owen) becomes the protector of Kee (Clare-Hope Ashitey), a woman who holds the secret to continuing life. *Universal/UIP/The Kobal Collection/Jaap Buitendijk*

The world is ending. The U.K. is the only world power still standing, and it has descended into a police state. There is hardly a happy moment to be found in *Children of Men*, aside from select uses of art and music that seem to momentarily wash sadness away. This film is about the terror of seeking hope in a dismal world.

In the year 2027 humanity has lost its ability to conceive children, and no one knows why. The whole world, it seems, has plunged into depression. Main character Theo Faron (Clive Owen), a British bureaucrat, has been pulled into a plan to obtain a travel permit for a young woman. He soon learns that the aptly named woman, Kee (Clare-Hope Ashitey), holds the secret to continuing life on Earth.

Children of Men must be one of the most suspenseful sci-fi movies ever made. The film's quintessential example of this is a masterful four-minute single-shot scene in which Faron, Kee, and a few members of the underground group facilitating Kee's border-crossing are ambushed by

a group of fanatics. During this scene, the camera gently moves around inside the characters' car like a human head until the attack begins, resulting in mayhem upheld for most of the four minutes, and ending in tragedy. The realism with which the scene plays out is enhanced by the lack of camera cuts. This is but one example of this technique being used in the film.

The suspense and tension built up throughout *Children of Men*, coupled with its dreary hues and wet environments, force viewers to feel the same anxiety to which Faron is continually subjected. It is difficult to allow yourself to have hope during dark times because you may, as in the case of some of these characters, be setting yourself up for disappointment and, thus, increased dismay. However, if there is something that allows optimism to survive in even the worst scenarios, it is the beauty that the world has to offer. The film presents us these moments of beauty in rare, isolated circumstances.

Children of Men can be difficult to watch. Despite the fact that its violence is not excessive and that its plot is, though saddening, not overly harrowing, it is portrayed so realistically that the violence and sadness that is present has an immediate impact. However, its ability also to find moments of happiness hidden amidst its events makes it a rewarding experience.

The Host

YEAR 2006

COUNTRY South Korea

RUNTIME 1 hr. 59 min.

RATED R; creature violence, language

DIRECTED BY Joon-ho Bong

WRITTEN BY Joon-ho Bong, Chul-hyun Baek, Won-jun Ha

STARRING Kang-ho Song, Ah-sung Ko, Hie-bong Byeon, Hae-il Park

SIMILAR SCI-FI *Cloverfield*, *Godzilla* (1954), *Godzilla vs. Hedorah*, *Mothra*, *Super 8*, *Yongary: Monster from the Deep*

Coming from South Korea, *The Host* may be the best giant monster movie of modern time. It not only has a dynamic monster but an involving story to go with it. This is not an id-pleaser focused on watching a creature cause destruction. This is a film designed to resonate with our sense of humanity.

When an American scientist forces a Korean assistant to dump bottles and bottles of formaldehyde down a drain that leads to a river frequented by the locals, he inadvertently creates a giant mutant amphibian that begins terrorizing the residents of the area. Luckily (read: unluckily), the United States government steps in to fix everything. We follow the Park family through this scenario as the daughter of Gang-Du Park (Kang-ho Song) is captured by the monster and as Gang-Du himself is quarantined by the military, as he is feared to have been exposed to dangerous parasites with which the creature is supposedly infested.

Though it contains a healthy dose of political commentary, *The Host* is primarily about family. Gang-Du is hopelessly apathetic, but when he

The Host is a top-notch giant monster movie designed to resonate with our humanity.
Chungeorahm Film/The Kobal Collection

learns that his daughter is alive and is basically being held captive in a sewer, he discovers a desperation and drive he has never known. When the Parks break Gang-Du from the government's grasp, the laughs are as numerous as the thrills. In a memorial service for those lost in the monster attack, the Parks break into an all-out fight with each other and are left lying on the ground, beaten and crying in front of everyone.

"HAVE ANY OF YOU HEARD IT? THE HEARTBREAK OF A PARENT WHO'S LOST A CHILD... WHEN A PARENT'S HEART BREAKS, THE SOUND CAN TRAVEL FOR MILES...."

-PARK HIE-BONG

The movie has won several awards including Best Film at the Asian Film Awards.
Chungeorahm Film

What's surprising about *The Host* is how consistently and effortlessly it moves among its scenes of thrills, horror, and humor. There is excitement as the Parks flee the government, there is horror when the monster rampages through Han Lake, there are laughs at the family's dysfunctional nature, and there is outright dismay at elements of Gang-Du's quarantine—particularly when he is operated on with a diluted anesthetic. It is this ability to encompass what feels like every major emotion of the human experience that makes *The Host* a great film.

The common theme running through *The Host*'s various elements is that of responsibility. Just as Gang-Du is redeemed through his acceptance of responsibility for his daughter, the U.S. is demonized for its refusal of responsibility, passing off horrible mistakes as the result of "misinformation." The monster almost falls to the sideline in this movie. It is a catalyst for examining the ways we react to disaster.

28 Weeks Later

YEAR 2007

RUNTIME 1 hr. 39 min.

RATED R; strong violence/gore, language, some sexuality/nudity

DIRECTED BY Juan Carlos Fresnadillo

WRITTEN BY Rowan Joffe, Juan Carlos Fresnadillo, E.L. Lavigne, Jesus Olmo

STARRING Robert Carlyle, Rose Byrne, Jeremy Renner, Catherine McCormack

SIMILAR SCI-FI *28 Days Later*, *Aliens*, *Cloverfield*, *The Crazies* (1973)

A victim of the zombie plague peeks in on a survivor (Emily Beecham). *Fox Atomic/DNA Films/UK Film Council/The Kobal Collection/Susie Allnut*

In 2002, Danny Boyle's *28 Days Later* injected the ailing zombie subgenre with an artistic view and an energy that few could have anticipated. Five years after that, Juan Carlos Fresnadillo took the reins of the sequel and managed to uphold the virtue of this new, science fiction-bound approach to zombiedom. This sequel, *28 Weeks Later*, is an exercise in creating both breathtaking thrills and moral dilemmas that instill a horror greater than that of a raging zombie horde.

28 weeks after the viral outbreak of the first film, the United States has stepped in to help secure and rebuild Great Britain, which has fallen to the zombie plague. It is not long before the U.S. claims "mission accomplished," and a part of London is partially repopulated in towering apartment buildings with a boatload of security measures to guard against another outbreak. Unfortunately, no plan is fool-proof, and the exact circumstances that could contribute to another outbreak indeed fall into place. Now the virus is loose, newly zombified residents are rampaging through the established safe zone, and the U.S. military is ordered to fire on anything that moves.

The most horrifying thing about *28 Weeks Later* is the necessity of the evils committed. It is not long before the outbreak gets to the point that the soldiers firing on those running loose in this small sector of London are unable to discriminate between the infected and the healthy, and plenty of innocent lives are lost in the mayhem. However, we can't blame these soldiers for their actions. If they spent time trying to tell human from zombie, which are indiscernible in the chaos following the outbreak, they would have no chance of eliminating the zombie threat. And if they don't eliminate the zombie threat, the entire continent of Europe is at risk of infection.

Throughout this story, we follow two children who lost their mother in the first outbreak, and Fresnadillo confronts us with nonstop horrific scenarios as they try to escape the city. There is a masterful scene near the end of the film, in which we follow the children and one soldier as they walk through an unlit subway system inhabited by roaming zombies. Our sight is confined to

the limited view of the soldier's night vision scope. If we look in the distance, we can't see the children. If we watch the children, we can't see what's out there. It doesn't get much tenser than this.

Fresnadillo takes the *28 _____ Later* mythology and brings it to its visceral and moral extremes. There are plenty of sci-fi fans whose loyalty lies unwaveringly with the first film in the franchise. If you wanna pick a fight, though, there are arguments to be made for the superiority of this sequel.

"ABANDON SELECTIVE TARGETING. SHOOT EVERYTHING. TARGETS ARE NOW FREE. WE'VE LOST CONTROL."
-STONE

WARNING!

28 WEEKS LATER

MAINTAIN THE QUARANTINE

DEADLY FORCE WILL BE USED TO PROTECT THIS AREA

MAY 11, 2007
FOXATOMIC.COM

It's been reported that a possible third installment of the film will happen. *Fox Atomic/DNA Films/UK Film Council*

District 9

YEAR 2009
COUNTRY New Zealand, South Africa
RUNTIME 1 hr. 52 min.
RATED R; bloody violence, pervasive language
DIRECTED BY Neill Blomkamp
WRITTEN BY Neill Blomkamp; Terri Tatchell
STARRING Sharlto Copley, Jason Cope, Vanessa Haywood, Nathalie Boltt
SIMILAR SCI-FI *E.T.: The Extra-Terrestrial, Super 8, The Fly* (1986)

A government agent (Sharlto Copley, middle) is tasked with rounding up and relocating aliens that have landed in South Africa. *Key Creatives/The Kobal Collection*

Director Neill Blomkamp's breakthrough feature effort, *District 9*, is arguably the best science fiction film of its decade. It seems to pull us in every emotional direction, but it always feels cohesive as a story. Placing its main character in the most terrifying of circumstances, this is a film that can force even hardened pessimists to pray for a positive outcome.

In Johannesburg, South Africa, aliens have arrived. They are not here to invade or communicate, however. They are lost, disoriented, and confused. As the director of a government agency tasked with keeping the millions of prawn-like aliens confined to a slum, Wikus van de Merwe (Sharlto Copley) is put in charge of an effort to relocate them to what amounts to a prison camp. Something goes wrong, though, and during the mass eviction, Wikus comes into contact with a strange substance that causes him to slowly morph into one of the aliens.

The film begins with a documentary style and retains a similar realism throughout. Because of this, *District 9*'s focus remains on its characters (primarily Wikus), and the film doesn't devolve into a simple "humans vs. aliens" thriller. Even during the movie's action-oriented sequences, at the forefront is not the action itself but rather the emotional trauma of the situation, signified by the gore and death surrounding Wikus. The special effects are superb, but they don't exist to be showcased. They are used to strengthen an engaging story.

More than anything else, *District 9* is an emotionally distressing film. From Wikus' grotesque metamorphosis to his desperate attempt to regain normalcy, the movie's chief concern is demonstrating that no matter how hard he fights, Wikus has little hope of ever returning to his normal life. He has turned into that which he despises, and there's probably nothing he can do about it.

It's easy to pass *District 9* off as a simple apartheid analogy, but its concerns are much broader than that. This is a film about the horror of great change.

It is about being placed in a situation so dire that all you can do is fight, even though there's virtually no chance of escape. It is about hope and the disappointment of hope unfulfilled.

"WHEN DEALING WITH ALIENS, TRY TO BE POLITE, BUT FIRM. AND ALWAYS REMEMBER THAT A SMILE IS CHEAPER THAN A BULLET."
-AUTOMATED MNU INSTRUCTIONAL VOICE

The movie received an Academy Award nomination in 2010 for Best Picture.
Key Creatives/Heritage Auctions

Moon

YEAR 2009
COUNTRY United Kingdom
RUNTIME 1 hr. 37 min.
RATED R; language
DIRECTED BY Duncan Jones
WRITTEN BY Duncan Jones, Nathan Parker
STARRING Sam Rockwell, Kevin Spacey, Dominique McElligott, Kaya Scodelario
SIMILAR SCI-FI *2001: A Space Odyssey*, *Solaris* (1972), *Solaris* (2002), *Source Code*, *Sunshine*

Moon, the first feature film by director Duncan Jones, did not get a wide release, but it did turn out to be a breakthrough aesthetic and critical success. This movie takes full advantage of the science fiction genre, imagining an outlandish scenario in order to analyze the nature of man. Taking the quiet, contemplative route of classics like *2001: A Space Odyssey* and *Solaris*, *Moon* is a moving study of a man forced to face his multiple selves while living as far away from humanity as possible.

Sam Bell is the only man on the moon, responsible for the day-to-day maintenance and operation of a highly automated station that harvests Helium 3 and sends it back to Earth. Upon nearing the end of his three-year contract, he is knocked unconscious in an accident and wakes to an unprecedented realization (which shouldn't be spoiled). As a result of these events, Sam is forced to accept a new understanding of himself and the world.

Above all else, *Moon* is an emotional film. The truths that Sam discovers about his life and his identity are devastating, and he spends the latter two-thirds of the film wrestling with his conflicting beliefs in anger and resentment toward

Moon is inspired by such sci-fi classics as *2001: A Space Odyssey* and *Solaris*.
Liberty Films/UK

Sam (Sam Rockwell) faces a personal crisis as he nears the end of his three-year stint on the moon. *Liberty Films/UK/The Kobal Collection*

himself. Sam's longing to see his wife and daughter again is also present throughout the film, and one devastating call to his home on Earth is enough to move viewers to tears.

Sam Bell is played by Sam Rockwell, who invokes the perfect blend of quirkiness and melancholy to remain not altogether depressing but never fully happy either. When he lashes out at himself, he conveys more sadness than anger. When he breaks into dance, he seems more like he's trying to escape his problems than revel in high spirits. Sam Bell is almost the only character in *Moon*, but Rockwell brings enough energy and dynamism for a full cast.

Moon is a refreshing film, taking a subdued approach to science fiction when so many filmmakers think the genre requires action scenes of some sort. Jones realizes that characters are almost always the most important elements of cinematic works, so he spends an entire film focusing on one alone.

"THAT'S ENOUGH, THAT'S ENOUGH. ... I WANNA GO HOME." -SAM BELL

Inception

YEAR 2010
COUNTRY United States
RUNTIME 2 hrs. 28 min.
RATED PG-13; sequences of violence throughout
DIRECTED BY Christopher Nolan
WRITTEN BY Christopher Nolan
STARRING Leonardo DiCaprio, Ellen Page, Joseph Gordon-Levitt, Cillian Murphy
SIMILAR SCI-FI *The Cell*, *Dark City*, *Eternal Sunshine of the Spotless Mind*, *The Matrix*, *Solaris* (1972), *Solaris* (2002)

Christopher Nolan, the writer/director behind such films as *Memento*, *Batman Begins*, and *The Dark Night*, proves with *Inception* that he is a master of cinema. This is a film so cerebral that its description makes it sound like a film made by M.C. Escher. However, despite its complexity, it also does a superb job of upholding tension and remaining understandable.

Inception is based on the idea that with the right technology, you can force your way into the dreams of another and steal information or, in the rare circumstance, implant notions into another's psychology. In this story, a main character by the name of Cobb (Leonardo DiCaprio) attempts to enter a man's dreams and delve so deep within his psychology that he can plant an idea that will instantly blossom into a fundamental part of that man. Cobb's goal is to influence the subject's actions at a specific upcoming point in his life.

The film is nearly bewildering in its depiction of life-like dream states, dreams within dreams, and dreams within dreams within dreams. *Inception* imagines the forces present in a man's various levels of

The world of dreams creates many cerebral twists and trippy imagery in *Inception*.
Warner Bros./The Kobal Collection

"*THEY SAY WE ONLY USE A FRACTION OF OUR BRAIN'S TRUE POTENTIAL. NOW, THAT'S WHEN WE'RE AWAKE. WHEN WE'RE ASLEEP, WE CAN DO ALMOST ANYTHING*"
-COBB

conscious much like *TRON* imagined the inner workings of a computer system. This not only leads to some intriguing ideas regarding the nature of the subconscious and its relativity to any other given state of consciousness, but it also leads to some mind-twisting imagery, such as a city literally folding in on itself and a fight that takes place in a revolving hotel hallway.

One of the most impressive things about *Inception*, though, is Nolan's ability to keep its plot coherent. Nolan lays out the rules of dream travel in exposition hidden in scenes focused primarily on character development, and when we later descend the levels of the dream world, it is almost always clear which level we are on. That's not to say there aren't some elements that won't have you scratching your head, but it's no nest of confusion like it could have been.

Inception explores the relativity of every level of personal reality even while it provides thrilling sequences of mind-espionage. It is made great by its ability to provoke thought and excitement in equally high doses while delving into borderline surrealism and remaining comprehensible throughout. Few directors could pull off such a stunt.

It's survival of the fittest when cloned dinosaurs at a new theme park, including a T-Rex and raptors, go on a rampage in *Jurassic Park*.

Amblin Entertainment/Universal Pictures

CHAPTER 3

FURTHER ESSENTIALS

For any newcomer to science fiction, this chapter represents the final stretch of generally high-quality films that are required viewing before delving into the genre's more obscure delights. These are those movies that have done a lot for science fiction and have remained, on the whole, highly enjoyable throughout the years, but some aspect of them has kept them from being great. Still, there is no ignoring the impact they have had on the landscape of sci-fi cinema. Many of them are fan favorites themselves. They may be flawed, but they have still proven vital to the evolution of the genre and have provided tons of entertainment to sci-fi fans.

Some of these have strong stories that just don't feel quite as packed with meaning as the greats. *20,000 Leagues Under the Sea* (1954) is a presentation of a variety of character types faced with muddled morals and forced to navigate in dangerous ethical territory, but it occasionally stretches that theme out for slightly too long, during which time the characters cease to develop. *Transformers* (2007) is a blast to watch, with surprisingly intense robot battles and visual effects details, but its basic story of discovering one's inner strength, while competent, is not original.

Other movies in this chapter are more deficient in some areas but are especially innovative in others. *Predator* may contain a thin plot, but its monster and its near emasculation of the action hero archetype provided an experience unlike any other. *Superman* contains ridiculous villains and a plot that could never hold up to scrutiny, but its title hero is so inspiring and unforgettable that the movie's problems are almost irrelevant.

One or two films in this chapter are viewed by a significant number of film enthusiasts not to be of adequate quality to be considered "good," but they remain essential viewing in order to gain a full understanding of the genre's culture and history. *Star Wars: Episode I – The Phantom Menace* is the prime example of

When a shape-shifting alien invades an Antarctic research station, level-headed helicopter pilot R.J. MacReady (Kurt Russell) leads the charge against the creature in *The Thing*. *Universal Pictures/Heritage Auctions*

this. Many film fans outright hate *The Phantom Menace*, yet it has spurred such fiery debate in the science fiction community that anyone interested in the genre has to be familiar with it and the reasons it is so controversial.

Not all of these movies have significant problems. Some just feel like they could have contained more substance or appear to have gotten caught up in one element, like thrills or special effects, to the minor neglect of others, like story or emotion. Regardless of whatever holds them back from being greats, all of these films have contributed to science fiction in a notable, if not major, way.

It Came from Outer Space

YEAR 1953

COUNTRY United States

RUNTIME 1 hr. 21 min.

RATED Not Rated; may contain some scary images for younger children

DIRECTED BY Jack Arnold

WRITTEN BY Ray Bradbury (source story), Harry Essex

STARRING Richard Carlson, Barbara Rush, Charles Drake, Joe Sawyer

SIMILAR SCI-FI *Alien Trespass*, *The Day the Earth Stood Still* (1951), *The Earth Dies Screaming*, *Invaders from Mars*, *Invasion of the Body Snatchers* (1956)

It Came from Outer Space has not aged well in the sixty years since its release, but for the early 1950s it was an exceptional example of both thrilling and thoughtful sci-fi horror. Supported by its observation of our tendency to respond rashly to uncertainty, this movie tells a story about a misunderstood man seeking the truth about other misunderstood beings. There are numerous shortcomings in the details, but *It Came from Outer Space* remains a fun examination of the lengths of human xenophobia.

During a sappy night of stargazing, writer John Putnam (Richard Carlson) and his girlfriend Ellen Fields (Barbara Rush) witness something crashing to Earth. Upon investigating, Putnam discovers that it's an alien spaceship. Of course, it wouldn't be a 1950s sci-fi film if anyone believed him at all, so he's quickly branded a liar, out to seek publicity for his writing. When the visitors aboard the ship begin

"IT WASN'T THE RIGHT TIME FOR US TO MEET. BUT THERE'LL BE OTHER NIGHTS, OTHER STARS FOR US TO WATCH. THEY'LL BE BACK."
–JOHN PUTNAM

Shadowy figures lurk. *Universal Studios/The Kobal Collection*

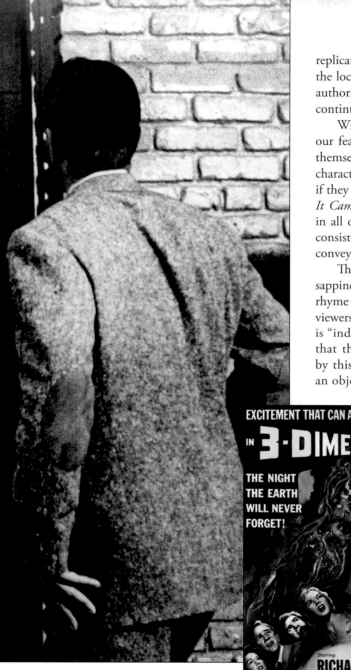

replicating townspeople and coming into town in human guise, though, the locals start to catch on. The problem now is that John has to keep the authorities from killing these aliens, who want only to leave so they can continue exploring the galaxy.

What's interesting about *It Came from Outer Space* is its portrayal of our fear of that which is different from us. These aliens eventually make themselves look exactly like us but are still hated for their otherness. The characters hate them solely because they don't understand them (granted, if they did see the creatures, the situation would probably be even worse—*It Came from Outer Space* boasts what might be the ugliest alien species in all of sci-fi cinema). Throughout the film, director Jack Arnold makes consistently creepy use of shadows, perspective, and open spaces, effectively conveying the characters' trepidation.

There are plenty of moments of cliché and simplicity, however, like the sappiness contained in the opening (Ellen recites the "Star Light, Star Bright" rhyme within the first couple of minutes), that mar the experience for modern viewers. At one point, one character disparagingly tells another that John is "individual and lonely, a man who thinks for himself." Even knowing that the line is supposed to portray individuality as underappreciated by this close-minded character (as opposed to being actually bad from an objective standpoint), it's difficult for modern viewers not to scoff at such dialogue.

Much of *It Came from Outer Space* is based on the mystery of the aliens and of the events surrounding the replicated characters' strange actions. Today anyone watching it will be at least two steps ahead of the plot at any given point, and the "thrilling" scenes are mostly just hokey, like the kind of stuff they play at the Sci-Fi Dine-In Theater at Disney World. Still, the film has enough merit to make it a worthwhile watch. This is required viewing for any fan of science fiction, especially those with proclivities for the Golden Age.

This was Universal's first movie to be filmed in 3D. *Universal Studios/Heritage Auctions*

20,000 Leagues Under the Sea

YEAR 1954
COUNTRY United States
RUNTIME 2 hrs. 7 min.
RATED G; some mild violence
DIRECTED BY Richard Fleischer
WRITTEN BY Jules Verne (source novel), Earl Felton
STARRING James Mason, Kirk Douglas, Paul Lukas, Peter Lorre
SIMILAR SCI-FI *The Black Hole*, *Fantastic Voyage*, *The Time Machine* (1960)

"I AM NOT WHAT IS CALLED A CIVILIZED MAN, PROFESSOR. I HAVE DONE WITH SOCIETY FOR REASONS THAT SEEM GOOD TO ME. THEREFORE, I DO NOT OBEY ITS LAWS." -CAPTAIN NEMO

This version of *20,000 Leagues Under the Sea* is a rare film that presents two opposing storytelling styles yet retains coherence. Wavering between Disney-naïve scenarios and unexplored moral territory, this movie tells the tale of characters venturing beyond the boundaries of society. It is in such an environment as this that we gain the clearest view of right and wrong—if such a view is to be found.

Set in a time predating modern submarine technology, *20,000 Leagues* follows a professor, his assistant, and a sailor as they find themselves as involuntary guests aboard the self-sustaining submersible of a possible madman, Captain Nemo (James Mason). This Nemo is accommodating enough, but it's impossible to pinpoint his motives. Once he has effectually befriended his guests, he commits a destructive act that challenges our understanding of him.

The film begins with a level of innocence that only Disney could get away with. For one, it contains the most stereotypical sailors you are ever likely to see, ones that wear striped muscle shirts and sing harmonious sea songs. Nemo himself is a bit of a stereotype as well, the gentlemanly captain who lives in large, plush quarters, dines on fine seafood, and always seems to have a philosophical speech prepared. Oh, there's also a pet seal that roams the sub freely and is trained to give kisses.

20,000 Leagues' innocent tone, however, functions as a softener for the morally uncertain scenarios with which we are presented as viewers. When Nemo commits the aforementioned controversial act, we are left to decide whether he is a morally good character. The characters have their own opinions of him, and those who most oppose his actions are also the least informed. This moral uncertainty is the point of the film.

The sub's pet seal gets friendly with Ned (Kirk Douglas). *Walt Disney/Heritage Auctions*

Sailors battle a giant squid attacking their submarine.
Walt Disney/Heritage Auctions

Taking place under the sea, it is about escaping society and its conventional ethical notions so that we can view the world free of the demands and expectations of civilization.

This movie is not only a literal adventure; it is a moral adventure. The characters, and we with them, are forced to face ambiguous moral situations, but we are afforded the opportunity to do so free of a pre-established moral code. Even as we are challenged, though, the film's prevailing innocence renders it as un-abrasive as a work with such goals can be.

Them!

YEAR 1954
COUNTRY United States
RUNTIME 1 hr. 34 min.
RATED Not Rated; some giant ant violence
DIRECTED BY Gordon Douglas
WRITTEN BY Ted Sherdeman, Russell Hughes, George Worthing Yates
STARRING James Whitmore, Edmund Gwenn, James Arness, Joan Weldon
SIMILAR SCI-FI *The Deadly Mantis*, *Empire of the Ants*, *Kingdom of the Spiders*, *Tarantula*

Mutated ants transform into giant man-eating monsters. *Warner Bros./The Kobal Collection*

You want giant killer insects? Start with the subgenre's seminal film: *Them!* This is a movie that seems to balance tension, story, and giant monsters perfectly. It is naturally a moral about atomic weaponry, but its screenplay and pacing keep it fresh even for modern viewers.

Two police officers find a little girl in shock in the desert. Then they discover a trailer with walls broken out from the inside. A nearby general store exhibits the same type of destruction. It doesn't take long for world-renowned myrmecologist Harold Medford (Edmund Gwenn) to confirm his unlikely suspicion: this is the doing of giant ants, mutated by the radiation from atomic bomb tests. After some further investigating by Medford and the FBI, they discover something even more unsettling: these giant ants have made a home in the storm drainage system of Los Angeles.

Them! uses its setup to tell a story not only about monsters created by atomic bombs but about the government's tendency to go to any lengths necessary to avoid frightening the public. Along with their ongoing attempt to simply avoid revealing the presence of the giant ants, the FBI goes so far as to recommend that one ant-witness be detained in a mental health facility. The giant monster story itself is well-executed, too, with a focus on the horror of a potential city-wide attack. Sure, there are a few early attacks to up the ante (no pun intended), but the story is centered on the ants' migration and officials' attempts to quell the threat the creatures will eventually pose to the public on a large scale.

The giant ants themselves are both creepy and goofy—their goofiness enhancing their creepiness. While they look thoroughly fake, the giant,

Them! was the first movie to depict insects as monsters. *Warner Bros./Heritage Auctions*

clumsily moving heads of the insects convey an emotionlessness that is borderline terrifying. You know that when these things are trying to kill people, they are thinking nothing of it—kind of like when humans stomp the monsters' miniscule brethren.

"When man entered the atomic age, he opened a door into a new world. What he'll eventually find in that new world, nobody can predict." *Them!* ends with this line, which isn't exactly realistic coming from a myrmecologist but which sums up the point of the film. It succeeds in the sci-fi/horror subgenre not because of the terror it can manufacture but because of its observation that mankind is well capable of manufacturing terror on its own.

"WE HAVEN'T SEEN THE END OF THEM. WE'VE ONLY HAD A CLOSE VIEW OF THE BEGINNING OF WHAT MAY BE THE END OF US."
-DR. HAROLD MEDFORD

The Quatermass Xperiment

YEAR 1955
COUNTRY United Kingdom
RUNTIME 1 hr. 22 min.
RATED Not Rated; some mild horror
DIRECTED BY Val Guest
WRITTEN BY Richard H. Landau, Val Guest, Nigel Kneale
STARRING Richard Wordsworth, Brian Donlevy, Jack Warner, Margia Dean
SIMILAR SCI-FI *The Andromeda Strain*, *District 9*, *First Man into Space*, *The Fly* (1986)

Save for a handful of examples, it is not enough for a sci-fi/horror film to have a unique monster. The way that monster is approached or portrayed is what makes the movie. *The Quatermass Xperiment* is a prime example of this, with a man turned monster and an investigation that will require us to broaden the bounds of our assumptions about life and the universe.

The world's first manned spaceship has crashed back to Earth, and only one of the three astronauts is found inside. The one that is still there, Victor Carroon (Richard Wordsworth), is catatonic. After being taken in for an extended and secretive examination, Carroon is broken free. To the surprise of his wife, he then goes on an emotionless killing spree with the aid of a monstrously mutated arm. Carroon is not the man he used to be. In fact, he'll soon no longer be a man at all.

The interesting thing about *The Quatermass Xperiment* is its depiction of how exploration—in this case, space travel—can change us on a fundamental level. First, there is the physical

Astronaut Victor Carroon (Richard Wordsworth) is not the man he used to be after he returns to Earth. *Hammer Film Productions/ The Kobal Collection*

changing of Carroon, the result of his encounter with a sort of intangible life form in space. It is a change that affects his core being, altering not only his body but his identity and the way he lives (i.e. a purely predatory life).

More importantly, however, there is Professor Bernard Quatermass (Brian Donlevy), the scientist in charge of the exploration project, who is seeking an understanding of Carroon's metamorphosis in the first place. To do so necessitates a change in his understanding of the world. It has now become a place in which invisible, intangible living beings reside (in space) and, through a mere encounter, can drastically alter the course of one's life and possibly of a civilization. Our search for knowledge, our exploration, has brought only more uncertainty.

Quatermass's mindset throughout all of this, however, is arguably inhumane and, at the least, coldly objective. Through his character, the film posits a certain fear of scientific exploration. The only horror greater than Carroon's transformation is the fact that the only people who can help him are more interested in studying him. The rewards may be worth the risks, but discovery is no innocuous task.

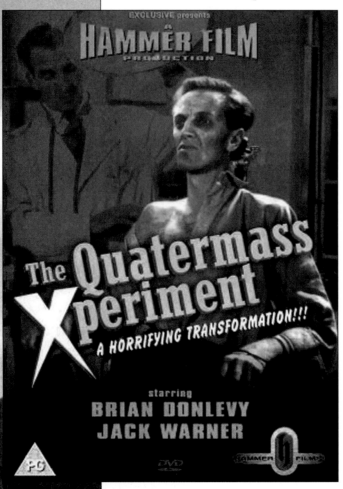

The movie's U.S. title is *The Creeping Unknown.* Hammer Film Productions

"I'M AN OLD-FASHIONED SORT OF CHAP. I DON'T KNOW MUCH ABOUT ROCKETS OR TRAVELING IN SPACE. I DON'T READ SCIENCE FICTION. I'M A PLAIN, SIMPLE BIBLE MAN. I HAVE A ROUTINE MIND, AND I HAVE TO DO ROUTINE THINGS."
-INSP. LOMAX

Earth vs. the Flying Saucers

YEAR 1956
COUNTRY United States
RUNTIME 1 hr. 23 min.
RATED Not Rated; some violence
DIRECTED BY Fred F. Sears
WRITTEN BY Major Donald E. Keyhoe (source novel), Curt Siodmak, George Worthing Yates, Bernard Gordon
STARRING Hugh Marlowe, Joan Taylor, Donald Curtis, Morris Ankrum
SIMILAR SCI-FI *20 Million Miles to Earth*, *Independence Day*, *The War of the Worlds* (1953)

Aliens launch an attack on Earth. *Columbia Pictures/Heritage Auctions*

In one sense, there's nothing special about *Earth vs. the Flying Saucers*. It's a straightforward UFO invasion flick with a happy ending and few surprises. However, it's the degree to which the filmmakers have dedicated themselves to the basics of the invasion that makes the film stand out. Watch this one not so much for the story but for the visuals.

Aliens in flying saucers have come to Earth, and scientist Russell Marvin (Hugh Marlowe) is involuntarily pulled into the ordeal when the aliens attempt to contact him directly. He misses their first communication, so the military, caught off guard, attacks the aliens immediately when they land. It doesn't seem to matter, though. They were pretty much here just to take over anyway. Laser—and sonic gun—battles ensue.

The special-effects work of the legendary Ray Harryhausen is what makes this film unique. The UFOs, though outdated, are impressive for their time—no visible strings and no wobbliness, and the effects are competent enough to hold up even in close-up shots. Furthermore, the destruction is taken to the fullest degree, with complete depictions of multiple national

Scenes of flying saucers were used in several other movies and a Three Stooges' short, "Flying Saucer Daffy." *Columbia Pictures/Heritage Auctions*

Things spiral out of control and lead to a full-scale invasion. *Columbia Pictures/Heritage Auctions*

"WHEN AN ARMED AND THREATENING POWER LANDS UNINVITED IN OUR CAPITOL, WE DON'T MEET HIM WITH TEA AND COOKIES!" -GEN. EDMUNDS

monuments being destroyed by the UFOs. We had seen massive, alien-induced devastation in *War of the Worlds* three years before, but *Earth vs. the Flying Saucers'* imagery of the destruction of such landmarks signifies not only death but the loss of culture and identity—a relevant fear for Americans in the 1950s.

At the end of the film, Dr. Russell's wife asks him whether he thinks there are more aliens, which might one day come back. Russell's response is simply that if there are more aliens they won't come today … because the weather is too pretty for an invasion. It's a facetious response, but it may also be the best. We have to enjoy what we have when we can, because who knows when those things might be taken away?

The Blob

YEAR 1958

COUNTRY United States

RUNTIME 1 hr. 22 min.

RATED PG; some mild scares

DIRECTED BY Irvin S. Yeaworth, Jr.

WRITTEN BY Kate Phillips, Irvine Millgate, Theodore Simonson

STARRING Steve McQueen, Aneta Corsaut, John Benson, Earl Rowe

SIMILAR SCI-FI *Beware! The Blob*, *The Blob* (1988), *Caltiki: The Immortal Monster*, *The Monolith Monsters*

After falling from the sky, a crashed meteor containing a small jelly-like blob is discovered by an unlucky first victim. *Paramount Pictures/The Kobal Collection*

The Blob makes its way through town, growing bigger with each body it absorbs. *Paramount Pictures*

The Blob is required viewing not for its general aesthetic success but for a number of specific elements that were executed particularly well—namely, the concept of the Blob itself and the special effects of the creature. The story is a sound one, but it trudges a bit too uneventfully during its non-Blob minutes, which are the vast majority of them. Still, *The Blob* has enough enjoyable elements to leave most any viewer wanting more.

In a stereotypical carefree 1950s town where the biggest worries are for teenagers competing in friendly drag races, a Blob has fallen from the sky and begun consuming people. A teenager named Steve Andrews (played by none other than Steve McQueen) is one of the first to see this thing and live, but he has a reputation as a mischief-maker, so no one will listen to him. Since this Blob grows larger with each body it absorbs, it might be too late by the time people start believing him.

For the 1950s, the special effects here are superb. The Blob is an actual gelatinous substance, not an animation or stiffly molded clay model. Moving smoothly and naturally, the Blob consistently looks like an actual predatory glob of goo. The shot of the creature pushing itself through multiple openings into a movie theater is classic. You'd be hard-pressed to find a more fun and unique monster.

There is one crucial problem with *The Blob*, though: there's not enough Blob! The eponymous mass gets less than three minutes of screen time, and the non-Blob portions of the film are spent doing uninteresting things like trying to convince police of the creature's existence. Doubtless this is to some extent due to the difficulty of creating Blob effects, but it's unfortunate that the movie consists of so much filler.

Teenager Steve (Steve McQueen) tries to get people to believe there's a big Blob on the loose before it's too late. *Paramount Pictures*

The Blob itself can be viewed as a metaphor for all the evil things in the world, as a shapeless mass that simply absorbs innocents and moves on, growing more powerful with each death. The uncertainty of the ending supports this understanding. We may be able to contain evil at times, and we can occasionally stop it cold, but there is always a chance that it will be revived. For this understanding of the film and for its special effects, *The Blob* is a classic. Newcomers should be warned, though: a briskly paced film this is not.

"HOW DO YOU GET PEOPLE TO PROTECT THEMSELVES FROM SOMETHING THEY DON'T BELIEVE IN?" -STEVE ANDREWS

First Man into Space

YEAR 1959
COUNTRY United States
RUNTIME 1 hr. 17 min.
RATED Not Rated; some mild violence
DIRECTED BY Robert Day
WRITTEN BY John C. Cooper, Lance Z. Hargreaves, Wyott Ordung
STARRING Marshall Thompson, Bill Edwards, Carl Jaffe, Marla Landi
SIMILAR SCI-FI *Destination Moon*, *Monster on the Campus*, *The Quatermass Xperiment*, *The Thing from Another World*

After a pilot bucks the rules and encounters strange cosmic dust, he disappears and a creature with a taste for blood takes his place. *Metro-Goldwyn-Mayer/Heritage Auctions*

In many ways, *First Man into Space* is a generic and predictable '50s "monster terrorizes innocents" flick. However, it uses that era's sci-fi/horror conventions in a premise that allows them to carry more meaning than typical monster fare. This is not just about the horror of a monster coming after you; *First Man into Space* is about the dangers of exploring the unknown.

The military is conducting the first launch of a manned vessel beyond the Earth's atmosphere. Lieutenant Dan Prescott (Bill Edwards) is the man chosen for the job, but his penchant for doing things his own way has consequences when he pilots his craft beyond the established flight plan. Upon doing so, he encounters a strange cosmic dust and crashes back to Earth. His body is nowhere to be found, but soon a hideously deformed monster begins roaming a village near the crash, killing cows and people. Could there be a connection?

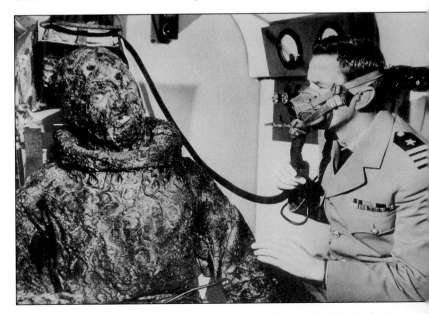

A lieutenant learns the hard way there's a big price to pay for wanting to be the first man to venture into space. *Metro-Goldwyn-Mayer/Heritage Auctions*

THE PICTURE THAT LEAPS AHEAD OF THE HEADLINES!

M-G-M presents

FIRST MAN INTO SPACE

The most dangerous and daring mission of all time!

Starring
MARSHALL THOMPSON and MARLA LANDI · JOHN C. COOPER and LANCE Z. HARGREAVES · Screenplay by
Produced by JOHN CROYDON and CHARLES F. VETTER JR. · Directed by ROBERT DAY · AN AMALGAMATED PRODUCTION

"THE CONQUEST OF NEW WORLDS ALWAYS MAKES DEMANDS OF HUMAN LIFE. AND THERE WILL ALWAYS BE MEN WHO WILL ACCEPT THE RISK."
-DR. PAUL VON ESSEN

Made before history's first human made it to space, *First Man into Space* demonstrates the potential horrors of unexplored frontiers. Even before Prescott's encounter with the space dust, his mere traveling to zero-gravity space has nearly disastrous consequences, as his mind and body do not know how to deal with this new state of being. Later, when he experiences the space dust travesty, the situation becomes outright grave. However, during the other characters' investigation of the mysterious bloodthirsty monster, we learn that Prescott had no regrets about his decision to launch as far into space as possible, even considering the horrible things he went through. There are dangers to be had when exploring any type of new territory, but there are also individuals whose thirst for knowledge outweighs consequences of any severity.

This film is a depiction of the price we are willing to pay for discovery. There are potentially horrible things to be found in the unknown, but even so, it is always worth looking to see. The desire to become the first man to do anything in particular is not selfish. It is bold.

These Are the Damned

YEAR 1963
COUNTRY United Kingdom
RUNTIME 1 hr. 27 min.
RATED Not Rated; nothing objectionable
DIRECTED BY Joseph Losey
WRITTEN BY Evan Jones, H.L. Lawrence (source novel)
STARRING Macdonald Carey, Shirley Anne Field, Oliver Reed, Viveca Lindfors
SIMILAR SCI-FI *The City of Lost Children, Village of the Damned*

Mysterious children held captive in a cave briefly escape and enjoy the sun and flowers for the first time, but are soon rounded back up again by men in radiation suits. *Hammer Film Productions/The Kobal Collection*

Two major components of production company Hammer Film's success during the 1950s and '60s were its movies' focus on characters and the filmmakers' willingness to take aesthetic risks. Hammer didn't require that all its stories be capped with a happy ending. What mattered was that the films were as engaging as possible. *These Are the Damned* (a.k.a *The Damned*) is a chief example of this approach to moviemaking.

These Are the Damned follows Simon Wells (Macdonald Carey), an American tourist in England who stumbles upon a group of children who live in a cave, have no body heat, communicate with a "teacher" via a television screen, and are visited periodically by men in hazmat suits. The plot of the film feels like a well-oiled trap. Once the first event—Simon being led to his mugging by a beautiful girl named Joan (Shirley Anne Field)—is triggered, a series of events involving the military, an overprotective brother, and a sculptor plays out while connections are drawn between various characters, all of which lead us down a path that drops us into the story of the children with us hardly expecting it.

Part of the reason the film is so efficient at getting us to an unexpected place is that it focuses heavily on the characters. Save for one scene, roughly the first two-thirds of the film play out like a straight up thriller, even sporting Hitchcockian overtones. The movie is completely devoted to fleshing out main characters Simon and Joan and establishing a peculiar relationship between the two. Because of this, when they meet the mysterious children, we can feel how shocked they are. These children, we learn, are a trump card for mankind's survival, but in order to remain as such, they have to live in a perpetual state of oblivion. There is nothing anyone can do to save them from the lot that life (and the government) has given them. You can bet, though, that Simon and Joan are going to try.

The film concludes with some of the bleakest developments possible and with the haunting repetition of a plea for help. This downbeat approach adds honesty to *These Are the Damned*. It is not meant to be a crowd-pleaser. It is meant to show how profoundly the powerful can affect the lives of the weak.

The film's tagline makes the children sound sinister, when in fact they're innocent victims.
Hammer Film Productions/Heritage Auctions

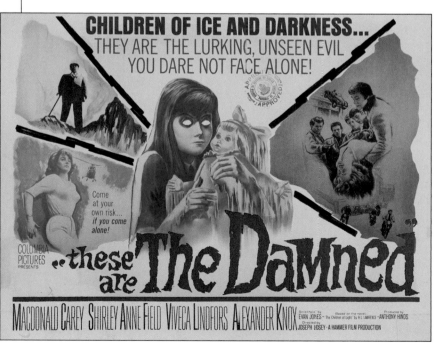

CHILDREN OF ICE AND DARKNESS...
THEY ARE THE LURKING, UNSEEN EVIL YOU DARE NOT FACE ALONE!

Come at your own risk... if you come alone!

COLUMBIA PICTURES PRESENTS

..these are The Damned

MACDONALD CAREY · SHIRLEY ANNE FIELD · VIVECA LINDFORS · ALEXANDER KNOX

THX 1138

YEAR 1971

COUNTRY United States

RUNTIME 1 hr. 28 min.

RATED R; some sexuality and nudity

DIRECTED BY George Lucas

WRITTEN BY George Lucas, Walter Murch

STARRING Robert Duvall, Donald Pleasance, Maggie McOmie, Don Pedro Colley

SIMILAR SCI-FI *A Clockwork Orange, Alphaville, Cube, Fahrenheit 451, Logan's Run*

A couple rebels against their rigidly controlled environment and android police.
American Zoetrope/Warner Bros./The Kobal Collection

The fact alone that *THX 1138* is the debut feature film of the director who gave us *Star Wars* is enough reason for it to be required viewing for any fan of science fiction. However, it also happens to be a pretty good movie. Filming *THX 1138* in a significantly more stylistic manner than he has since become known for doing, George Lucas crafts a story filled with silence, white spaces, and a bleak view of the direction to which consumerism and fear could steer society.

THX 1138 takes place in an underground society in which mandatory drugs have numbed us of any possible emotion and in which our sole and end purpose of life is to be productive. The world is as lifeless as it could be. The main character, THX (Robert Duvall), spends his days working at a factory, buying meaningless and functionless objects in his off hours, and occasionally visiting electronic confession booths. One day, he gets the notion to stop taking his drugs. Then something amazing happens: he finds himself with the will to escape this empty society.

This film is different from most other "mindless society" movies, though, in that the government is only mildly militaristic. Everyone, save for a select few individuals including THX, is fully given to this world's ideal. Imagine the comfort of not having to worry, of not having to consider ethical dilemmas, and of not needing to find meaning in life. That is the existence these people have achieved,

George Lucas developed this from his student film, *Electronic Labyrinth: THX 1138 4EB*.
American Zoetrope/Warner Bros./Heritage Auctions

constructing a society that allows them to vanquish such unpleasant aspects of life. The result is joyless contentment.

Lucas has said that he basically thought *THX 1138* would ruin his career, even as he filmed it. He was fine with that, though, because he was more interested in filming documentaries (crazy, right?). It's easy to see why he thought this might happen. *THX 1138* is not a blockbuster or crowd pleaser by any means. It is, rather, an interesting and important film—not just because it was made by George Lucas but because it was made by a director who had a unique vision and executed that vision with no fear of studio rejection or repercussion.

"LET US BE THANKFUL WE HAVE COMMERCE. BUY MORE. BUY MORE NOW. BUY MORE AND BE HAPPY."

–OMM 0000

The Crazies

YEAR 1973
COUNTRY United States
RUNTIME 1 hr. 43 min.
RATED R; bloody violence, language, brief nudity
DIRECTED BY George A. Romero
WRITTEN BY George A. Romero, Paul McCollough
STARRING Will MacMillan, Lane Carroll, Harold Wayne Jones, Lloyd Hollar
SIMILAR SCI-FI *28 Days Later*, *28 Weeks Later*, *The Crazies* (2010), *The Host*

Created by George Romero in the heyday of his zombie cinema revival, *The Crazies* takes a different approach to the "everyday humans turned into mindless monsters" theme of which Romero has demonstrated himself to be so fond. This film is not about the horror of turning into something else; it is about the horror of making difficult moral decisions. In this film, we are not confronted with the undead. We are confronted with ourselves.

A biological weapon, the Trixie virus, has gotten loose among the population of Evans City, Pennsylvania. Those infected by Trixie either die or go violently mad. The latter most often occurs. The government, realizing the massive problem it has on its hands, now has to determine how to contain the virus. The solution may involve destroying Evans City and everyone in it. It sounds evil, yes, but what are our other options?

What makes *The Crazies* special is that neither the townspeople nor the government are painted as good or bad. Even though the residents' lives are being flagrantly encroached upon, the military is carrying out what it sees as the only reasonable course of action. The antagonists and protagonists in this setup are spread among each side of the conflict. There are evil government personnel who could not care less about the fate of the town, and likewise there are civilians who seem to value personal rights over the chance to stop this virus from spreading throughout the world. It is not a situation in which we can choose a side; we have to root for humanity itself.

Whereas in Romero's zombie films, the undead form of the former humans creates a clear visual distinction between us and them, *The Crazies* portrays its unique brand of zombies, if they can be considered as such,

Regular civilians have to battle both "the crazies," as well as military soldiers told to shoot on sight.
Laurel/Libra/The Kobal Collection

exactly as living humans. This is unsettling. Without death serving as a barrier between the bloodthirsty and the (theoretically) humane, we are forced to accept evil as something that can infect us *as we are*. Somehow we all have the capacity to perform the acts committed by *The Crazies'* infected. All it takes is a certain impetus for us to begin doing so.

George Romero makes two cameos in the movie, including being seen on a monitor as the president of the United States. *Laurel/Libra/Heritage Auctions*

Godzilla vs. Mechagodzilla

YEAR 1974
COUNTRY Japan
RUNTIME 1 hr. 24 min.
RATED G; some monster violence
DIRECTED BY Jun Fukuda
WRITTEN BY Jun Fukuda, Shinichi Sekizawa, Masami Fukushima, Hiroyasu Yamamura
STARRING Masaaki Daimon, Kazuya Aoyama, Saeko Kaneshiro, Reiko Tajima
SIMILAR SCI-FI *All Monsters Attack*, *Godzilla: Final Wars*, *Godzilla Against Mechagodzilla*, *Godzilla vs. Hedorah*, *Godzilla vs. Mechagodzilla II*, *Terror of Mechagodzilla*

Honestly, there are probably about half a dozen Godzilla movies you could substitute for *Godzilla vs. Mechagodzilla* in a book such as the one you are reading, but this flick seems to find the quintessence of Godzilla's fun and goofy years. With over twenty-five movies to his name, Godzilla has been through a lot over time, and the monster has been treated more nebulously than perhaps any single character in cinema, but that inconsistency can be forgiven, for it led to films such as this.

Godzilla vs. Mechagodzilla is one of Godzilla's "hero monster" installments, in which Big G is not a menace but rather protects Japan against attacking monsters. It doesn't seem that way at first, though, when what appears to be Godzilla comes to town and immediately begins punching (yes, punching) buildings. We soon learn that this Godzilla is an impostor. Beneath the reptilian skin is a highly formidable robot monster modeled after Godzilla, built for a purpose that is not even worth getting into. But don't worry, Japan. Godzilla steps up to teach this giant robot a lesson, and he's even got some help from a friendly, doglike demon named King Caesar.

Boasting three of the coolest monsters in the Godzilla universe, some ridiculous visuals, and the franchise's trademark man-in-monster-suit effects, the entertainment level of *GvM* is hard to match. Some of the film's highlights include Mechagodzilla flying around like a fighter jet, Godzilla throwing his arm in frustration after a dodged attack, and King Caesar's ability to absorb Mechagodzilla's rainbow laser through one eye and shoot it back out the other. And wait till you see the magnetizing move Godzilla pulls out of nowhere. You get the point. The movie is as fun as it is dumb.

"MECHAGODZILLA WILL START ACTION AT 6 IN THE MORNING."
—ALIEN

Three monsters hanging out: King Caesar, Mechagodzilla, and Godzilla.
Toho/The Kobal Collection

Don't expect any sort of tie-in, thematically or plot-wise, to the first *Godzilla*, which is a masterpiece of giant monster horror. This piece of the franchise came during a time when the studio (Toho) was more interested in seeing what kind of kicks they could get out of the creature. *GvM* is an essential taste of this strange period of Godzilla's life.

Invasion of the Body Snatchers

YEAR 1978
COUNTRY United States
RUNTIME 1 hr. 55 min.
RATED PG; terror/violence, some disturbing images
DIRECTED BY Philip Kaufman
WRITTEN BY Jack Finney (source novel), W.D. Richter
STARRING Brooke Adams, Donald Sutherland, Leonard Nimoy, Jeff Goldblum
SIMILAR SCI-FI *Body Snatchers* (1993), *The Fly* (1986), *Invaders from Mars*, *The Invasion* (2007), *Invasion of the Body Snatchers* (1956), *It Came from Outer Space*

After Don Siegel's first adaptation of *Invasion of the Body Snatchers* in 1956, it would seem that no further versions would be necessary. However, director Philip Kaufman managed to take the story and create a film with comparable effectiveness. This time around, instead of using clever cinematography, lighting, and set design to evoke fear, the threat is presented more immediately, with some gross-out special effects and people who just won't listen.

You probably know the story. An alien plant life has invaded a city on Earth and is infecting residents one by one, organically replicating their bodies, disposing of and posing as the originals, and thereafter planting the means to snatch more bodies. We follow main character Elizabeth Driscoll (Brook Adams), who slowly catches on to the truth after her husband suddenly begins acting strange. But will anyone listen to her? And will it be too late by the time they do?

Whereas the first *Invasion of the Body Snatchers* is about paranoia and claustrophobia, this first remake (there are currently three remakes, plus the original), is about the need to ask outlandish questions in a society prone to accepting everything as ultimately normal, or explainable through pop psychology. Despite the evidence that mounts and mounts, others are slow to accept the possibility of a conspiracy such as that which Elizabeth

Matthew (Donald Sutherland) and Elizabeth (Brooke Adams) try to elude the aliens.
United Artists/The Kobal Collection

Matthew figures out what's going on, but officials tell him not to worry about it. *United Artists/Heritage Auctions*

This 1978 version has many similarities to the original from 1956, but is seen more as a satire of the "Me Decade." *United Artists*

suspects. Even when multiple characters have seen direct proof of the event, others pass off their claims as stemming from repressed feelings or simple delusion.

This film's most obvious distinguishing element from the first, though, is its body-birthing effects. As effective as the first film is, it is light on the grotesque. This one takes the opposite approach, showing the half-developed copies of humans in complete, slimy, disgusting detail while the real bodies are sucked dry. In the first film, we fear becoming part of a group consciousness. In this one, we fear the antagonists as monsters capable of spawning gruesome creations.

Sometimes bizarre and unexplainable things happen. These are the times when, contrary to what society teaches us, it pays to be paranoid. *Invasion of the Body Snatchers* is about the horror of having legitimate reason to suspect the worst but having no one to take you seriously. This disconnect is the result of one of history's most repeated mistakes: believing yourself to be safe from harm.

"THERE'S NO NEED FOR HATE NOW - OR LOVE."
-A PODPERSON

Superman: The Movie

YEAR 1978
COUNTRY United States
RUN TIME 2 hrs. 23 min.
RATED PG; for peril, some mild sensuality, language
DIRECTED BY Richard Donner
WRITTEN BY Mario Puzo, David Newman, Leslie Newman, Robert Benton
STARRING Christopher Reeve, Margot Kidder, Gene Hackman, Valerie Perrine
SIMILAR SCI-FI *Iron Man, Spider-Man, Superman II, Superman III, Superman IV: The Quest for Peace, Superman Returns*

Gene Hackman as Lex Luthor, Superman's arch nemesis. *Warner Bros./DC Comics/Heritage Auctions*

Superman: The Movie is the product of a mindset simpler than that of most modern day superhero movies. That is not a criticism. This film functions as pure dream fulfillment. Its presentation of a morally pure superhero righting wrongs in a world of clear-cut morality is something that gives us all what we want: a hero that not only trumps evil but that does so with an understanding of good that is unanimously agreed upon.

As nearly the entire world knows by this point, the Superman mythology goes like this: One day, the faraway planet Krypton began to literally crumble. In the final seconds of the planet's life, one Kryptonian placed his infant son in a space pod and, to save his life, shot him off to a planet called Earth. This human-looking alien landed on the farm of an old Kansas couple who would go on to raise him as their son, naming him Clark Kent. When Clark grew, he quickly realized that the Earth's sun has an effect on his body that grants him a myriad of superpowers, most notably super strength, invulnerability, and flight. With these powers, he becomes known as Superman, fighting evil to better the lives of humanity.

This film is largely concerned with watching Superman simply play the

"I'M HERE TO FIGHT FOR TRUTH, AND JUSTICE, AND THE AMERICAN WAY." -SUPERMAN

The late Christopher Reeve was a nearly unknown actor when cast in the role that catapulted his career. *Warner Bros./DC Comics/Heritage Auctions*

role of hero. We watch him perform a range of acts from fighting crime to getting cats down from trees. In most movies, this strategy would become tedious. However, thanks to the acting of Christopher Reeve in the title role, the character becomes one that does not have to do interesting things in order to remain appealing. Reeve devotes himself so straightforwardly to the role of the benevolent hero that we are forced to accept the character as such, and not as a juvenile creation. Because of his acting, even his famous line, "I'm here to fight for truth, and justice, and the American way," manages to come across as inspiring rather than cheesy.

When the movie does bring in a central conflict for Superman to overcome, it loses speed. The fully human villain Lex Luthor (Gene Hackman) and his henchman Otis (Ned Beatty) are goofy and cartoonish, qualities which in no way complement the seriousness of Superman. Furthermore, their "destroy ninety percent of California and sell the remaining real estate for billions" master plan sounds like something you would find in a *Teenage Mutant Ninja Turtles* cartoon. Ironically, *Superman* works better when it is going nowhere in particular than when it injects an antagonist to spur the main character forth.

Superman shows signs of age, for sure, but its hero wish remains unadulterated. In 2001, an episode of the live-action, Superman-based TV series *Smallville* dedicated an episode to Reeve. After the credits, a message read, "He made us believe a man could fly." That is precisely what he did in the four *Superman* films between 1978 and 1987. And no one could have done it better.

The Thing

YEAR 1982
COUNTRY United States
RUNTIME 1 hr. 49 min.
RATED R; bloody violence, grisly and disturbing images, language
DIRECTED BY John Carpenter
WRITTEN BY John W. Campbell, Jr. ("Who Goes There?" source story), Bill Lancaster
STARRING Kurt Russell, A. Wilford Brimley, T.K. Carter, Keith David
SIMILAR SCI-FI *Alien*, *The Blob* (1988), *Invasion of the Body Snatchers* (1956), *Invasion of the Body Snatchers* (1978), *Re-Animator*, *The Thing from Another World*

Showing more influence from *Invasion of the Body Snatchers* than from *The Thing from Another World* (the film from which it gets its name), *The Thing* is director John Carpenter's exercise in paranoia, suspense, and the grotesque. This film is unrelenting in its goal of creating unease by not knowing who the enemy is. It also has some of the sci-fi/horror subgenre's most creative visuals.

One day at an Antarctic research facility, a group of researchers are confronted with a life form not of this world: a creature that devours other animals, assumes their form, mixes in with other like creatures, and repeats the process until everything is taken over. Oh, and this process happens to be as gruesome as you can imagine. As the characters attempt to destroy the thing before it can reach Earth's population, they soon realize it is emulating them, and they immediately become suspicious of one another. Anyone can be the enemy.

Smartly, Carpenter relies more on the building of tension than on its release. Even upon multiple viewings, the alien's body-takeovers and the characters' various plans to determine whose body has been appropriated are paced slowly enough to create suspense but quickly enough to remain interesting. This method is applied to the plot itself as well as individual scenes, the best of which must be a unique sort of blood test the characters implement while the suspected are tied to a couch. No matter how many times you see it, *The Thing* never loses its thrill factor.

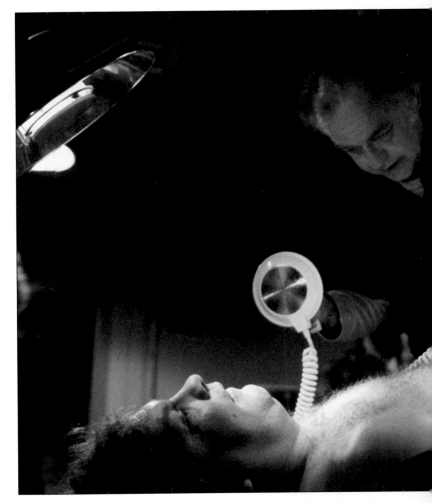

Dr. Cooper (Richard Dysart) attempts to revive Norris (Charles Hallahan) after he suffers a heart attack. *Universal Pictures/The Kobal Collection*

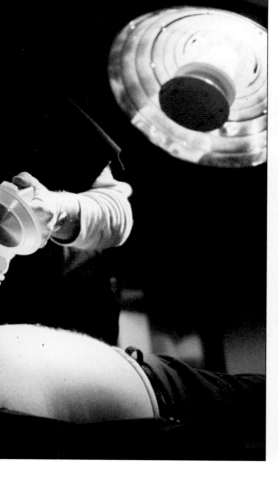

The gruesome nature of the alien's body takeovers elevates *The Thing* from effective thriller to sci-fi/horror classic. This alien takes over creatures in some incredibly disgusting ways, resulting in such images as numerous tendrils darting from the body of a dog whose face has split in four, and one character's stomach opening into a mouth and biting the arms off another. The stuff of pleasant dreams this is not.

Though the main character, a J&B-swilling, bearded roughneck named R.J. MacReady (Kurt Russell), seems to be taken from thriller hero stock, *The Thing* is a prime example of how to keep viewers enthralled through fear. Too many similar movies are told as though a monster alone makes them worth watching. It takes a hand like Carpenter's to use such things effectively.

The alien in the middle of a grotesque transformation. *Universal Pictures*

TRON

YEAR 1982
COUNTRY United States
RUNTIME 1 hr. 36 min.
RATED PG; some mild virtual-world violence
DIRECTED BY Steven Lisberger
WRITTEN BY Steven Lisberger, Bonnie MacBird
STARRING Jeff Bridges, Bruce Boxleitner, David Warner, Cindy Morgan
SIMILAR SCI-FI *The Lawnmower Man*, *The Matrix*, *TRON: Legacy*, *THX 1138*

Around the dawn of the modern computer era, the film *TRON* was made. It was a technological breakthrough in cinema. Like the computers that were made at the same time, it has also aged immensely in the years since. However, there is so much originality to be found in this movie that it is required viewing for any film fan, especially those with proclivities for science fiction.

In *TRON*, computer genius and arcade wizard Kevin Flynn (Jeff Bridges) finds himself sucked into a computer system, inhabiting it among the system's programs, all of which are portrayed by human actors. The computer's goal: to make Flynn battle the programs in gladiatorial games. Flynn's goal: to get the heck out of the computer!

The film's combination of animated, computer-animated, and live-action visuals is by far its most notable aspect. By today's standards these visuals are, honestly, lame, but in their time they signified great technological prowess and imagination. Furthermore, in a pre-*Neuromancer*, pre-Windows, and pre-*Matrix* world, *TRON* dared to imagine the inner workings of computers in terms to which we can relate. For every otherworldly component of *TRON*'s computer world,

there is something familiar, something onto which we can grasp.

Perhaps because of *TRON*'s focus on visuals, there is not much story. The story that is there, though, is interesting, as it presents the following question: To what extent are computer programs like people? And, conversely, to what extent are people like computer programs? This computer system is a world where programs not only carry out tasks but compete with one another for power and even ask theological questions. It's too bad the overwhelming majority of the

Video game heroes Yori (Cindy Morgan) and Tron (Bruce Boxleitner).
Walt Disney Pictures/The Kobal Collection

movie is concerned purely with Flynn's contests.

Even though *TRON* today looks like a bad '80s music video, it still holds a certain charm. Things like the famous light cycle contest and the flying-disc stand-off have struck a geek crowd chord that continues to resonate today. Ultimately, though, you have to appreciate this one for what it was, not what it is.

"WON'T THAT BE GRAND? ALL THE COMPUTERS AND THE PROGRAMS WILL START THINKING AND THE PEOPLE WILL STOP." -DR. WALTER GIBBS

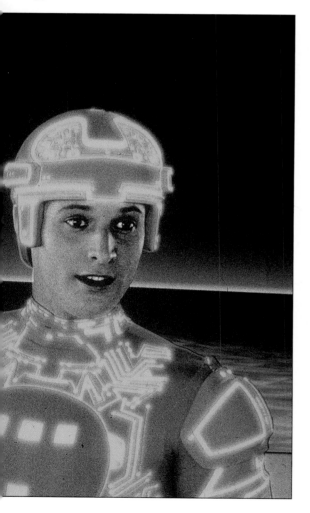

Walt Disney Pictures/Heritage Auctions

Back to the Future

YEAR 1985

COUNTRY United States

RUNTIME 1 hr. 56 min.

RATED PG; mild violence, language

DIRECTED BY Robert Zemeckis

WRITTEN BY Robert Zemeckis, Bob Gale

STARRING Michael J. Fox, Christopher Lloyd, Crispin Glover, Lea Thompson

SIMILAR SCI-FI *Back to the Future Part II, Back to the Future Part III, Bill & Ted's Excellent Adventure, Futurama: Bender's Big Score, Hot Tub Time Machine*

Back to the Future has a special kind of charm. It's not deep, and it's not particularly exciting, but there's no denying that it tells a moving story with an energy like that of someone who just had a great epiphany. Driven by the charisma of Michael J. Fox and a scenario involving a character ensuring that his own parents fall in love, *Back to the Future* can be watched over and over by anyone, sci-fi fan or not.

Marty McFly (Fox) finds himself in quite a predicament when he accidentally travels to the 1950s via a time-traveling DeLorean built by his friend Dr. Brown (a.k.a. "Doc"). Not only does he not have the required fuel source to get him back to the future; he has also, through a chance encounter, altered the course of his future-parents' lives. Now Marty has to play matchmaker to his mom and dad in order to ensure he is one day born, and he and a thirty-year-younger Doc (Christopher Lloyd) have to find a way to harness the 1.21 gigawatts required to send him back to 1985.

Every bit of this movie is fun, from the opening scenes of Fox skateboarding through town against a Huey Lewis soundtrack, to Marty's continual need to rebuff the advances of his 1950s mother (Lea Thompson), who, not knowing he is her future son, has fallen in love with him. The most rewarding aspect of it, though, is Marty's instillation of self-confidence into his father, George (Crispin Glover), who is bullied even when he's an adult. This plot seems to touch on some universal truth. There are times when we must look after our parents, but we can never let them know when we do. Marty is in this kind of situation. The

Doc (Christopher Lloyd) and Marty (Michael J. Fox) with the DeLorean Doc has turned into a time machine. *Amblin Entertainment/Universal/The Kobal Collection*

only difference is that his existence is what's at stake.

In the end, it is clear that George's problem was that he always just went along with things. Sometimes it's temptingly easy to continue down the path on which the past has placed you. *Back to the Future* shows how great it feels to do the opposite—not to fall in line with events but to set them in motion.

This movie was the top-grossing release of 1985.
Amblin Entertainment/Universal/ Heritage Auctions

Brazil

YEAR 1985
COUNTRY United States
RUNTIME 2 hrs. 12 min.
RATED R; some strong violence
DIRECTED BY Terry Gilliam
WRITTEN BY Terry Gilliam, Tom Stoppard, Charles McKeown
STARRING Jonathan Pryce, Kim Greist, Robert De Niro, Michael Palin
SIMILAR SCI-FI *Sleeper*, *THX 1138*

Imagine an entire country run like the DMV. Now you have a pretty good idea of what the world of *Brazil* is like. *Brazil* is a quirky satire set in a society that has become a bureaucratic hell. This film is packed with unforgettable imagery and the sense of just how bad things can be when man becomes slave to the laws and processes he creates.

A simple bureaucrat named Sam Lowry (Jonathan Pryce) is sent on a job to deliver a check of reimbursement to a woman whose husband was executed because someone's typewriter accidentally typed a "B" instead of a "T." Strangely, while attempting to deliver said check, Lowry, who regularly experiences hallucinatory daydreams of rescuing a woman in distress, meets the exact woman who appears in his dreams. When this woman (Kim Greist) attempts to prove the innocence of her neighbor's husband, she is deemed a terrorist. Luckily, Lowry is able to accept the precise governmental position to allow him to clear this Good Samaritan's name, but the girl is not quite ready to trust someone from the government.

In *Brazil*, one of the results of society's reliance on paperwork as the word of truth is a systemic

Sam Lowry (Jonathan Pryce) has frequent daydreams of saving a beautiful maiden.
Universal/Embassy/The Kobal Collection

inefficiency not only of government but of technology. This is the chief source of the film's satire. Twelve-inch-thick ducts run through the middle of every room, tractor-trailers are driven as simple taxis, and even bathtub stoppers appear to be designed by Rube Goldberg. Every piece of technology seems like its inventor ran full speed with the most preliminary of ideas. Additionally, as Lowry attempts to free the woman of his dreams from this bureaucracy, he hardly comes across an individual whose life is not dictated by etiquette, protocol, or paperwork. This is a society so absorbed in convention that the status quo has become its god.

Brazil suffocates the viewer with visions of a world that has rendered itself absurd, just as that world's government suffocates its citizens' ability to think. This is the kind of movie you laugh at until you realize it could potentially become non-fiction. Then, you become somewhat terrified.

"INFORMATION TRANSIT GOT THE WRONG MAN. I GOT THE RIGHT MAN. THE WRONG ONE WAS DELIVERED TO ME AS THE RIGHT MAN; I ACCEPTED HIM ON GOOD FAITH AS THE RIGHT MAN. WAS I WRONG?" -JACK LINT

Sam's mother, Ida (Katherine Helmond), goes through plastic-surgery torture to preserve her looks. *Universal/Embassy*

Re-Animator

YEAR 1985

COUNTRY United States

RUNTIME 1 hr. 35 min.

RATED R; extreme horror violence/gore, nudity, sexuality

DIRECTED BY Stuart Gordon

WRITTEN BY H.P. Lovecraft (source story), Dennis Paoli, William J. Norris, Stuart Gordon

STARRING Jeffrey Combs, Bruce Abbott, Barbara Crampton, David Gale

SIMILAR SCI-FI *Beyond Re-Animator, Bride of Re-Animator, Frankenstein, The Return of the Living Dead, Weird Science, Young Frankenstein*

Re-Animator has one of the most wildly macabre senses of humor you will find in a movie. If it was toned down, it might well become straight-up sci-fi/horror, but as it is, its gore and depictions of scientific monstrosities are so extreme that laughter is the only possible response. This is indeed a funny movie, but the laughter it provokes is probably also

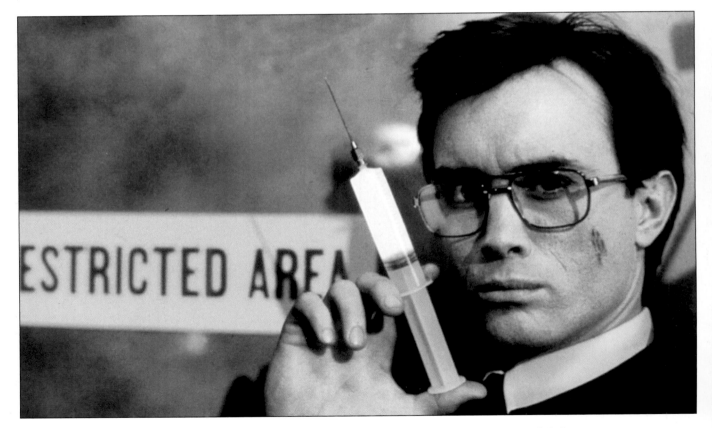

Herbert West (Jeffrey Combs) has a talent for bringing dead things back to life. *Re-Animated Productions/Empire/The Kobal Collection*

the result of mild hysteria.

Herbert West (Jeffrey Combs), a bright but defiant and radical student of medicine, is bent on essentially becoming the next Dr. Frankenstein. With the university unwilling to condone his theories of revitalizing clinically dead bodies, he is forced to experiment in the basement of his roommate's house. It's hard to say exactly where things start to go wrong. Maybe it's when he revitalizes his roommate's dead cat (which he *promises* he didn't kill). Maybe it's when he breaks into the hospital morgue and brings a bodybuilder back to life. One thing is for sure, though: West's science has opened pandemonium upon the Miskatonic University hospital.

Fueled by the hilariously calm madness of West and by scenes depicting preposterous levels of gore, *Re-Animator* is consistent in its ability to perpetuate the absurd. The clean-cut young man hides only his experiments themselves, not his eccentricity. However, even his experiments surface roughly halfway through the film. From there, his need to

carry out reanimations becomes pathological.

The reanimations provide the bulk of the film's dynamics. For whatever reason—maybe it's like an extreme version of morning grumpiness—West learns that people (and animals) tend to be particularly ill-tempered when woken from death. This leads to a seemingly endless stream of grisly events, of which West's thrusting a bone-saw through the torso of a resurrected man is only the beginning. By the end of the movie, dead bodies are carrying their own heads around, launching intestines around West's neck, and performing laser-lobotomies on the living.

Re-Animator begins in one of the most audacious ways possible for a movie with horror elements—with an opening credits homage to Alfred Hitchcock's *Psycho*. For a movie based on a character so bold as to bring dead bodies back to life, that is probably fitting. This is a work that, instead of feeling out its boundaries and attempting to tell a story within them, is concerned only with taking things as far as it can.

The Return of the Living Dead

YEAR 1985
COUNTRY United States
RUNTIME 1 hr. 31 min.
RATED R; strong zombie violence/gore, nudity, pervasive language
DIRECTED BY Dan O'Bannon
WRITTEN BY Dan O'Bannon, Rudy Ricci, Russell Streiner
STARRING Thom Mathews, James Karen, Don Calfa, Linnea Quigley
SIMILAR SCI-FI *Day of the Dead*, *Re-Animator*, *Slither*

The Return of the Living Dead is like an ice-breaker for thinking about death. In a world where death is the most solemn concept you can consider—if you are willing to think about it at all—this movie not only treats it with a sense of humor, it never lets up in doing so.

When Frank (James Karen), the foreman at a medical supplies facility, shows off some secret government chemical containers to a new employee, Freddy (Thom Mathews), the former accidentally lets loose the gas therein. Unfortunately for them, this secret gas ends up reanimating the cadavers in the facility and the corpses in the nearby cemetery. Frank and Freddy also happen to get a face-full of the stuff, which quickly causes some alarming health effects. They respond to these events as anyone would—with extreme and prolonged hysteria. And the punk-rebel kids who happen to be partying in the cemetery at the time? They're in for a surprise.

The events in *The Return of the Living Dead* seem geared only toward heightening the chaotic state of mind in which the main characters find

Exposure to poisonous gas turns Freddy (Thom Mathews) into a brain-eating zombie.
Orion/The Kobal Collection

"SEND MORE PARAMEDICS."
-ZOMBIE

themselves. Among other things, we are subjected to a naked cadaver running around without a head, a half-dog brought back to life, and one particularly memorable reanimated body that seems to consist half of bones and half of tar. The zombies that eventually rise are uniquely intelligent. After ambushing an ambulance and eating the paramedics, one zombie picks up the radio and requests, "Send more paramedics."

With the cemetery gang, the film provides a look at death from the opposite viewpoint, in a female character named Trash. Trash is so infatuated with death that she is sexually aroused by it, stripping completely naked and dancing around the graveyard while openly pondering what it would be like to be eaten alive by… old men. Judging by the reaction of her friends, this is normal behavior for Trash. Interestingly, however, the character's obsession with death seems to be no less intense than Frank and Freddy's fear of death. Even when death produces opposite reactions, it still takes us to extremes.

The thing about *The Return of the Living Dead* is that most of its comedic parts could conceivably be realistic insofar as they take place in an event involving the dead coming to life. It's our own reaction to the events that makes it funny. Maybe it's not so hard to find humor in death after all.

Predator

YEAR 1987
COUNTRY United States
RUNTIME 1 hr. 47 min.
RATED R; bloody violence, grisly images, language
DIRECTED BY John McTiernan
WRITTEN BY Jim Thomas, John Thomas
STARRING Arnold Schwarzenegger, Carl Weathers, Bill Duke, Jesse Ventura, Kevin Peter Hall
SIMILAR SCI-FI *Alien, Aliens, Predator 2, Predators*

On the surface, *Predator* is simply the kind of manly action movie that was commonplace in the day of actors like Arnold Schwarzenegger and Carl Weathers. This one improves upon the standard action film formula, however, in that it flips the odds against the main characters with an otherworldly foe. In *Predator*, even a Green Beret team led by Schwarzenegger is barely a match for the threat dreamed up by the film's creators.

About half a dozen of these elite soldiers land in the jungle of the fictional country of Val Verde to help rescue a cabinet member lost behind enemy lines. When they arrive, however, they find much more than they expected: an alien that seems to want little more than to kill them—and that is well equipped to do so. What appears to be a team of immortal action heroes is soon cut down to size by a single opponent with some powerful weaponry and adept hunting skills.

Structurally, the struggle against this alien is *Predator*'s biggest differentiation from other action films. Usually in these types of movies, we watch immensely powerful characters lay waste to bad guys and possibly face one foe of a somewhat equal power level in the end, only to defeat that enemy as

Kevin Peter Hall as the menacing Predator. *20th Century Fox/The Kobal Collection*

well. In *Predator*, our characters, as powerful as they are, find themselves being picked off one-by-one by the creature hunting them. Especially since the characters are realized with believable and distinct personalities, this threat becomes one we can feel.

The alien itself, the Predator, is what elevates *Predator* from distinguished sci-fi/action to a sci-fi/action classic. Revealed little by little—first through its own peculiar point-of-view, later while wearing an invisibility cloak, and eventually in its full, unmasked glory—the Predator is one of the most startling-, menacing-, and disgusting-looking creatures in science fiction. Add to its design some

"IF IT BLEEDS, WE CAN KILL IT." -DUTCH

weaponry that would make Iron Man proud, and you've got a thoroughly enjoyable monster.

The Predator is iconic enough to have been included in a direct sequel, a (disappointing) two-film crossover with the *Alien* franchise, a recent pseudo-reboot, and numerous comics (sometimes even facing off against Batman and Superman). None of these works, however, recapture the thrill of the original. With this monster, you just can't do better than to pit it against ultra-muscular '80s action stars.

RoboCop

YEAR 1987
COUNTRY United States
RUNTIME 1 hr. 43 min.
RATED R; graphic brutal violence, language, drugs
DIRECTED BY Paul Verhoeven
WRITTEN BY Edward Neumeier, Michael Miner
STARRING Peter Weller, Kurtwood Smith, Miguel Ferrer, Nancy Allen, Ronny Cox
SIMILAR SCI-FI *Predator 2, RoboCop 2, RoboCop 3, Surrogates, Terminator 2: Judgment Day*

Though *RoboCop* has shortcomings as a story, it is a smartly made film. It is packed with stock bad guys and pushes through key elements with a lack of logic, but it primarily functions as an affirmation of the inability to fully lose one's identity. Based on a man trying to regain his life and self after being commoditized by a mega-corporation, *RoboCop*'s appeal is built into its formula.

In the crime-torn city of Detroit, a company called Omni Consumer Products has stepped in to finance the police force…under the condition that they also manage it. One day, when an officer is ambushed and shot into a coma, OCP decides to turn him into an armed and armored cyborg, erasing his memory in the process to make him more efficient. However, RoboCop (Peter Weller) soon begins to remember who he was—something that should not happen. With memories slowly returning, he sets out to kill the criminals who ruined his life.

Despite plentiful explosions and in-your-face violence, the allure of *RoboCop* is RoboCop himself. This is an honest man who has been forced to live as a machine with virtually no hope of a human lifestyle. Somehow, though, he does begin to rediscover a sense of humanity. When he does, we watch him seek personal justice and, in doing so, affirm that our identities can never be completely taken away. Of course, the explosions and totally sweet handgun (and thigh that doubles as a holster!) don't hurt the film's allure, either.

RoboCop does have several problems that can detract from the experience, however. The most prevalent issue is the clichéd nature of the villains. These characters are way overblown, dressing like street thugs from a children's cartoon and laughing insanely at the slightest bit of humor. More importantly, though, as far as the story of RoboCop is concerned, his ability to remember his past is a huge stroke of convenience. There's no logic behind it other than the fact that it fits the movie's theme. You have to take everything for face value here. Once you start questioning too much, holes begin to show.

Despite its flaws, *RoboCop* presents a unique character in a dilemma that is relevant to any human: the loss of identity. Whatever the flaws of the film are, we have to root for the main character. If we don't, we admit our mutability.

RoboCop (Peter Weller) apprehends crime boss Clarence Boddicker (Kurtwood Smith). *ITV Global// Orion/Heritage Auctions*

Heroes Barf (John Candy) and Captain Lone Star (Bill Pullman) rescue Princess Vespa (Daphne Zuniga) and Dot Matrix (voiced by Joan Rivers).
Metro-Goldwyn-Mayer/The Kobal Collection

Spaceballs

YEAR 1987

COUNTRY United States

RUNTIME 1 hr. 36 min.

RATED PG; crude humor, some sci-fi violence

DIRECTED BY Mel Brooks

WRITTEN BY Mel Brooks, Thomas Meehan, Ronny Graham

STARRING Bill Pullman, John Candy, Rick Moranis, Mel Brooks, Daphne Zuniga, Joan Rivers

SIMILAR SCI-FI *Family Guy: Blue Harvest*, *Family Guy: Something, Something, Something Dark Side*, *Hardware Wars*, *Robot Chicken: Star Wars – Episode III*, *Young Frankenstein*

Villains Colonel Sandurz (George Wyner), Dark Helmet (Rick Moranis), and President Skroob (Mel Brooks). *Metro-Goldwyn-Mayer*

> *"EVIL WILL ALWAYS TRIUMPH ... BECAUSE GOOD IS DUMB."*
> **-DARK HELMET**

Just look at the title of this movie, and you know what you're getting into. The humor in *Spaceballs*, Mel Brooks' spoof of *Star Wars* (and occasionally other films), seems to come from everywhere—dialogue, sight gags, character qualities, names, and so on. This film is an endless stream of silly jokes in a world that vaguely resembles the fictional one we so love.

In a galaxy "very, very, very, very far away," the princess of Druidia (Daphne Zuniga) has run out on her arranged marriage. In another part of the galaxy, the wasteful planet Spaceball has run out of air. Lucky for the Spaceballs, they are able to capture this princess and hold her hostage, with the demand that Druidia give them all of their air. However, the king of Druidia is able to fight back, hiring a certain Lone Starr (Bill Pullman) and his half-man-half-dog co-pilot Barf (John Candy) to save her. You get the idea. The plot is little more than an excuse to give our main characters some obstacles to progress through while we watch them do and say ridiculous things and use ludicrous technology.

Most of the jokes are almost childish in their blatancy. One moment you'll be watching the villain Dark Helmet (played by Rick Moranis—who else?) confuse a coffee maker with a radar, the next you'll see a short, shriveled, wizard called Yogurt (Mel Brooks) talk about *Spaceballs* merchandising. There are subtler jokes to be found, however, such as when the Spaceball military commences their ship's "metamorphosis," and one character says to another, "Ready, Kafka." A few jokes come from other movies as well. One of the film's best gags involves actor John Hurt reprising his role as Kane from *Alien*—with a slightly altered outcome.

Spaceballs is the first non-short *Star Wars* parody, and while it may arguably be no longer *the* best, its consistent, innocent humor remains laudable. Nowadays we have *Family Guy* characters injecting their crude sensibilities into *Star Wars* (see P. 166), and we've got *Robot Chicken* taking basic aspects of the saga and running wild with them. Back in the '80s, we had bad guys incensed because their radars were jammed with strawberry jam or because they got caught playing with dolls. Choose your poison.

Akira

YEAR 1988
COUNTRY Japan
RUNTIME 2 hrs. 7 min.
RATED R; violence, mature themes, brief nudity
DIRECTED BY Katsuhiro Ôtomo
WRITTEN BY Katsuhiro Ôtomo, Izô Hashimoto
STARRING Mitsuo Iwata, Nozomu Sasaki, Tarô Ishida, Mami Koyama
SIMILAR SCI-FI *Cowboy Bebop: The Movie*, *The Fly* (1986), *Metropolis* (2001), *Neon Genesis Evangelion: Death and Rebirth*, *Scanners*

Sometimes movies don't have to be totally comprehendible to be good. Such is the case with the animated Japanese film *Akira*. The imagination and ideas contained within are so wild that they are often beyond full comprehension, but that is part of their allure, as if its creators are venturing beyond the understandable in search of a fundamental truth of the universe.

A heavily abbreviated adaptation of the manga by the same name, *Akira* takes place in a future "Neo-Tokyo" and is about a teenage motorcycle gang which is one day involved in an incident resulting in one of them, Tetsuo (Nozomu Sasaki), acquiring some sort of psychokinetic cosmic power. The military has several similar individuals already under their control, out of fear of what their powers could lead to, but something about Tetsuo is special, and this boy can't be reined in. When Tetsuo goes in search of Akira, an entity that seems to be the source of these powers, he begins losing control of himself. The result is a standoff, with this boy of godlike strength facing off against the military and some of his friends.

Akira is best appreciated for its story about power. Supernatural phenomena aside, this film is at its root concerned with Tetsuo's acquiring of his abilities and his lack of control over them. Accustomed to being the weakling of any particular group, Tetsuo's pent-up anger seems to find the perfect escape through these unprecedented abilities. In the final standoff, when Tetsuo's best friend, Kaneda (Mitsuo Iwata), tries to kill him, Kaneda's attempt to do so is genuinely for his friend's own good. He knows Tetsuo is not evil, just overcome with power.

The film utilizes dynamic visuals all the way through, from Kaneda's *TRON*-like motorcycle to the shriveled children that were born with psychokinetic abilities. There is one nightmare sequence that makes haunting use of stuffed animals, and viewers are treated to some insane imagery during Tetsuo's final standoff. If one thing can be said for *Akira*, it is that it never becomes boring.

Akira may take a few viewings to warm up to, but that is only because it doesn't spell out the answers to its mysteries. In fact, it only partially seems to care. Many of the details of the events are esoteric in their logic, but they are of secondary importance to the overarching story.

Kaneda (Mitsuo Iwata) takes aim at his best friend, Tetsuo. *Akira Committee Company Ltd./The Kobal Collection*

原作・監督 ■ 大友克洋

ネオ東京にシグナル、感知！

Akira's Japanese poster. *Akira Committee Company Ltd./Heritage Auctions*

The Abyss

YEAR 1989
COUNTRY United States
RUNTIME 2 hrs. 51 min.
RATED PG-13 for some scenes of action, language
DIRECTED BY James Cameron
WRITTEN BY James Cameron
STARRING Ed Harris, Mary Elizabeth Mastrantonio, Michael Biehn, Todd Graff
SIMILAR SCI-FI *2001: A Space Odyssey*, *Close Encounters of the Third Kind*, *The Day the Earth Stood Still* (1951), *Destination Moon*, *Sunshine*

Vastness. Emptiness. Blackness. These are the characteristics of an abyss. In his third major feature film, director James Cameron explores such a place to prove that even when we think we're staring into an abyss, there is something, some truth, hidden somewhere within. And, in typical Cameron fashion, he pushes the boundaries of special effects as he does so.

When a U.S. submarine is sunk in the Caribbean, the Navy enlists a group of deep-sea drillers with a mobile underwater oil rig to help them investigate the vessel and determine what happened. With tensions high between the U.S. and Russia, the military is quick to jump to the most obvious conclusion. During their investigation thousands of feet below the surface, though, the drillers and the military are forced to rule out any such suspicion, as they find something that is neither Russian nor human.

For the most part, *The Abyss* is a non-stop action thriller. The tension between the drillers

and the Navy Seals in charge of the operation starts high and continues to intensify as the commanding Naval officer gradually goes mad. This tension is heightened further by the close quarters of the underwater rig. Before long, the characters also find themselves confronted by a series of events that threaten to plunge the rig to depths that would kill them all. Between the military conflict and the efforts to maintain functionality of the facility's life support systems, moments of respite during the film are rare and brief.

On top of the plot's action sits the alien element. Though we don't get to see them often, these iridescent, water-manipulating creatures represent not only beauty but hope. The film's final moments paint the world as a figurative abyss comparable to physical abyss of the sea in which the characters have been struggling. However, just when we find this amazing life form in the water, we also find hope in a world overrun by crime, war, and hate. Add some special effects work that was unprecedented in its time, and these elements combine to create a classic.

The Abyss tells a simple story but an effective one. At times it can seem too concerned with providing thrills rather than analyzing the ideas at

Lindsey (Mary Elizabeth Mastrantonio) and Bud (Ed Harris) meet an aquatic alien. *20th Century Fox/The Kobal Collection*

hand, but that is the point. When one sets out to explore a philosophical abyss, to test whether there is any meaning in life, the process can be jarring and painful, just as these events are to the characters. When we find something within, though, it becomes more meaningful than we could have imagined.

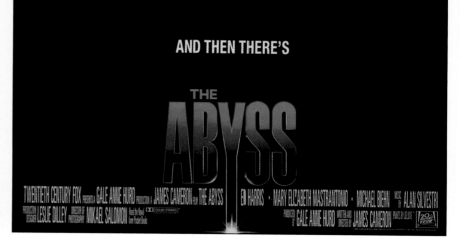

The movie won the 1990 Oscar for Best Visual Effects. *20th Century Fox/Heritage Auctions*

Jurassic Park

YEAR 1993
COUNTRY United States
RUNTIME 2 hrs. 6 min.
RATED PG-13; intense sci-fi terror
DIRECTED BY Steven Spielberg
WRITTEN BY Michael Crichton, David Koepp
STARRING Sam Neill, Laura Dern, Richard Attenborough, Jeff Goldblum
SIMILAR SCI-FI *Jurassic Park III*, *King Kong* (1933), *King Kong* (2005), *The Land Unknown*, *The Lost World* (1925), *The Lost World: Jurassic Park*

In Steven Spielberg's alien science fiction, he expresses wonder at what could be out in the unknown. In *Jurassic Park*, he expresses wonder at what we know existed long ago. This dinosaur film is a moral about the consequences of playing God, but it is heightened by an infusion of admiration for the beauty and power of nature.

Philanthropist John Hammond (Richard Attenborough) has funded an operation to clone dinosaurs from DNA found in the bellies of sixty-five-million-year-preserved mosquitoes and to keep them on an island-turned-amusement park. After a fatal accident involving a velociraptor, he invites two paleontologists, a mathematician, a lawyer, and his grandchildren to confirm the safety of the park and the excitement it has to offer. Unfortunately, it turns out that safety can never be guaranteed, and several of the characters find themselves stranded in the elements with dinosaurs loose all around them.

Spielberg's foremost concern in *Jurassic Park* is to thrill us, and he succeeds greatly. Once the plot gets rolling, it basically turns into a long string of dinosaurs hunting, chasing, and attacking the main characters. Spielberg achieves terrifying levels of tension through impressive visual effects, even more impressive sound effects, and dinosaurs that are designed so that we never know quite what they are thinking, even when they stare us in the face. At some points the thrills are so intense you could classify the film as horror.

What makes *Jurassic Park* a beautiful film, though, is that throughout

The game warden (Bob Peck) has a showdown with a tyrannosaurus.
Amblin Entertainment/Universal Pictures/Heritage Auctions

it all, even during the more visceral scenes, the dinosaurs are presented with a sense of majesty, facilitated greatly by the score of legendary composer John Williams. The characters occasionally stop to gaze at the more docile dinosaurs, and their love for the creatures is contagious. This is the film's most commendable accomplishment: its evocation of a childlike sense of awe.

In *Jurassic Park*, Spielberg doesn't resurrect dinosaurs just to scare us with them. He does so because they are just as amazing, if not more so, than any creature science fiction can dream up. Because of this, the film is more than entertainment; it is a statement of respect for the glory of nature.

Drs. Ellie Sattler (Laura Dern) and Alan Grant (Sam Neill) tend to an ailing dinosaur.
Amblin Entertainment/Universal Pictures/Heritage Auctions

The City of Lost Children

YEAR 1995

RUNTIME 1 hr. 52 min.

RATED R; disturbing images of violence

DIRECTED BY Marc Caro, Jean-Pierre Jeunet

WRITTEN BY Gilles Adrian, Jean-Pierre Jeunet, Marc Caro, Guillaume Laurant

STARRING Ron Perlman, Judith Vittet, Daniel Emilfork, Dominique Pinon, Joseph Lucien

SIMILAR SCI-FI *Alien: Resurrection*, *Dark City*, *Fantastic Planet*

Director Jean-Pierre Jeunet has a knack for making movies that don't just utilize unique visuals but that revolve around them. *Amélie* may be his most famous achievement in this regard, but as far as science fiction goes, *The City of Lost Children* (co-directed with Marc Caro) is his most exemplary work. This is a darkly whimsical film about the ugliness of valuing dreams more than the joys of everyday life.

In some strange, foggy city near the water, a mad scientist with the power to create life has spawned a woman, a talking brain, a brilliant inventor named Krank (Daniel Emilfork), and six copies of himself. All of these creations happen to come with flaws, though, and the inventor's flaw in particular has led to a big problem in the city. Due to his inability to dream, Krank has established an operation in which children are kidnapped on a regular basis so that he can steal their dreams. When Denree (Joseph Lucien), the little brother

Mad scientist Krank (Daniel Emilfork). *Claudie Ossard/ Constellation/The Kobal Collection*

of a carnival strongman named "One," (Ron Perlman) is kidnapped, One sets out to bring down Krank with the help of a thieving orphan girl (Judith Vittet).

Though the plot itself is important to the film as a whole, the focus is primarily on the visuals. In *The City of Lost Children*, Jeunet, through bizarre imagery coupled with green and rusty hues, creates a frequently nightmarish dream world. Many of the characters alone look bizarre, such as Krank with his birdlike face and large, bald head, or the six clones who seem to make contorting facial expressions endlessly. Other memorable images are the shots of the talking brain in green, bubbling liquid; a scene of Krank dressed as Santa Claus and singing to a room of horrified, crying babies; and close-ups of specially trained assassin fleas administrating poison to their targets. There is hardly an ordinary moment in the film.

Ultimately, *The City of Lost Children* is about the problem inherent

in attempting to achieve dreams or goals at the expense of the present. The figurative dream world—the state of being in which one has essentially reached perfect contentment through the achieving of goals—is shown to be an echo of the literal dream world, a well-reputed but sordid place painted with a kind of ugly beauty. Krank is evil because he views Denree in terms only of how Denree can help him complete his life. One, on the other hand, values Denree for who he inherently is. One's dream is not to find something that he feels will complete his life; he just wants to make life generally happier. It's more fulfilling to live with joyful incompletion than to die with no desires.

"YOU ARE THEIR NIGHTMARE. YOU COULD PERSECUTE ALL THE CHILDREN IN THE WORLD, BUT THERE'S ONE THING YOU'LL NEVER HAVE ... A SOUL."
- L'ONCLE IRVIN (TO KRANK)

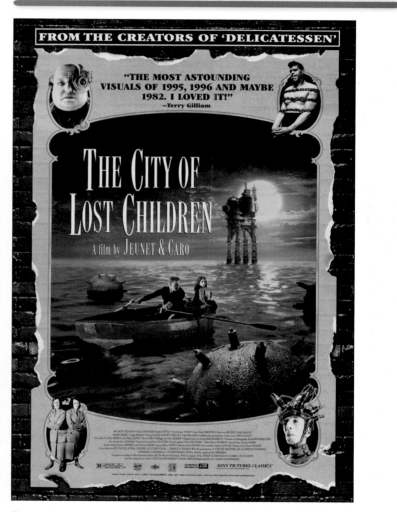

The movie spawned a video game released in the U.S. and parts of Europe for the PC and PlayStation console. *Heritage Auctions*

Ghost in the Shell

YEAR 1995

COUNTRY Japan

RUNTIME 1 hr. 23 min.

RATED Not Rated; some strong sci-fi violence, nudity, some language

DIRECTED BY Mamoru Oshii

WRITTEN BY Kazunori Itô, Masamune Shirow (source manga)

STARRING Atsuko Tanaka, Aiko Ôtsuka, Tamio Ôki, Iemasa Kayumi

SIMILAR SCI-FI *Cowboy Bebop: The Movie, Ghost in the Shell 2: Innocence, Neon Genesis Evangelion: Death and Rebirth, RoboCop*

"That's the only thing that makes me feel human: the way I'm treated." Set in a world in which cybernetic enhancements are commonplace, *Ghost in the Shell* presents an existential crisis with this statement, spoken by an individual who is more machine than human. At what point, once we begin altering ourselves, is the original us no longer there?

Ghost in the Shell presents a labyrinthine plot involving cyborgs, government agencies, political espionage, and a hacker who is trying to take over the mind of a government cyborg. Even if you keep track of the various interests at play, they are of only of minor importance. The story's chief concerns lie in Motoko Kusanagi (Atsuko Tanaka), a cyborg agent who, when the aforementioned hacker targets a peer's brain, begins questioning her status as a living being.

The film is primarily concerned with notions of the self and life. The characters posit the idea that memories are what make up the individual's

Cyborg agent Motoko Kusanagi. *Manga Entertainment/The Kobal Collection*

identity and sense of self, but what happens when memories are manipulated—or completely replaced?

Once cybernetic enhancements are so ubiquitous as to be applied to the brain, this becomes a serious question. And what constitutes life anyway? With super-advanced programs—some of which have all the attributes of a personality—roaming various networks, is a human body even necessary in order to be alive? These are the ideas of *Ghost in the Shell*, complete with the kind of cyborg visuals for which anime is known and which science fiction fans love.

Concepts like the transferability of consciousness or the technological altering of identity can sound unnecessarily far-fetched. That is part of the beauty of *Ghost in the Shell*. It anticipates far-away existential dilemmas in order to question fundamental assumptions about life. As outlandish as it may be, its core concerns are always relevant.

Neon Genesis Evangelion: Death & Rebirth

YEAR 1997
COUNTRY United States
RUNTIME 1 hr. 41 min.
RATED Not Rated; violence, language, brief nudity
DIRECTED BY Hideaki Anno, Masayuki, Kazuya Tsurumaki
WRITTEN BY Hideaki Anno
STARRING Yûko Miyamura, Megumi Ogata, Megumi Hayashibara, Kotono Mitsuishi
SIMILAR SCI-FI *Akira*, *The End of Evangelion*, *Evangelion 1.11: You Are (Not) Alone*, *Evangelion 2.22: You Can (Not) Advance*

Neon Genesis Evangelion: Death & Rebirth is an awesome film, but it is tiringly difficult to follow. However, that also accounts for some of its allure. Beneath the frequently incomprehensible plot of giant robots fighting giant aliens, the film's symbolism and humanism seems to represent some hyper-aware understanding of the universe that is only half-possible to grasp.

Death & Rebirth is actually an anthology of two related films, *Neon Genesis Evangelion: Death* and *Neon Genesis Evangelion: Rebirth*. Each revolves around a military-like operation called Marduke, which has developed giant half-organic robot-like weapons with which specially selected children from a young age are trained to psychically fuse in order to pilot them. These machines, called "Evangelions" ("Evas" for short), are derived from one of the aforementioned giant aliens, known as "Angels," and are used to thwart off attacks by those aliens. *Death* primarily follows the attempts of the Marduke children to fight off invading angels. *Rebirth* covers a certain institute's attempt to combine the entire race into a single being. If you want to understand more about the plot, you're best off turning to the television series.

On a visceral level, the Eva-Angel fights are stunning. The designs of these monstrous forces pull from various anime conventions, yet the outcomes are unique, with the Angels having nearly indefinable forms and the Evas being just organic enough to instill a sort of horror at their very existence. When the beings are thrown together, the result is never just a city-leveling brawl; the at times animal-like emotion exhibited by the Evas and Angels makes the conflicts approach unsettling levels of intensity.

It's up to some young pilots to stop super-powered Angels from bringing about an event that has the capability of destroying all human life.
Production I.G/Gainax Company

Though there is thick religious symbolism present in *Death & Rebirth*, the film is at its core, perhaps surprisingly, about the inability of men and women to understand each other. The movie presents the Eva-Angel conflict as parallel to the ongoing conflict between the two sexes (a parallel that is too involved to illuminate in this space). Though some indefinable force always attracts us to each other, we are also, at a seemingly fundamental level, perpetually at odds with each other. The only way to resolve this conflict, it seems, is through cataclysm.

At one point in *Death & Rebirth*, a character explains that "understanding one hundred percent of anything is impossible." That is both a reason for the Angel-Eva/male-female conflict and an explanation for its elusiveness. It also seems to be the philosophy under which the story was written: if this work is difficult to understand, that's because the world itself is, too.

"AFTER ALL WE'VE BEEN THROUGH, OUR FINAL ENEMY IS OUR FELLOW MAN." -FUYUTSUKI

The Iron Giant

YEAR 1999
COUNTRY United States
RUNTIME 1 hr. 26 min.
RATED PG; fantasy action, mild language
DIRECTED BY Brad Bird
WRITTEN BY Brad Bird, Tim McCanlies, Ted Hughes (source novel)
STARRING Eli Marienthal, Vin Diesel, Jennifer Aniston, Christopher McDonald
SIMILAR SCI-FI *CJ7, The Day the Earth Stood Still* (1951), *E.T.: The Extra-Terrestrial, Transformers*

The Iron Giant must be the world's most touching giant robot movie. In a medium in which the term "giant robot" is practically synonymous with "destroyed city," the creators of this animated film use such an element not for action and thrills but to create a unique friendship. *The Iron Giant* is about the sadness of responding to perceived threats with violence.

In Rockwell, Maine during the Cold War, a boy named Hogarth discovers a giant robot, whose origin remains unknown but who demonstrates himself to be far friendlier than one would expect a giant robot to be. This robot doesn't quite know how things work (when he becomes hungry for railroad tracks, the results are nearly catastrophic), but Hogarth manages to teach him some basics of life on Earth. Unfortunately, a government agent has shown up in Rockwell and is bent on finding this robot and bringing it down simply because it's a giant robot.

Always aware of the time period in which it is set, *The Iron Giant* becomes a statement about the distrust that arises when dealing with that which we don't understand. The government's response at merely hearing about this robot is to track it down and kill it. Hogarth seems to understand this instinctually, knowing from the second he meets the robot that it must be kept a secret.

The robot is not immune to this kind of thought, either. When it at one point sees Hogarth wield a toy gun, it automatically, and with no apparent voluntary decision, arms itself and attempts to eliminate the boy. Sometimes it is difficult to escape our inclination for responding with aggression, but Hogarth shows us there's a simple trick to fixing that: free will.

When we feel threatened we tend to respond with emotion, not thought. *The Iron Giant* takes that idea and watches it play out in a world facing an unprecedented discovery. The result is an expression of sadness at our intolerance for the unknown and of optimism at our capacity to control ourselves.

"ALL I KNOW IS WE DIDN'T BUILD IT, AND THAT'S REASON ENOUGH TO ASSUME THE WORST AND BLOW IT TO KINGDOM COME!"
-KENT MANSLEY

Hogarth and the giant robot spend some time bonding. *Warner Bros./The Kobal Collection*

The Matrix

YEAR 1999
COUNTRY United States
RUNTIME 2 hrs. 16 min.
RATED R; sci-fi violence, brief language
DIRECTED BY Andy Wachowski, Larry Wachowski
WRITTEN BY Andy Wachowski, Larry Wachowski
STARRING Keanu Reeves, Laurence Fishburne, Carrie-Ann Moss, Hugo Weaving
SIMILAR SCI-FI *Dark City*, *The Matrix: Reloaded*, *The Matrix: Revolutions*, *TRON: Legacy*, *X-Men*

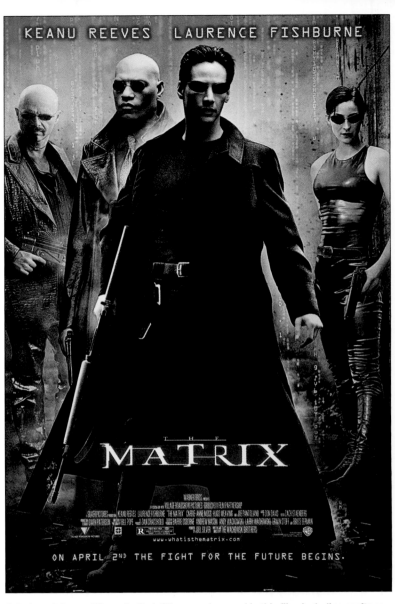

Sets from fellow sci-fi movie *Dark City* were also used in this film, including rooftops.
Warner Bros./Heritage Auctions

When *The Matrix* came out in 1999, there was almost nothing like it. Few movies are capable of remaining so superficially entertaining while provoking so much thought. It also utilized visual techniques that would influence the landscape of action film cinematography. This is required viewing for everyone, not just fans of science fiction.

A hacker known as "Neo" (Keanu Reeves) has been searching for something called the Matrix. He doesn't know what it is, but he knows that it's big, that it's secret, and that it exists. One day, someone contacts Neo directly through his computer's operating system, claiming to have the answers. Neo soon learns that the Matrix is much closer and bigger than he thought. The bad part is that the agents that guard and police the Matrix are practically omnipotent, and they don't want anyone finding out about it.

It's difficult to discuss the full aesthetic success of *The Matrix* without spoiling a vital twist. It must suffice to say simply, then, that despite the extent to which the events in the film become fantastical, they are always solidly grounded in science fiction. Because of the nature of the Matrix, those who are privy to its secrets are able to manipulate the world around them. They can run on walls, float in the air, dodge bullets, you name it. And the filmmakers know exactly how to maximize the potential for these elements.

> *"EVERY MAMMAL ON THIS PLANET INSTINCTIVELY DEVELOPS A NATURAL EQUILIBRIUM WITH THEIR SURROUNDING ENVIRONMENT, BUT YOU HUMANS DO NOT. YOU MOVE TO AN AREA, AND YOU MULTIPLY, AND YOU MULTIPLY, UNTIL EVERY NATURAL RESOURCE IS CONSUMED. THE ONLY WAY YOU CAN SURVIVE IS TO SPREAD TO ANOTHER AREA. THERE IS ANOTHER ORGANISM ON THIS PLANET THAT FOLLOWS THE SAME PATTERN. DO YOU KNOW WHAT IT IS? A VIRUS." –AGENT SMITH*

What makes all of this so cool is the cinematography. *The Matrix* made breakthroughs in the use of bullet time and time slice camera techniques, slowing everything to a crawl, and at times to a stop, then moving the camera freely around in order to fully show off the feats the characters perform. Naturally, this magnifies the effect of the film's already awesome action scenes.

At the core of *The Matrix* are questions of reality. What is it, how do we know that we are living in it, and if we're *not* living in reality, do we really want to discover the potentially ugly truth? These are questions with which Neo is directly confronted, as he learns things that few of us would want to know and fights to expose the truths of the world. Who says action films have to be mindless?

There are those who argue against the unoriginality of *The Matrix*, as most of its basic ideas have been posited before. To make such an argument, however, is to forget one key truth: never before have these ideas been presented in such an entertaining manner. This is a film that's unafraid to combine action and thought—two elements that we so often consider incompatible. It also excels at presenting both. How often does that happen?

Neo (Keanu Reeves) squares off against nemesis Agent Smith (Hugo Weaving). *Warner Bros./Heritage Auctions*

Star Wars Episode I – The Phantom Menace

YEAR 1999
COUNTRY United States
RUNTIME 2 hrs. 13 min.
RATED PG; sci-fi action and violence
DIRECTED BY George Lucas
WRITTEN BY George Lucas
STARRING Liam Neeson, Ewan McGregor, Jake Lloyd, Natalie Portman
SIMILAR SCI-FI *Star Wars: Episode II - Attack of the Clones, Star Wars: Episode III - Revenge of the Sith, Star Wars: The Clone Wars*

Star Wars: Episode I – The Phantom Menace, the film that kicked off the long-awaited prequel trilogy to the original *Star Wars* films, is essential viewing for any sci-fi fan not because it is good and not because it is bad, but because it is so polarizing. Released sixteen years after the greatest sci-fi saga ever put to film, *The Phantom Menace* was one of the most highly anticipated movies of all time. When it finally hit theaters, though, fans did not get what they expected—and many were disappointed.

Going back to the beginning of the Empire's rise to power, we follow Obi-Wan Kenobi as a Jedi student embarking on a mission to settle a trade dispute and thereafter stumbling upon Anakin Skywalker, a slave boy fated to become one of

The high point of the movie is the epic lightsaber duel between Obi-Wan (Ewan McGregor), Darth Maul (Ray Park) and Qui Gon (Liam Neeson, not pictured).
Lucasfilm/The Kobal Collection

the most powerful Jedi ever. With this setup, the plot at times loses focus on the significance of the characters and gets more caught up in show, but we always eventually return to Anakin and the potential benefits and dangers of training someone

so naturally powerful. In the end, we get both a trademark final lightsaber duel and a full-scale battle between two armies.

Problems with the film are found in its style, characterizations, plot, and even its treatment of the mythology of the Force. Whereas one of the most notable qualities of the original trilogy was its presentation of a used, gritty world, *The Phantom Menace* is pristinely polished and at times cartoonishly colored. Many of the main characters are one-dimensional, speaking lines that do little more than advance the plot. There are also a number of holes in the plot, including the unnecessarily roundabout method the characters use to leave a planet on which they become stranded. By the time the previously mystical nature of the Force is explained in scientific terms, many fans of the original films are alienated. Finally, the infamous Jar Jar Binks may be the single largest misstep of the film and of the entire prequel trilogy. The creature's slapstick clumsiness and juvenile manner of speaking may garner some high-pitched giggles, but for virtually any viewer in adolescence or beyond, Jar Jar has no redeeming qualities. Ultimately, most have to agree, *The Phantom Menace* was aimed not at the legions of preexisting *Star Wars* fans but at children, in order to create a whole new generation of fandom.

Still, there is a case to be made for *The Phantom Menace*. The massive success the film had in capturing younger audiences is evidence that the movie is successful on at least some level. Also, though plot holes do exist in the movie, many *Star Wars* fans forget that the original films were not perfectly ironed out themselves (there were hundreds of stormtroopers stationed on the Death Star, but only a dozen or so TIE fighters were available to fend off an attack?). Furthermore, there's no denying that some scenes in *The Phantom Menace* are simply awesome—most notably, the final lightsaber duel, in which two Jedi battle Darth Maul, an animalistic dark Jedi with a double-bladed lightsaber. This fight is almost universally acknowledged as being stunningly choreographed, and, at face value, it may be the best duel of all the *Star Wars* movies.

The prequel debate, starting with *The Phantom Menace*, lives on after a decade and will likely continue for much longer. Surely, many criticisms of the film are the result of *Star Wars* fans simply getting something much different from what they expected. In these cases, the core issue becomes one of respect, as fans of the originals have felt betrayed by *Star Wars* creator George Lucas. There are others who feel that there is nothing significantly wrong with the prequels, just that they are different in a neutral way. Regardless of one's position on the matter, no fandom of the genre is complete without a familiarity of *The Phantom Menace* as, if nothing more, the science fiction culture's biggest point of contention.

Metropolis

YEAR 2001
COUNTRY Japan
RUNTIME 1 hr. 53 min.
RATED PG-13; violence, images of destruction
DIRECTED BY Rintaro
WRITTEN BY Katsuhiro Ôtomo, Osamu Tezuka (source comic)
STARRING Kei Kobayashi, Yuka Imoto, Tarô Ishida, Kousei Tomita, Kôki Okada
SIMILAR SCI-FI *A.I.: Artificial Intelligence*, *Astro Boy*, *Steamboy*

An adaptation of the comic inspired by Fritz Lang's *Metropolis* (see P. 10), director Rintaro's *Metropolis* is significantly different from the 1927 film. It is an anime with elements of Lang's masterpiece, but it combines them in vastly altered proportions and plays them out in a style that is the polar opposite. It is an expression of longing for a world in which every human and otherwise sentient being is accepted and loved.

When private investigator Shunsaku Ban and his nephew Kenichi (Kei Kobayashi) attempt to track down an organs smuggler, they become caught up in a debacle involving Duke Red (Tarô Ishida), an aristocrat attempting to gain absolute power; Rock (Kôki Okada), Duke Red's pseudo-adopted but unwanted son; and Tima (Yuka Imoto), an android that thinks she's human. Rock, a hunter of robots who act outside of their given parameters, is homicidally jealous of Tima, which Duke Red had built to fill the void left by his deceased daughter

With its vibrant color palette and beauty, this movie is a visual treat. *Bandai/Toho/The Kobal Collection*

and to power a massive military weapon. After befriending Tima, Kenichi takes up the task of protecting her against Rock and whatever insidious intents Duke Red has in mind for her.

Despite being a bit convoluted, *Metropolis* is a beautiful film in every sense of the word. Nearly every plot point is somehow concerned with the joy to be found in simple kindness or the societal damage caused by those who harm others. This idea is present specifically in Tima's story as well. The only thing non-human about Tima is that she is made of metal, and we are made to care just as much for her—and other robots—as for the human protagonists. *Metropolis* does not discriminate between the organic and the mechanical.

The movie's beauty also pervades its visuals. Its childlike character designs, sugary color palette, and mixture of 2D and 3D animation make *Metropolis* a pure visual joy. The city of Metropolis is filled with a vibrancy and imagination that is rarely achieved.

Though the film's plot is more complex than it needs to be, its story remains touching and even enthralling. Its characters evoke sympathy, and its animation inspires wonder. It is a fundamentally charming and endearing film.

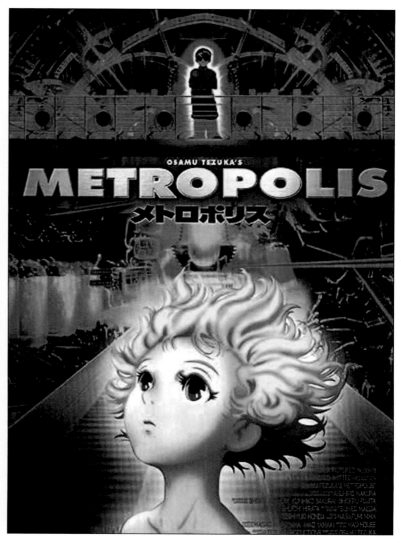

This movie draws some aspects of its storyline from the 1927 *Metropolis.* *Bandai/Toho*

Minority Report

YEAR 2002
COUNTRY United States
RUNTIME 2 hrs. 25 min.
RATED PG-13; violence, brief language, some sexuality and drug content
DIRECTED BY Steven Spielberg
WRITTEN BY Philip K. Dick (source story), Scott Frank, Jon Cohen
STARRING Tom Cruise, Max von Sydow, Neal McDonough, Colin Farrell
SIMILAR SCI-FI *Blade Runner, Repo Men, Total Recall*

The things we see are always witnessed in the context of who we are. That is the point of *Minority Report*, though it's often easy to get too caught up in its surface elements to notice much else. With this film, Steven Spielberg has created a sci-fi experience that is simultaneously thoughtful and exciting.

John Anderton (Tom Cruise) is a police officer in Washington D.C.'s "precrime" division, a young but politically championed operation centered on the ability to detect murders before they take place. This is made possible by three individuals with uncanny predilections for pattern recognition. When a future murder is predicted, the police force swoops in, arrests the would-be killer, and locks him away in a semi-comatose state. All is good and well…until Anderton receives a precognitive report of a murder committed by himself.

The movie sets itself up as a hypothetical scenario in which we ponder the solidity of the future. If we apprehend murderers before they actually commit murder, haven't we then apprehended innocents? And furthermore, how do we know that the events foreseen by the "precogs," as they are known, are unchangeable? Wouldn't this negate any notion of free will?

Spielberg takes his story deeper than these perhaps unanswerable questions, though. With the director's use of the eye (and the removal thereof) as a recurring theme, *Minority Report* becomes a film about seeing. Whether it's a literal sight, a vision of the future, or something less concrete like a world view, nothing seen by any given individual can be deemed absolute. Notice how Anderton's fugitive state corresponds with his seeing the world through someone else's eyes. Notice how taking a different view of things (by donning glasses) provides one early character with a mindset that justifies murder.

At the same time, *Minority Report* is successful as a straight-up thriller/mystery. Anderton's flight from the police at the same time that he is trying to solve the mystery of the future murder for which he has been framed (or has he?) is no less engaging than similar films like *The Fugitive*. The plot contains action, suspense, and plenty of events that are simply painful to imagine (as you may guess, given the film's emphasis on eyes). It may at times become sidetracked from its larger concerns, but the film constantly upholds its sense of urgency.

Minority Report can be appreciated by virtually anybody. For the more demanding viewer, however, the film has multiple layers which may not be apparent upon a casual viewing. It meets modern visceral demands without sacrificing depth.

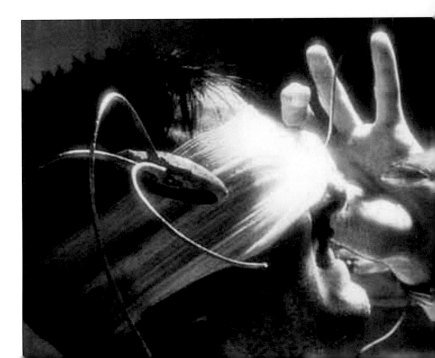

There's a lot of emphasis on eyes in the movie.
20th Century Fox/Dreamworks

John Anderton (Tom Cruise) kidnaps one of the precogs (Samantha Morton). *20th Century Fox/Dreamworks/ The Kobal Collection*

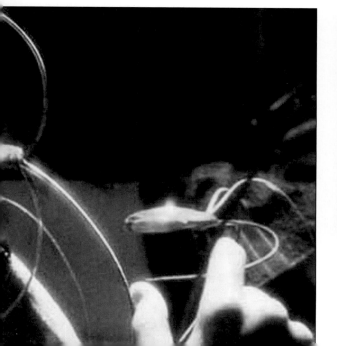

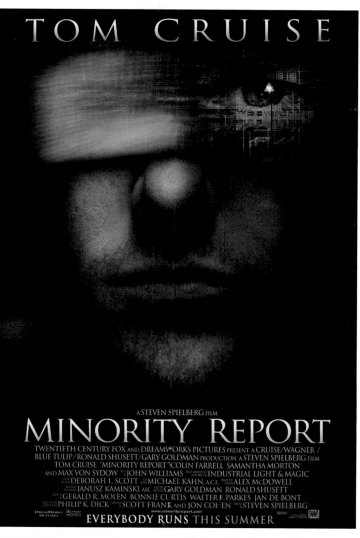

The movie has received critical acclaim and is thought to be one of Steven Spielberg's best. *20th Century Fox/Dreamworks/Heritage Auctions*

The Incredibles

YEAR 2004
COUNTRY United States
RUNTIME 1 hr. 55 min.
RATED PG; action violence
DIRECTED BY Brad Bird
WRITTEN BY Brad Bird
STARRING Craig T. Nelson, Holly Hunter, Spencer Fox, Samuel L. Jackson, Jason Lee
SIMILAR SCI-FI *Astro Boy*, *Despicable Me*, *Megamind*, *Monsters vs. Aliens*, *Spider-Man*, *X-Men*

A kid-friendly, eye-popping, CG-animated film about a mildly dysfunctional family of superheroes—it almost seems too easy. *The Incredibles* does what all movies should do: it entertains superficially at the same time that it tells a story with which virtually anyone can identify. This is one of those films that calls into question the sanity of anyone who claims to dislike it.

The Parrs, a family of four that closely resembles the Fantastic Four in their superpowers, lives in constant suppression of their abilities after the government has outlawed super-vigilantism. This is detrimental to the spirits of Mr. Parr (a.k.a. Mr. Incredible), a man of superhuman strength who is forced to stamp insurance claims papers all day, and his speed-powered son Dashiell (a.k.a. "Dash"), who has to suffer high school without taking advantage of his potential to excel at every sport imaginable. One day, however, Mr. Parr (Craig T. Nelson) receives a message that will eventually draw the whole family into an all-out super-powered fight against Syndrome, a villain who presents a threat to the whole city.

As *The Incredibles* progresses, we are treated to the types of visuals that appeal to any lover of science fiction. All characters have numerous opportunities to show off their abilities, including Mr. Incredible stopping an escape car with an uprooted tree, his wife (Holly Hunter) stretching into a parachute to slow the fall of a newborn, his son (Spencer Fox)

Former Mr. Incredible fan Buddy reinvents himself as the superhero's foe, Syndrome, bent on revenge. *Pixar/Walt Disney Pictures/Heritage Auctions*

racing through woods to escape bladed helicopter drones, and his daughter (Sarah Vowell) producing force fields to protect her family from explosions. Naturally, there's also a giant robot that attacks the city.

The Incredibles is most enjoyable, however, for its core story. This film contrasts the misery of living an inauthentic life with the thrill of accepting yourself. Before they are forced to once again don costumes to fight off Syndrome (Jason Lee), the Parrs' lives are so ordinary as to be torturous. When they are able to utilize their natural-born talents, they find a happiness they had long forgotten. Not surprisingly, these parts of the film are the most rewarding.

Some superhero movies begin with the benefit of a well-known franchise yet fail to deliver the elements for which those franchises are so loved. The Incredibles is the opposite. This is a story spawned by a writer who, though showing obvious influence from other properties, does not rely on a pre-established name to draw fans but instead on a fun story with relatable characters. It seems so simple, yet it far surpasses so much superhero cinema.

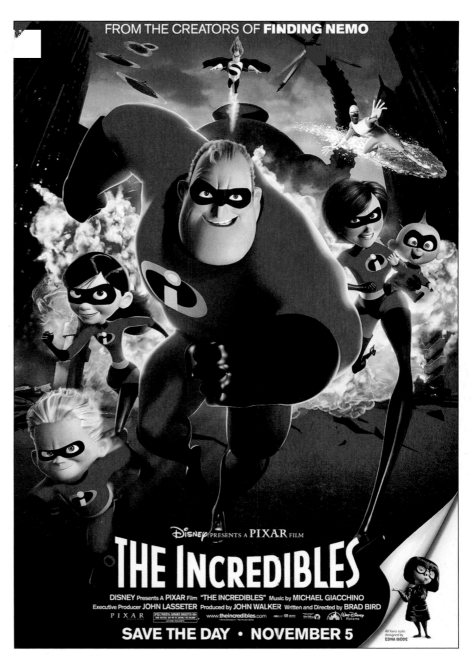

The film won the Academy Award in 2004 for Best Animated Feature.
Pixar/Walt Disney Pictures/Heritage Auctions

Stewie as Darth Vader and Lois as Princess Leia, with stormtroopers. *20th Century Fox*

Family Guy: Blue Harvest

YEAR 2007
COUNTRY United States
RUNTIME 48 min.
RATED Not Rated; some animated cartoon violence, some language
DIRECTED BY Dominic Polcino

WRITTEN BY Seth MacFarlane, David Zuckerman, Alec Sulkin
STARRING Seth MacFarlane, Seth Green, Alex Borstein, Mike Henry
SIMILAR SCI-FI *Family Guy: Something, Something, Something Dark Side*, *Family Guy: It's a Trap!*, *Hardware Wars*, *Robot Chicken: Star Wars – Episode III*, *Spaceballs*

If there has been one proven formula for parody, it is this: never cease to respect the source material, even while you poke fun at it. Mel Brooks' *Young Frankenstein* is a paragon of this philosophy. For a modern example, you need look no further than Seth MacFarlane's mash-up of *Star Wars* with his own *Family Guy* series. The result is *Family Guy: Blue Harvest*, a parody that is rarely surpassed in demonstrating a love for the original and that also provides laughs all the way through.

Sticking strictly to *Star Wars: Episode IV* for this forty-five-minute film (Episodes V and VI are tackled in subsequent installments), *Blue Harvest* follows a condensed version of the events while inserting *Family Guy* characters as "actors" in the main roles (Peter, voiced by Seth MacFarlane, is Han Solo; Chris, voiced by Seth Green, is Luke Skywalker, and so on). It's a given that the plot plays out almost identically to *Star Wars*, with Luke learning to use the Force, making some lifelong friends, and attempting to destroy the Death Star. However, one of the most impressive aspects of *Blue Harvest* is the degree to which the parody stays true to its source work beyond the plot alone. For many scenes and even for quick, inconsequential shots, the movie uses the precise camera angles used in the original. Visual details remain the same, too. One comically repeated clip recreates the exact way Han is unable to hit a TIE fighter with laser blasts from the *Millennium Falcon*, and even the cantina bartender is drawn with the same facial expressions and mannerisms

as he has in the original film. Because of this obvious love the movie demonstrates for its source, the parody is always endearing.

Above all, though, *Blue Harvest* provides the trademark humor that has made *Family Guy* so popular. Quick jabs at the source work account for much of the comedy. When Luke expresses disappointment with Han for not believing in the Force, Han responds, "Oh, you mean the thing you just found out about three hours ago and are now judging me for not believing in?" Other humor comes from injections of the mundane into the goings on of the original film, such as Han's receiving a gift basket for helping Princess Leia (Alex Borstein) escape the Death Star, and Leia's inability to email the Death Star plans to Obi-Wan because R2-D2's operating system is too complicated to deal with.

There seems to be no middle ground of opinions concerning the *Family Guy* series as a whole. This film, however, should be appreciated by any fan of *Star Wars*. When it comes to parodies of that galaxy far, far away, *Blue Harvest* is one of the best.

20th Century Fox

Sunshine

YEAR 2007

COUNTRY United States

RUNTIME 1 hr. 47 min.

RATED R; violent content, language

DIRECTED BY Danny Boyle

WRITTEN BY Alex Garland

STARRING Cillian Murphy, Cliff Curtis, Chris Evans, Rose Byrne

SIMILAR SCI-FI *2001: A Space Odyssey*, *Solaris* (1972)

Sunshine has all the makings of an adventure-oriented thriller. It presents a scenario in which the world is at risk of destruction and a team of astronauts has one chance to save the planet. However, instead of devising obstacles that provide thrills in seeing how characters overcome them, *Sunshine* creates the most adverse circumstances it can in order to observe its characters' emotional reactions to the direst of situations.

Though the plot premise is not explained thoroughly, it is encapsulated in the opening line of the film, spoken by Dr. Robert Capa (Cillian Murphy): "Our sun is dying." The solution to this problem is essentially to restart the sun, by setting off something akin to a massive nuclear explosion in its core. The first ship to attempt this feat, the *Icarus I*, was never heard from after passing the range of communication with the Earth. The team of the *Icarus II*, with Dr. Capa accompanying, is now the Earth's last hope, as they carry the last

Searle (Cliff Curtis) in the Icarus II's observation room.
Fox Searchlight/The Kobal Collection

bomb of this nature that can be created with the resources our planet has to offer.

During the many dilemmas the crew faces on their mission, the focus is never on any action. Indeed, save for a misstep in the final act, most of the thrills are free of action scenes. Instead, the film is committed to the emotions the characters experience. Thanks to the acting of the main players, these emotions create a far more engaging experience than any action-oriented movie could provide. Because they are the product of such an imminent life-and-death scenario, the emotions present—which range from rapture to despair—seem to represent the most basic feelings of the human experience.

> *"AT THE END OF TIME, A MOMENT WILL COME WHEN JUST ONE MAN REMAINS. THEN THE MOMENT WILL PASS. MAN WILL BE GONE. THERE WILL BE NOTHING TO SHOW THAT WE WERE EVER HERE BUT STARDUST."*
> *– PINBACKER*

One imagistic theme, that of the eye, adds meaning to the film's examination of these emotions. Along with the movie's many close-ups of characters' eyes, even the *Icarus II* itself resembles a giant retina. The eye, an instrument of seeing, represents the acquisition of knowledge. Likewise the sun, that ultimate source of light, represents the perfect illumination of truth.

One of the theatrical posters. *Fox Searchlight*

Therefore, the characters' plight to restart the sun becomes symbolic of a search for knowledge of absolute truth. For at least one character, his unprecedented proximity with the sun becomes a near-religious experience.

Placed in the context of the themes of knowledge and truth, the emotional focus of *Sunshine*'s story represents our reactions not only toward impending death but toward enlightenment. It is something for which some are desperate and of which others are fearful. If we are defined by our feelings, perhaps humanity as a whole can be defined by the intensity of its feelings. This is the scenario in which those emotions shine the brightest.

Transformers

YEAR 2007
COUNTRY United States
RUNTIME 2 hrs. 23 min.
RATED PG-13; intense sequences of sci-fi action and violence, brief sexual humor, language
DIRECTED BY Michael Bay
WRITTEN BY Robert Orci, Alex Kurtzman, John Rogers
STARRING Shia LaBeouf, Megan Fox, Peter Cullen, Josh Duhamel
SIMILAR SCI-FI *The Iron Giant, Iron Man, Transformers: Dark of the Moon, Transformers: Revenge of the Fallen, Transformers: The Movie* (1986)

Director Michael Bay does not have a good reputation among most film critics and enthusiasts. So many of his movies seem to consist of little more than save-the-world plots infused with generic dialogue and surrounded by explosions. However, with *Transformers*, his knack for blockbuster filmmaking pays off. Fueled by giant robots (that transform into sweet cars!), huge action scenes, and, yes, plenty of explosions, *Transformers* may not be highbrow, but it is a ton of fun.

The plot could hardly be simpler. Two warring species of alien robots—the Autobots (the good guys) and the Decepticons (the bad)—are after a cube that contains the power of the universe. Lucky us, this cube lands on Earth, the robots come to our planet to fight over it, and an adolescent boy named Sam Witwicky (Shia LaBeouf) gets caught in the fray. Bottom line: In *Transformers* you get to watch giant robots kick each others' asses.

It is a universal fact that fighting robots are

awesome. What makes *Transformers* such an exceptional example of fighting-robot cinema is the realism, power, and agility with which they fight. Swinging from buildings, leaping over missiles, and pounding each other to scrap metal, these are some of the most entertaining computer-generated creations ever placed in a movie. Furthermore, the action is edited in such a way that we can clearly follow what is going on, and the robots themselves

"FATE HAS YIELDED ITS OWN REWARD: A NEW WORLD TO CALL HOME. WE LIVE AMONG ITS PEOPLE NOW, HIDING IN PLAIN SIGHT, BUT WATCHING OVER THEM IN SECRET, WAITING, PROTECTING. I HAVE WITNESSED THEIR CAPACITY FOR COURAGE, AND THOUGH WE ARE WORLDS APART, LIKE US, THERE'S MORE TO THEM THAN MEETS THE EYE." -OPTIMUS PRIME

are so intricately designed that we believe these things could plausibly have been the vehicles they morph to and from. Add to that the straightforward heroism of the Autobots, and there are so many things to like that any flaws seem negligible. (Did I mention they transform into sweet cars?)

Transformers surpasses generic action films by providing action that is displayed proudly with some of the coolest fighting machines conceivable, yet there are those who consider the movie mediocre due to its lack of intelligence. If you can't enjoy watching a semi-trailer change into a giant robot on the freeway and duke it out with an armored vehicle that has done the same, I don't think I can help you.

The movie features plenty of high-adrenaline, rollicking robot action. *Dreamworks/The Kobal Collection*

The high-tech suit of Iron Man (Robert Downey Jr.) comes with a repulsor in the palm.
Marvel Enterprises/The Kobal Collection

Iron Man

YEAR 2008
COUNTRY United States
RUNTIME 2 hrs. 6 min.
RATED PG-13; some intense sequences of sci-fi action and violence
DIRECTED BY Jon Favreau
WRITTEN BY Mark Fergus, Hawk Ostby, Art Marcum, Matt Holloway
STARRING Robert Downey Jr., Jeff Bridges, Gwyneth Paltrow, Terrence Howard
SIMILAR SCI-FI *Iron Man 2*, *RoboCop*, *Spider-Man* (2002), *Superman*, *Transformers (2007)*, *X-Men*

Iron Man is paragon of modern sci-fi action. This movie has one of the most awesome characters the genre has ever seen, and it features him doing things that rival his own demonstrations of coolness at every turn. *Iron Man*'s plot is about a man deciding to take responsibility for his creations, but the film as a whole is about the exploits of one of the few heroes with a narcissism that is probably warranted.

Based, of course, on the Marvel comic, *Iron Man* is about a celebrity genius and weapons designer named Tony Stark. Stark, after witnessing first-hand the ways that some of his weapons have come to be used, decides to become a proactive agent of justice. So, he creates for himself the most awesome weapon imaginable: the Iron Man suit. And you thought utility belts were cool.

The hot rod-colored, evil-looking, seemingly

"IF I WERE IRON MAN, I'D HAVE THIS GIRLFRIEND WHO KNEW MY TRUE IDENTITY. SHE'D BE A WRECK. SHE'D ALWAYS BE WORRYING I WAS GOING TO DIE, YET SO PROUD OF THE MAN I'VE BECOME. SHE'D BE WILDLY CONFLICTED, WHICH WOULD ONLY MAKE HER MORE CRAZY ABOUT ME..." -TONY STARK

all-powerful Iron Man suit is presented just as it is in the comics: not only as an effective weapon but as a weapon that is incredibly fun to watch. The film could have survived if all it did was showcase Stark using the suit's mini-missiles, repulsors, flamethrower, and ability to fly. One of the most exciting involves Ironman sparring with two F-22s. By that point, there's nothing you can do but sit back and let the movie continue to wow you.

Believe it or not, though, the Iron Man suit is not the star of the show. That title goes to Robert Downey Jr. himself, who plays Tony Stark and somehow pulls out such a charismatic performance that he's just as entertaining out of the Iron Man suit as in it. Constantly demonstrating his elocutionary wit and frequently womanizing, even when his body isn't encased in metal armament, there's very little this guy can't accomplish.

Watching *Iron Man* is like watching the world's greatest athlete compete in his prime. You get no tension over the possibility that he might not come out on top. Instead, you simply watch an amazing character best every type of opponent in the most entertaining ways possible.

Marvel Enterprises/Heritage Auctions

WALL-E

YEAR 2008

COUNTRY United States

RUNTIME 1 hrs. 38 min.

RATED G; contains nothing objectionable

DIRECTED BY Andrew Stanton

WRITTEN BY Andrew Stanton, Pete Docter, Jim Reardon

STARRING Ben Burtt, Elissa Knight, Jeff Garlin, Sigourney Weaver

SIMILAR SCI-FI *A.I.: Artificial Intelligence, Metropolis* (2001), *Silent Running, Short Circuit*

On paper, *WALL-E* sounds impossible. It's a robot love story with a theme of environmentalism. Somehow, though, through the title robot's subtle body language, infantile command of spoken language, and infatuation with another mechanical being whose directive is to determine the survivability of the deserted planet Earth, director Andrew Stanton is able to combine robot love with environmental overtones in a way that feels effortless.

It is the twenty-eighth century, and Earth, drowning in trash, has been abandoned for hundreds of years. In order to try to control the planet's waste problem, humans at one point invented "Waste Allocation Load Lifter—Earth Class" robots to roll around, gather trash, compact it into cubes, and stack it, but that only helped for so long. When we left to live on a self-sustaining spaceship, one of these robots (the title character, voiced by Ben Burtt) apparently remained activated by accident and has continued to roam Earth, packing trash ever since. When a robotic probe from the humans' vessel comes down to search for plant life as a sign of sustainability, however,

WALL-E falls quickly in love. At the same time, the probe discovers that humanity stands a chance to return to its home planet – if they're not too lazy.

WALL-E is established from the start as a fully living character that is

WALL-E and EVE's relationship is based on love and environmentalism.
Pixar/Walt Disney Pictures

impossible not to care about. His lone wandering of the wasteland of Earth is both saddening and endearing as, through simple body language, he alternatingly expresses the desire for companionship

and curiously plays with the junk we left behind. When he meets the probe, EVE (Elissa Knight), which becomes his love, the dynamic of the interaction is identical to that of any budding relationship between an infatuated boy and an at-first-uninterested girl. This is the film's greatest accomplishment, to evoke feeling and sympathy for a rusty, square robot, at times even to the extent of producing tears.

The environmental aspect of the film plays out similarly, as if humanity is the uninterested party on the receiving end of the Earth's desire for affection. In *WALL-E*, the megacorporation that ruined the world has so desensitized us from the virtues

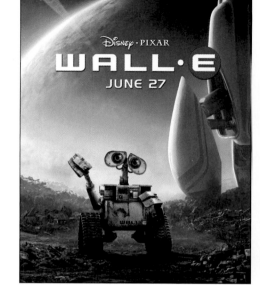

The movie makes viewers care about a rusty, square robot. *Pixar/Walt Disney Pictures*

of nature that we live a meaningless, consumerist, and sedentary existence. We have tried to create our own pleasures, and they have in turn caused the deterioration of our race. In the distance, the Earth sits dirty and alone, waiting for us to return.

WALL-E is equally beautiful, heartwarming, and frightening. At the same time, the feelings it evokes for its main character machine constitute something of an artistic feat. This is one of science fiction's animated greats.

"... OH, I SEE THE SHIP'S LOG IS SHOWING THAT TODAY IS THE 700TH ANNIVERSARY OF OUR FIVE-YEAR CRUISE. WELL, I'M SURE OUR FOREFATHERS WOULD BE PROUD TO KNOW THAT 700 YEARS LATER WE'D BE... DOING THE EXACT SAME THING THEY WERE DOING...." -CAPTAIN

Avatar

YEAR 2009
COUNTRY United States
RUNTIME 2 hrs. 42 min.
RATED PG-13; intense battle sequences and warfare, sensuality, language
DIRECTED BY James Cameron
WRITTEN BY James Cameron
STARRING Sam Worthington, Zoe Saldana, Sigourney Weaver, Stephen Lang
SIMILAR SCI-FI *The Abyss*, *King Kong* (2005), *Star Wars*

Avatar reached *Phantom Menace* levels of hype leading up to its release. Mega-director/producer (and writer) James Cameron pushed moviemaking technology to its bleeding edge to realize his vision of a film featuring the most realistic computer-generated characters possible. In the end, *Avatar* turned out to be one of cinema's greatest visual achievements with a story that, though clichéd, plays meaningfully into its dazzling visuals.

In the year 2154, paraplegic Marine Jake Sully (Sam Worthington) has agreed to take part in the "Avatar Program" on a moon, Pandora, in a distant star system. In this program, individuals train to be remote operators of fully organic, artificially developed replications of the moon's natives, a blue-skinned species of tribal humanoids called the Na'vi. When Sully, living via this avatar, falls in love with a female Na'vi, he has to make the choice between remaining loyal to the increasingly aggressive U.S. forces or helping the Na'vi defend their home.

Neytiri (Zoe Saldana) teaches Jake (Sam Worthington) the Na'vi's ways. *20th Century Fox*

Simply put, this film's visuals are stunning. Utilizing 3D technology to endow it with a natural depth (not to jut objects at the audience), *Avatar* is currently as immersive a cinematic experience as you can find. Furthermore, no matter how fantastical the imagery gets, from the otherworldly creatures to the luminescent plant life, it always looks entirely real. Even the obscenely large and destructive vehicles of the humans have their own beauty. Unfortunately, when viewing the film in 2D, the immersive nature of these visuals is significantly diminished, even though they still look great.

Since *Avatar* is about learning to see the world from the point of view of those different from you, the movie's visual immersion strengthens its theme. Just as Sully experiences life among the Na'vi via his avatar, we experience life on Pandora in as immediate an experience as a film can create. Unfortunately, practically every element of the story is predictable, and Cameron still falls for the military clichés to which he succumbed so heavily in *Aliens*. The visuals are the priority here, working to heighten a somewhat generic story, not to illustrate an original idea.

Pushing the medium to its limit, Cameron created a cinematic milestone with *Avatar* and helped to legitimize 3D filmmaking. There's a reason why, despite containing a stock plot, this is the highest-grossing film of all time.

The fearsome thanator is one of the many creatures Jake encounters on Pandora.
20th Century Fox/The Kobal Collection

Star Trek

YEAR 2009

COUNTRY United States

RUNTIME 2 hrs. 6 min.

RATED PG-13; sci-fi action and violence, brief sexual content

DIRECTED BY J. J. Abrams

WRITTEN BY Robert Orci, Alex Kurtzman

STARRING Chris Pine, Zachary Quinto, Karl Urban, Leonard Nimoy, Eric Bana

SIMILAR SCI-FI *Star Trek: The Motion Picture, Star Trek VI: The Undiscovered Country, Star Trek II: The Wrath of Khan, Star Wars*

Kirk (Chris Pine) and Spock (Zachary Quinto) discuss some matters with villain Nero (Eric Bana). *Paramount/Bad Robot/The Kobal Collection*

In 2009, director J.J. Abrams did the unthinkable. He made *Star Trek* cool. In his reboot of the famous franchise's original series, Abrams not only stays true to the characters that *Trek* fans so love, he puts them in a story that is packed with energy from beginning to end.

When a Romulan named Nero (Eric Bana) travels back in time to kill Spock, deeming him responsible for the destruction of Romula, the freshman crew of Jim Kirk (Chris Pine), Spock (Zachary Quinto), Leonard McCoy (Karl Urban), etc., turns out to be the only crew in the fleet in a position to take Nero on. We watch them confront this threat and, in doing so, fall into the roles—as Starfleet officers and as companions—for which they were meant. The plot itself does not matter so much. The focus of the film is on the characters and their plight.

This *Star Trek* is about individuals fulfilling their destinies. Though, as Spock points out, their existence constitutes a reality that is separate from their alternate timeline originals, there is never a question that they are meant for the same greatness

as their parallel predecessors. This film sees them fight Nero, plausibility, and even each other in their quest to achieve the things for which they have been fated. While it all plays out, the score and the cinematography convey a sense of awe at these young heroes, who seem to exist outside the usual bounds of human capability.

There is never a dull moment in Abrams' *Star Trek*. It seems to revel in the classic characters' trademark attributes, showcasing Kirk's bravado, Spock's struggle to subdue his emotions, and McCoy's bitterness and sarcasm. Even the actors' mannerisms and facial expressions remain true to their original counterparts. The film also has plenty of straight-up action, which always carries a sense of weight and urgency. Top it all off with some humor (Simon Pegg plays Scotty for goodness' sake), and *Star Trek* is no longer for only die-hard sci-fi fanatics. This movie is for everyone.

Star Trek is a rare instance in which a reboot not only pays tribute to but improves upon the elements of the original. Abrams manages to keep every positive aspect of the classic series and to improve upon its shortcomings. The result is the most fun *Star Trek* film yet.

An incensed Spock chokes Kirk after Kirk mocks his lack of emotion. *Paramount/Bad Robot*

H.G. WELLS'
"THINGS TO COME"
An
ALEXANDER KORDA
PRODUCTION
with RAYMOND MASSEY · RALPH RICHARDSON · SIR CEDRIC HARDWICKE · PEARL ARGYLE
MARGARETTA SCOTT
and a cast of 20,000
Directed by WILLIAM CAMERON MENZIES
A LONDON FILM Released thru UNITED ARTISTS

CHAPTER 4

LESSER-KNOWN GEMS

Once an aspiring sci-fi film enthusiast has made it through all the best, most influential, and most famous sci-fi movies, it's time to explore the genre's lesser-known gems. These are the ones the layman doesn't know about. This is the penultimate step of completing one's genre fandom.

Note that not all of these films are necessarily "hidden" or "obscure." Some of them, like *Invaders from Mars*, are well known by most serious film fans of any genre preference but seem simply to have escaped widespread recognition. Others, like *Cube*, are less broadly recognized on the whole but have developed a cult following throughout the years.

A few of these are best appreciated for their historical value as opposed to their inherent quality. "A Trip to the Moon" (1902) might be the first sci-fi film of all time and thus is naturally a required film for any fan of the genre. *Things to Come* is similar. Though it lacks the aesthetic value of many of its counterparts in this chapter and though it came after the genre had already produced a number of masterpieces, it is notable for approaching certain issues, including the interaction of war and technology,

far before they would become common in science fiction.

Still, there are a number of films in this chapter that even some of the most die-hard science fiction fans may be unfamiliar with. The French short "La Jetée," an apocalyptic time travel story told by narrator over a slideshow of images, is one of these. *The American Astronaut* is another, a movie that seems destined for cult status but that hasn't quite picked up an adequate following even to be deemed a cult film.

Some of the films in this chapter are well known in certain circles. Others have yet to be dug up even by sci-fi fanatics. The common theme, here, is that none of them are household titles. Sure, any film student recognizes *Dark Star* as John Carpenter's (and writer Dan O'Bannon's) first feature effort, and anyone entrenched in the foreign film scene will be familiar with *Stalker* and *Alphaville*, but for anyone coming into science fiction, it can be a while before these titles start to show up on the radar. Generally speaking, these are the movies you don't hear about, much less see, until you're well into your exploration of the genre.

Preceding page: *Things to Come* serves as a warning against perceiving technology as being inherently bad. *ITV Global/Heritage Auctions*

This page: *Fantastic Planet* is a bizarre and semi-surrealistic sci-fi film. *Les Films Armorial*

A Trip to the Moon

YEAR 1902
COUNTRY France
RUNTIME 14 min.
RATED Not Rated; nothing objectionable
DIRECTED BY Georges Méliès
WRITTEN BY Georges Méliès, Victor André, Bleuette Bernon
STARRING Henri Delannoy, Jeanne d'Alcy, Bleuette Bernon, Georges Méliès
SIMILAR SCI-FI *Aelita: Queen of Mars*, *Destination Moon*, "*Frankenstein*" (1910), *Robinson Crusoe on Mars*, *Things to Come*, *Woman in the Moon*

"A Trip to the Moon" is one of the first sci-fi films of all time, and it is best appreciated as such. It is difficult, at times, to tell how much of the film director Georges Méliès believes is plausible as it shoots through scenario after trippy scenario. Because of this, "A Trip to the Moon" is an endearing and often amusing cinematic artifact, based not so much on imagining the possibilities of science as on dreaming up as crazy an experience as possible.

This gem tells the story of a group of scientists suddenly deciding they should go to the moon and, with hardly an expenditure of brainpower, devising the means to do so: a large gun that shoots a bullet-shaped pod literally into an eye of the moon's face. When they arrive, the first thing they do is…well, they take a nap. But then they start exploring, and the things they come across seem straight out of a Lewis Carrol novel.

The film is most notable for its imagery and its early yet competent visual effects, including its wild moon sets, an image of stars with female heads gazing at the moon's visitors, and a shot of the distant Earth from the moon's surface. When the scientists begin exploring the moon (no helmets necessary, by the way), they encounter such things as snow, giant mushrooms, and moon-natives that act so strange that one of them moves around like a dog with worms. As the film runs a mere fourteen minutes, to give any more away would be to spoil nearly the entire thing. Needless to say, it is an enjoyable fourteen minutes, and it's capped off by an event you could only have thought possible up until the mid-1400s.

As evidenced by the fact that it is meant to be screened with spoken narration that does no more than describes the events on screen, "A Trip to the Moon" is obviously the product of a time that did not quite understand how best to utilize the cinematic medium. But boy did Méliès try. This is a director running loose with his imagination. How often do we see such things nowadays?

The movie has fantastical imagery and imagination. *Méliès/The Kobal Collection*

Frankenstein

YEAR 1910
COUNTRY United States
RUNTIME 15 min.
RATED Not Rated; the creation process and monster might be frightening for young viewers
DIRECTED BY J. Searle Dawley
WRITTEN BY J. Searle Dawley, Mary Shelley (source novel)
STARRING Augustus Phillips, Charles Ogle, Mary Fuller
SIMILAR SCI-FI "A Trip to the Moon," *Bride of Frankenstein*, *Curse of Frankenstein*, *Frankenstein* (1931)

The first cinematic recreation of Mary Shelley's "Frankenstein" does not receive a fraction of the attention it deserves. Known only to die-hard sci-fi, horror, and silent-film fans, this fifteen-minute production (by Thomas Edison's studio, no less) has little story to tell, but it features what is arguably the most horrifying iteration of the Frankenstein monster in any movie. If you think Universal International or Hammer Film's Frankenstein monsters are frightening, wait till you see this guy.

Only a handful of title cards assist the telling of this story, and, largely because of the limited time it has to be told, the plot is thin. Three of the first five cards, spread over a couple minutes' worth of footage, read, "Frankenstein leaves for college," "Two years later Frankenstein has discovered the mystery of life," and "Instead of a perfect human being the evil in Frankenstein's mind creates a monster." Then we see a hellish creation scene, followed by several minutes of the monster terrorizing Frankenstein (Augustus Phillips) and his fiancée (Mary Fuller). The ending, while metaphorically appropriate, makes no literal sense at all and borders on the fantastical.

But if you come into this film expecting layered storytelling, you've come to the wrong place. The thing that makes this "Frankenstein" so famous is the monster itself, played by Charles Ogle. Varying drastically from any version of the monster since, this one is a hunched, hulking, white-faced beast with wild hair and twig-like fingers. Instead of lumbering like a zombie, this monster outright chases characters around the room. Even its creation process is disturbing. In this telling of the story, the monster is created not on a laboratory table but in a vat in a giant oven-like room. Alchemically, Frankenstein mixes some substances together and starts a fire, and through a hatch we see the being slowly assemble to a vague skeleton and finally to its full-bodied final form, all the while covered in flame. It is truly the stuff of nightmares.

Edison's "Frankenstein" has been in the public domain for decades, but because of a somewhat unreasonable film collector who owned the only extant copy of the movie, the full work was not available for wide viewing until the 2000s, with mostly just stills and excessively watermarked copies available before then, and even those were rare. Now, however, the full film has been loosed upon the public for viewing by anyone with interest. Seek this one out. Just don't do it near bedtime.

"*INSTEAD OF A PERFECT HUMAN BEING THE EVIL IN FRANKENSTEIN'S MIND CREATES A MONSTER.*"
-TITLE CARD

This shot of the monster (Charles Ogle) is the most well known. *Edison/The Kobal Collection*

Things to Come

YEAR 1936
COUNTRY United Kingdom
RUNTIME 1 hr. 40 min.
RATED Not Rated; nothing objectionable
DIRECTED BY William Cameron Menzies
WRITTEN BY H.G. Wells
STARRING Edward Chapman, Raymond Massey, Ralph Richardson, Cedric Hardwicke
SIMILAR SCI-FI *The Day the Earth Stood Still*, *Destination Moon*, *Woman in the Moon*

Things to Come is an early "futuristic society" film about the merits and ills of technological progress. Focusing on the relationship between technology

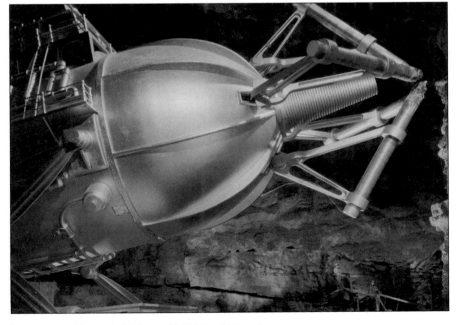

Immense machines rebuild the world. *ITV Global/Heritage Auctions*

and conflict, it depicts the full irony of war, as war is the result of aversion to progress even as it utilizes and promotes the progress of technology. The resulting work is like a compressed epic, abbreviating a repeated cycle of history over the span of a century into ninety minutes.

The irony of war is ubiquitous throughout the film and is inherently tied into its plot. Near the beginning of the movie, a soldier of the 1940s gas-bombs a village, lands, helps a wounded enemy, and then rescues a young girl who otherwise would have been one of his victims. The film continues into a society that generally shuns the technologies that once devastated them through war, that embraces those same weapons when they allow the people to maintain an isolated peace, and that rejects others who use similar technology, even if they do so for good. The movie further progresses to an age ruled by peace, prosperity, and technological advancement but that one day sees a rebellion when its citizens suddenly deem a particular technological achievement to be potentially dangerous and, thus, a social evil.

Depending on your proclivities, the dated style of *Things to Come* can be either endearing or off-putting. It is the kind of film that envisions a future world in which everyone dresses ridiculously and almost identically, and some of its technologies are downright silly from a modern viewpoint. When this future utopia develops a means of sending man to the moon, for instance, it is done by shooting a spaceship out of an enormous machine called a "space gun." This is about as vintage as it gets.

In the end, *Things to Come* is an optimistic film, but it is also a warning against perceiving technology as inherently bad. Those who do so are portrayed as having nonsensical mindsets, too frightened by risk to try to achieve a better existence. It is also one of science fiction's first utopia/dystopia films and an influence on later greats like *The Day the Earth Stood Still*. It may not be a must-see for the casual movie fan, but for sci-fi fanatics, it is required viewing.

"BUT... WE'RE SUCH LITTLE CREATURES. POOR HUMANITY'S SO FRAGILE, SO WEAK. LITTLE... LITTLE ANIMALS." -RAYMOND PASSWORTHY

John Cabal (Raymond Massey) represents freedom and intellectual curiosity. *ITV Global/Heritage Auctions*

Invaders from Mars

YEAR 1953
COUNTRY United States
RUNTIME 1 hr. 18 min.
RATED Not Rated; some imagery might frighten younger viewers
DIRECTED BY William Cameron Menzies
WRITTEN BY Richard Blake
STARRING Jimmy Hunt, Helena Carter, Arthur Franz, Leif Erickson
SIMILAR SCI-FI *Alien Trespass*, *The Day the Earth Stood Still* (1951), *The Earth Dies Screaming*, *Invasion of the Body Snatchers* (1956), *Invasion of the Body Snatchers* (1978), *It Came from Outer Space*

One of the first ever alien mind control paranoia movies, *Invaders from Mars* imbues a campy plot with bizarre elements. This particular film is also unique as compared to those that it inspired in that it follows a young boy as the main character, trying to save his town from the invaders. This is a story of the childlike disorientation experienced when confronted with an unprecedented event.

David Maclean (Jimmy Hunt), a boy in a small town, witnesses a UFO landing practically in his back yard. Before long, his family, friends, and neighbors fall periodically into a hole near the landing, only to later return with no emotion other than anger, no desire other than carry out the will of the aliens. Martians are controlling the minds of the townspeople, and it's up to David to convince others of the truth so they don't

The Martian mastermind. *20th Century Fox/The Kobal Collection*

all fall under the invaders' control.

While the story is straightforward (save town from alien invasion), the film is unique enough to make up for any shortcomings. As David runs around trying to alert everyone, doors seem as tall as buildings, police desks sit atop podiums, and hallways are exhaustingly long. These elements impress upon viewers David's perspective as a child, thus emphasizing the newness of the event.

When we do go underground and explore the UFO, the imagery becomes wild. Walls bubble like infected flesh, green humanoids traverse hallways with emotionless purpose, and the head Martian is literally a head (from which stem impractically short tentacles). The alien imagery looks as if taken directly from the classic sci-fi magazines David likely reads, in which science fiction is frequently little more than an attempt to ground surrealism in something concrete.

With plenty of "Aw, jeez" lines, soldiers who look like they've never had

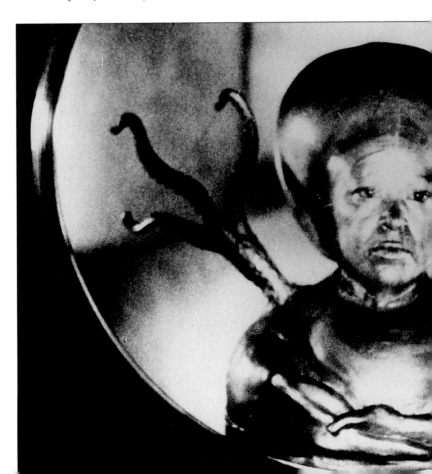

SCI-FI MOVIE FREAK

a day of exercise, and a military willing to launch a full-scale assault on a hole in the ground based on the warnings of a child, *Invaders from Mars* shows obvious age. It remains, however, a sci-fi/horror classic. This is an odd blend of expressionism and surrealism that offers things not even more masterful similar films like *Invasion of the Body Snatchers* accomplish.

"PLEASE GOD, LET THEM FIND MOM AND DAD BEFORE SOMETHING BAD HAPPENS. I DON'T WANT THEM TO DIE TOO." -DAVID MACLEAN

Child star Jimmy Hunt plays the police chief in a 1986 remake.
20th Century Fox/Heritage Auctions

The Killer Shrews

YEAR 1959
COUNTRY United States
RUNTIME 1 hr. 9 min.
RATED Not Rated; some of the shrew attacks might frighten younger viewers
DIRECTED BY Ray Kellogg
WRITTEN BY Jay Simms
STARRING James Best, Baruch Lumet, Ingrid Goude, Ken Curtis
SIMILAR SCI-FI *Kingdom of the Spiders*, *Night of the Lepus*, *Tarantula*

A giant shrew takes a bite out of a leg. *Hollywood Pictures/The Kobal Collection*

If *The Killer Shrews* had not been *just* good enough to make it into the "Lesser-Known Gems" category of this book, it would almost definitely have been included in the next chapter, "The Failures." This little 1950s flick has visual effects that are beyond laughable. However, if you can manage to look past the failed visuals (which, granted, is a tall order), there is a solid story structure to be found.

Captain Thorne Sherman (James Best) has made a supplies delivery to an island inhabited by a handful of researchers who are performing experiments with shrews. The research, led by Dr. Marlowe Craigis (Baruch Lumet), is aimed at finding a way to shrink humans to 50 percent of their natural size in order to stave off food shortages resulting from overpopulation. Unfortunately, one failed experiment results not in shrunken shrews but enlarged ones, which quickly escape, reproduce, and eat up all food sources on the island. Now they come out at night in search of human-sized snacks.

The pacing and structure of the story is actually effective. The shrews do not begin making visual appearances in the film until about the halfway point.

During the time leading up to their appearance, the film builds anxiety and tension by hinting at their terror and showing how deeply the researchers fear the creatures. When one character says simply, "A shrew got in the house," we can feel the characters' horror, despite the fact that the movie itself is not actually scary.

Unfortunately, everything good about *The Killer Shrews* is overshadowed by one fact: the giant shrews are obviously, to the most casual observer, dogs dressed in rat costumes. Not only that, but the dogs, which are supposed to appear as evil beasts, seem quite happy ninety percent of the time. Sure, there is the occasional close-up in which a full-blown giant rat head is shown gnashing at a character, and those instances can actually be kinda

"IF WE WERE HALF AS BIG AS WE ARE NOW, WE COULD LIVE TWICE AS LONG ON OUR NATURAL RESOURCES."
-DR. CRAIGIS

Tiny shrews grow to exactly the size of sheep dogs. *Hollywood Pictures*

This is often double billed with *The Giant Gila Monster*, **also directed by Ray Kellogg.**
McLendon Radio Pictures/Heritage Auctions

creepy, but for most of the time that the killer shrews are on screen, we are treated to scenes of excited dogs running around, probably wondering why they're dressed in such strange costumes.

The Killer Shrews might be the only movie that is simultaneously "so bad it's good" and actually not all that bad. If it weren't for its schlock factor, it would have been doomed to an existence as a competent but non-noteworthy film. Because of its ridiculous dog-rats, though, it will live forever. Watch this for any reason you like.

La Jetée

YEAR 1962

COUNTRY France

RUNNING TIME 28 min.

RATED Not Rated; nothing objectionable for mature viewers

DIRECTED BY Chris Marker

WRITTEN BY Chris Marker

STARRING Davos Hanich, Hélène Chatelain, Jacques Ledoux, Jean Négroni

SIMILAR SCI-FI *12 Monkeys, Alphaville, Solaris* (1972)

A twenty-eight-minute short by writer/director Chris Marker, "La Jetée" is a philosophical sci-fi romance drama executed in a style of which only the French must be capable. Understated yet always carrying a sense of importance, this film is confident to eschew thrills, mystery, and action in favor of contemplation. It seems to care so deeply about its main character that it approaches his every action as inherently important.

In the near future, World War III has transpired, and nuclear weaponry has killed off nearly everyone. The few survivors of the apocalypse live underground. We follow an unnamed prisoner of this underground world (Davos Hanich), who has been enlisted in an experiment. The goal: send him through time into the past and future in order to find someone who can help humanity out of its current, dismal state. While traveling to the past, however, the man finds something better: love.

"La Jetée" is told entirely through narration over a slideshow of still images. The resultant feeling is that we are traveling not through a presently unfolding story but through a man's memories. The point is that images, like photographs, are our connection to the past. Indeed, it is the exceptional vividness of the main character's memory that allows him to be the only successful time traveler in the first place. Furthermore, the specific images that we retain—an incidental facial expression, an uncommon object—reveal that which is important to us, even if we don't realize it at the time that they are captured.

This film demonstrates that memories, in the form of images, are the most intimate things you can have. Because of this, "La Jetée," though simple, dry, and straightforward, is also profoundly emotional. We are not just watching a man fall in love while traveling through time. We are gaining access to the instances of life so personally salient that his mind took them for its own. In the end, these images add up to nothing, but that is okay; the simple fact that these moments in time occurred and were chosen for keepsake gives them an importance and a relevance unsurpassed by functionality.

"NOTHING TELLS MEMORIES FROM ORDINARY MOMENTS. ONLY AFTERWARDS DO THEY CLAIM REMEMBRANCE, ON ACCOUNT OF THEIR SCARS." -NARRATOR

The prisoner (Davos Hanich) meets the woman from his memory (Hélène Chatelain). *Argos Films/The Kobal Collection*

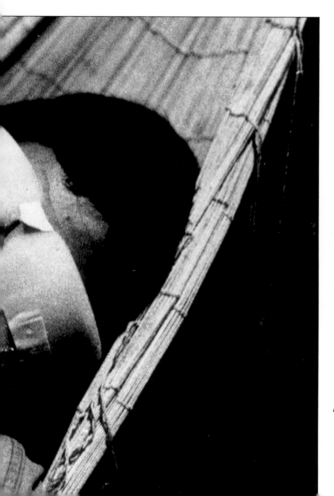

In 2010, *Time* magazine ranked this No. 1 in its list of Top 10 time travel movies. *Argos Films/Heritage Auctions*

A prisoner (Davos Hanich) is the test subject of a time-travel experiment. *Argos Films*

Alphaville

YEAR 1965
COUNTRY France
RUNTIME 1 hr. 39 min
RATED Not Rated; nothing objectionable for mature viewers
DIRECTED BY Jean-Luc Godard
WRITTEN BY Jean-Luc Godard
STARRING Eddie Constantine, Anna Karina, Akim Tamiroff, Howard Vernon
SIMILAR SCI-FI *Dark City*, *Fahrenheit 451*, "La Jetée"

Alphaville is a peculiar film and one that can be difficult to like. It contains computer-governed societies and intergalactic espionage, yet it never looks like anything but a quirky film noir. Famed French director Jean-Luc Godard fashioned this film to be as superficially unassuming as possible. At its core, however, lies a beautiful, sci-fi-powered presentation of humanist philosophy.

The planet Alphaville, which lies at the center of the civilized world, is governed solely by a computer. This computer, Alpha 60, runs the planet via probability calculations with the goal of maintaining a society in strict correspondence to the workings of the universe. The citizens of Alphaville no longer have a say in their own destiny. Unfortunately for the outlying galaxies, Alpha 60 has recently determined that their societies need to be wiped out. Now, secret agent Lemmy Caution (Eddie Constantine) has traveled from the "Outland" to take down the supercomputer.

Simply looking at the film, it would be impossible to realize that it falls under the science fiction genre. All set pieces are obviously from the sixties (the era the film was made), even though it takes place far in the future. For some, this can be a turn-off. However, the consciously low-budget, even anachronistic, look of *Alphaville* actually strengthens the film, conveying the feeling that its story is so worth telling that it doesn't matter whether the visuals are up to par. This is all part of Godard's style.

Caution's wading through the strange but supposedly ideal society of Alphaville and his budding relationship with the daughter of Alpha 60's creator lead the film to a glimpse of the significance of human life. In traversing a dull, emotionless world, we learn that it is art and beauty that make us who we are and may be our very sources of emotion. They

"YES, I'M AFRAID OF DEATH, BUT FOR A HUMBLE SECRET AGENT, THAT'S A FACT OF LIFE, LIKE WHISKEY. AND I'VE DRUNK THAT ALL MY LIFE."
-LEMMY CAUTION

Lemmy Caution (Eddie Constantine) and Natacha (Anna Karina) fall in love. *Chaumiane/Filmstudio/The Kobal Collection*

are also the two things that will save us from the chains of a strictly mathematical existence.

It may take a few tries to enjoy this movie, but if you are able to accept it fully for what it is, the result is rewarding. Its generally bland visuals are often the hardest obstacle to overcome. Once you're able to latch onto its ideas, though, *Alphaville* becomes a rich film. It just happened to be made by a particularly eccentric director.

The French movie poster. *Chaumiane/Filmstudio/Heritage Auctions*

Fantastic Planet

YEAR 1973
COUNTRY France
RUNTIME 1 hr. 11 min.
RATED PG; fantasy violence, animated nudity
DIRECTED BY René Laloux
WRITTEN BY Stefan Wul (source novel), Roland Topor, René Laloux
STARRING Eric Baugin, Jennifer Drake, Jean Topart, Jean Valmont
SIMILAR SCI-FI *The City of Lost Children, Dark City*

One of the weirdest sci-fi movies to be found is the pseudo-surrealistic animated French film *Fantastic Planet*. Its story takes place on another planet, but it feels like another universe. Nothing quite makes sense in this film, but in a story designed to evoke feelings of confusion and of being lost, that only adds to its effectiveness.

On a strange planet populated by giant, blue, wide-eyed beings called Draags, pockets of humans (called "Oms") roam in the wild like rodents, having been brought back from expeditions to the planet Terra (Earth). Occasionally these Oms are captured and taken in as pets. Due to their increasing numbers, however, the Draags plan to exterminate them. When the Oms learn to educate themselves via a Draag learning device, they become more empowered to fend for themselves, and the conflict between the two life forms escalates to the point of either compromise or all-out war.

The point of the film is to disorient the viewer's sense of place in the universe. This is a planet on which not only has our concept of human dominion been subverted, but so has logic. Not even nature makes sense in this place. There is one creature that appears to thrive off of simply killing other species and letting them die without ingesting them. The Draags' mating ritual consists of them meditating, during which process their heads separate from their bodies, travel to a nearby planet, settle on top of headless human statues, and mate with beings from other planets who are performing the same meditation. The score complements the feeling of confusion evoked by the events, as it seems to wander in a vast, unknown place without ever finding an endpoint.

The biggest problem in trying to relate to *Fantastic Planet* is not the result of the film's surrealism. It is the lack of an emotional arc, which is the movie's primary flaw. Regardless of this misstep, however, *Fantastic Planet* remains an intriguing and even mystifying viewing experience. It presents an existence in which the viewer has no bearings, in which we are forced to experience life with

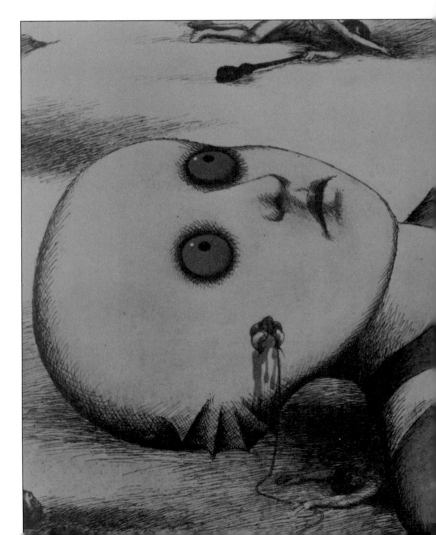

no sense of superiority over other species. Perhaps it is through such an experience that we learn the most about what the world fundamentally is like.

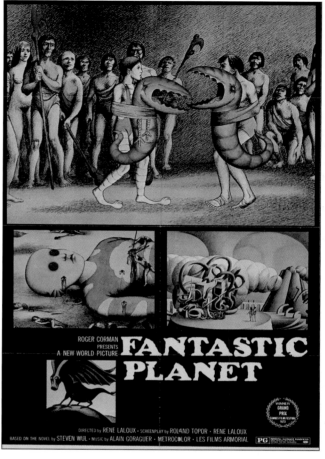

The film won the special jury prize at the 1973 Cannes Film Festival. *Les Films Armorial/Heritage Auctions*

Despite the lack of an emotional arc, the movie is still a mystifying viewing experience with its surreal imagery. *Les Films Armorial/Heritage Auctions*

Dark Star

YEAR 1974
COUNTRY United States
RUNTIME 1 hr. 22 min.
RATED G; some mild comic violence
DIRECTED BY John Carpenter
WRITTEN BY Dan O'Bannon, John Carpenter
STARRING Dan O'Bannon, Brian Narelle, Cal Kuniholm, Dre Pahich
SIMILAR SCI-FI *The Hitchhiker's Guide to the Galaxy, Sleeper, Spaceballs*

After a mishap, Commander Powell (Joe Saunders), spends his days cryogenically frozen. *Jack H. Harris Enterprises/The Kobal Collection*

There are a number of reasons to watch *Dark Star*. None of them, however, are because it's particularly good. A low-budget freshman filmmaking effort by director John Carpenter and writer Dan O'Bannon, *Dark Star* is, regardless of its overall quality, an essential artifact of science fiction history. It's also pretty funny.

The plot centers on a group of lackadaisical hippie astronauts tasked with seeking out unstable planets and blowing them up. We don't, however, see them performing their job so much as we watch them trudge through daily life on a spaceship, living as unproductive an existence as they probably could in such a situation. The most pressing concerns to these guys are the ship's defunct toilet and minor disagreements with one another.

Dark Star is little more than a string of ridiculous events and dialogue. During one video-journal entry, a character complains, "Doolittle treats me like an idiot, and Boiler punches me in the arm when no one is looking." One of the film's more memorable moments is a snail-paced thrill sequence in which a character is nearly killed by an alien with the exact likeness of a beach ball (plus webbed feet). The movie

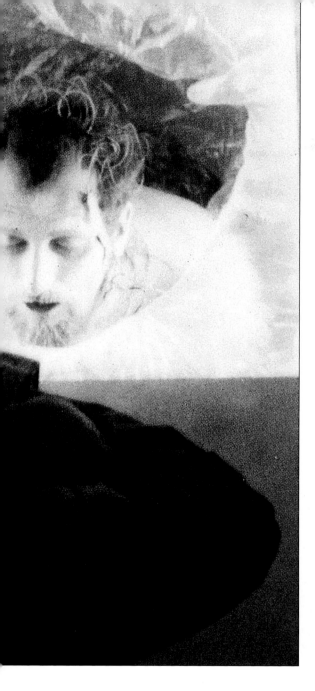

DAVID GRANT presents
A JOHN CARPENTER film

From
ALAN DEAN FOSTER
FIRST
2001: A SPACE ODYSSEY
THEN
THE POSEIDON ADVENTURE
NOW
DARK STAR A

DS-1

bombed out in space
with a spaced out bomb!

An OPPIDAN ENTERTAINMENTS Release of a JACK H. HARRIS Production Starring DAN C'BANNON and BRIAN NARELLE Produced & directed by JOHN CARPENTER

John Carpenter has described the movie as "Waiting for Godot in space." *Jack H. Harris Enterprises/The Kobal Collection*

reaches its climax, both of plot and of humor, when one crew member is forced to talk phenomenology with a bomb to convince it not to explode while attached to the ship.

Sometimes the film gets a little too ridiculous, though…as in, no longer funny. Some of the dialogue, coming from characters who have reached extremes of indolence, is simply boring. Also, while O'Bannon demonstrated throughout his career that he certainly could write (and even, as *The Return of the Living Dead* demonstrates, direct; see P. 137), *Dark Star* shows us that he may have been a little too stiff for acting. Regardless of its problems, however, the film remains fun to watch in a historical context.

In the end, the fact that *Dark Star* actually seems to have a worthwhile theme in mind (the conflation of life-fulfillment and death—we'll have to discuss that some other time) does not have much effect on either the positive or negative aspects of the film. With this film, you get to spend eighty-two minutes watching two eventual experts of science fiction make occasionally successful jokes while finding their cinematic footing.

"DON'T GIVE ME ANY OF THAT INTELLIGENT LIFE CRAP, JUST GIVE ME SOMETHING I CAN BLOW UP."
-DOOLITTLE

Stalker

YEAR 1979
COUNTRY Soviet Union
RUNTIME 2 hrs. 43 min.
RATED PG; some mild language, some scenes may be intense for younger viewers
DIRECTED BY Andrei Tarkovsky
WRITTEN BY Arkadi Strugatsky, Boris Strugatsky
STARRING Aleksandr Kaidanovsky, Anatoli Solonitsyn, Nikolai Grinko, Alisa Frejndlikh
SIMILAR SCI-FI *Solaris* (1972)

If you've made it through *Solaris* (1972) and you want more science fiction from Andrei Tarkovsky, it's time for *Stalker*. *Stalker* is another long, slow-paced, meditative film, and though it doesn't reach the mastery of *Solaris*, its sci-fi-infused examination of dream fulfillment is profound and haunting.

Some vague cosmic event has occurred and has transformed a wooded area in the Soviet Union into a sentient place referred to as "The Zone." The reality of the Zone, however, is based on a strange set of rules. The geography of the area is ever-changing, but this change is never seen. To get from point A to point B, the most roundabout of paths must be taken, or the Zone will kill you. If you make it to the center of the Zone, there is a room that grants your deepest wish. Naturally, the government fears this place more than anyone and guards it with lethal force. Two men, known only as "Professor" and "Writer," hire another man, called a Stalker, to sneak them into the Zone and lead them to its fabled room.

Throughout this protracted experience we follow Professor, Writer, and the Stalker sneaking into the Zone and working their way toward the

"IT'S BETTER TO HAVE A BITTER HAPPINESS THAN A DULL, GREY LIFE."
-"MONKEY"

middle. As the men circle in on their destination, they pause frequently to rest and to discuss philosophical matters. Even in the midst of dialogue there are long pauses as they spend time weighing the meaning of their own questions and answers.

As the characters approach their destination, the things they encounter become increasingly unsettling and confounding. Tension reaches its height when they come to realize that they might not even know what their innermost wishes are. People can have extremely unexpected subconscious desires, some of which they would not consciously want fulfilled. Yet, even after such a realization, something compels them to proceed.

Trepidation is felt in every step of *Stalker*, not only at the dangers of the Zone but at the very concept of achieving one's true dreams. The characters may move slowly, but their doing so only magnifies this tension. Like *Solaris*, this is a film for the patient, but it is as rewarding as it is long.

The Writer (Anatoli Solonitsyn). *Mosfilm Studios/The Kobal Collection*

The Brother from Another Planet

YEAR 1984
COUNTRY United States
RUNTIME 1 hr. 48 min.
RATED R: language, brief nudity, some drug content
DIRECTED BY John Sayles
WRITTEN BY John Sayles
STARRING Joe Morton, Daryl Edwards, Rosanna Carter, Bill Cobbs
SIMILAR SCI-FI The Man Who Fell to Earth

The Brother from Another Planet is an enigma of a film, not because it is difficult to follow but because its precise purpose is difficult to pinpoint. The story lacks impetus, and the film lacks flair, but once it's over it feels like a poignant experience. It's like some sort of Zen parable with sensibilities aimed at race and class conflicts.

An escaped alien slave who looks exactly like a human African American (except for his feet) lands on Earth. This character never talks and only occasionally acknowledges others who talk to him, but in Harlem he manages to make some friends who accept him for who he is. We watch this character as he walks silently through our world, casually observing those around him and occasionally being

"WHITE FOLKS GET STRANGER ALL THE TIME." -SMOKEY

chased by his (white) alien slavers.

There are times at which *The Brother from another Planet* feels like a way for us simply to listen to the socially oppressed. The people the brother encounters seem more than happy to share their thoughts, their woes, and their stories. Yet, near its end, the film becomes intent on making a point. The alien performs an act of vengeance in a situation involving one of society's highest forms of depravity: the upper class feeding off the desperation of the downtrodden. After this incident, it's almost like the brother has found purpose.

In the end, perhaps what is most important about *TBFAP* is its focus on kindness. It is heartwarming to see characters befriend the alien despite his inability to communicate with them. At the same time, the main character clearly comes to care for those around him, even those who hurt him. In fact, that explains his muteness – another example of his thorough selflessness.

While on Earth, the Brother (Joe Morton) develops a relationship with a singer (Dee Dee Bridgewater). *A Train/Cinecom C/The Kobal Collection*

Cube

YEAR 1997
COUNTRY United States
RUNTIME 1 hr. 30 min.
RATED R; strong sci-fi violence and gore, language
DIRECTED BY Vincenzo Natali
WRITTEN BY Vincenzo Natali, André, Bijelic, Graeme Manson
STARRING Maurice Dean Wint, Nicole de Boer, Nicky Guadagni, David Hewlett
SIMILAR SCI-FI *THX 1138*

"What does it want? What is it thinking?" So asks a character about the labyrinth in which she and a handful of others are trapped in *Cube*, and in doing so, she poses a philosophical question about the world. It's something we've all asked at one point: Why are we here?

With no warning or explanation whatsoever, about half a dozen individuals wake up in perfectly cubic rooms, each adorned with six doors, one each on the walls, floor, and ceiling. They all lead to more rooms, some of which are safe, some of which are fatally booby-trapped. Most of the characters we see find each other. Others die almost immediately. Those who live are left with nothing more than the faintest possibility that they might find a way out.

Given this setup, *Cube* is a metaphor for life. We are tossed into this world with no instruction and no explanation. You take a wrong step, you die. If you're resourceful (and a little lucky), you survive a while longer. The characters spend virtually the entire film questioning the purpose of the maze they are in and trying to determine what they should be doing. Just like any of us.

Boasting some particularly brutal traps, *Cube*

A group of strangers faces a seemingly endless Kafka-esque maze filled with deadly traps. *Feature Film Project/The Kobal Collection*

establishes a pervading sense of dread at what might happen if the next room is not safe. Most traps consist of razor-sharp wires slicing the unfortunate into pieces. Others are more straightforward, like the nozzle that gives one character a face-full of acid. Even when you're pretty sure the next room is going to be safe, there's always tension because if there *is* danger ahead, it's so horrific you don't want the characters to fall to it. And that's not even taking into account the threat that the characters eventually pose to each other.

Cube is a rare work that can be so heavily metaphorical yet remain immediately intense. It has several notable flaws (the foremost of which is the acting), but it accomplishes its goal effectively, and it is one of the more unique sci-fi films to be found. That goes a long way.

FEAR PARANOIA
SUSPICION DESPERATION

CUBE

"ONLY THE GOVERNMENT COULD BUILD SOMETHING THIS UGLY."
-HOLLOWAY

The American Astronaut

YEAR 2001
COUNTRY United States
RUNTIME 1 hr. 31 min.
RATED Not Rated; some sexuality, some language
DIRECTED BY Cory McAbee
WRITTEN BY Cory McAbee
STARRING Cory McAbee, Rocco Sisto, Gregory Russell Cook, Tom Aldredge
SIMILAR SCI-FI *Barbarella*, *Christmas on Mars*, *The Hitchhiker's Guide to the Galaxy*, *The Rocky Horror Picture Show*

If you think *The Rocky Horror Picture Show* is the only sci-fi musical worthy of attention, then you haven't seen *The American Astronaut*. Written by, directed by, and starring Cory McAbee of the band The Billy Nayer Show, this little niche piece is as competent in its music as it is surreal in its story. It may not be as good as *Rocky Horror*, but in its attempt to have fun beyond the limits of reason, it upholds the proud history of the sparsely populated realm of musical science fiction.

Not that the plot makes any sense, but here goes a rundown: Samuel Curtis (McAbee) is an interplanetary trader who mostly seems interested in live goods, such as an adolescent boy, a cat named Monkeypuss, and a girl in a briefcase (girls, it seems, are particularly rare finds these days). While trying to carry out a string of trades that will supposedly result in lots of money, Curtis is being hunted down by a "birthday boy," whatever that means. This birthday boy, Professor Hess (Rocco Sisto), wants to forgive Curtis so that he can kill Curtis. We have to take Curtis' word for

The movie's tagline is, "Space is a lonely town."
BNS Productions/Commodore Films

it when he explains that this makes perfect sense.

This film is best approached as you would approach poetry. Don't focus on making direct meaning of everything (or anything) that happens, and instead just feel it as an experience. When viewed in this way, *The American Astronaut* becomes an unlikely moving story about the bond that has developed between Curtis and Hess. It also becomes, through its music, a simply fun space romp punctuated by moments of silliness and even glee.

The music of *The American Astronaut* is as bizarre and intriguing as the film itself. Though it's frequently as difficult to decipher

as the story, it is also easy to enjoy without an understanding of its meaning. Ranging from country henchmen breaking into dance in a bar bathroom, to a teenage boy singing about vowels, to Curtis himself singing a magnetic tune about a character's "demure" anatomy, the music is often as catchy as it could possibly be within the bounds of such an off-the-wall work of art.

When Curtis utters lines like, "My father taught me to kill the sunflower," it's almost impossible to imagine the dialogue containing any inherent meaning. However, what's important in *The American Astronaut* is that its elements have meaning for the characters themselves. We can't fully understand why they do the things they do, but we can see that those things are important to them. Isn't that what ultimately matters?

Cory McAbee was nominated for the 2001 Grand Jury Prize at the Sundance Film Festival. *BNS Productions/Commodore Films*

CHAPTER 5

THE FAILURES

No thorough understanding of any art form is complete without a knowledge of its worst failures. Luckily for anyone familiarizing themselves with such works, though, failure can be an entertaining thing. This chapter is dedicated to the most essential and hilarious of these botched attempts at art.

Any film enthusiast will recognize *Plan 9 from Outer Space* as the oft-hailed worst movie ever made. However, as this chapter will demonstrate, there are a number of movies that present *Plan 9* with competition for that title. Perhaps the strongest contestant is *Robot Monster*, a thoroughly nonsensical sci-fi/horror flick that features a man in a gorilla suit and scuba helmet as the title monster (which actually is not a robot at all).

While other titles in this chapter might not be the caliber of *Plan 9* and *Robot Monster*, they are still tons of fun to watch. *Gammera the Invincible*, for example, is an ill-fated attempt to cash in on Asia's giant monster craze, featuring one of the dumbest giant monsters in cinema history and endowing it with such bizarre attributes that it would be difficult to make a more absurd monster if you tried.

Of course, many of the films in this chapter contain a significant "What were they thinking?" factor. *Howard the Duck* ranks particularly high in this aspect, as a Lucasfilm-produced comedy-thriller about an anthropomorphic duck from outer space. A more modern example of bafflingly bad science fiction is *Battlefield Earth*, a film that raises questions concerning not only its many enormous plot holes but the fact that the script made it past a producer without being immediately set aflame.

We can deride these movies endlessly; however, many of them are so incompetent they become endearing. There's something special about bad science fiction. With all the dynamics involved in the genre, its disasters are often far more fun to watch than, say, bad romance comedies. Viewing these films is not just a way to deepen your understanding of what does and doesn't work in science fiction. Doing so can also be extremely amusing.

An anthropomorphic duck from another planet befriends a rocker girl in *Howard the Duck.* Lucasfilm/Universal

At left: Giant rabbits go on the attack in *Night of the Lepus.*
Metro-Goldwyn-Mayer/The Kobal Collection

The accidental detonation of an atomic bomb awakens a giant fire-breathing turtle in *Gammera the Invincible.* Harris Associates/National Telefilm Associates

Robot Monster

YEAR 1953
COUNTRY United States
RUNTIME 1 hr. 3 min.
RATED Not Rated; only the script is objectionable
DIRECTED BY Phil Tucker
WRITTEN BY Wyott Ordung
STARRING Gregory Moffett, George Nader, Claudia Barrett, George Barrows, John Mylong
SIMILAR SCI-FI *Attack from Space, Bride of the Monster, Plan 9 from Outer Space*

Most bad genre films from the 1950s can be understood as fast and easy attempts to cash in on the era's monster craze. A select few, though, are so thoroughly bad that they bewilder in their demonstrations of ineptitude.

An alien monster (who doesn't actually seem to be part robot) named Ro-Man (George Barrows) has invaded Earth and wiped out all of humanity except for one family that somehow survived. By complete coincidence (read: writer's convenience), this family was camping out about half a mile from the cave in which Ro-Man has set up shop, and they have since taken refuge in a nearby crater-like hole in the ground. The

"I CANNOT - YET I MUST. HOW DO YOU CALCULATE THAT? AT WHAT POINT ON THE GRAPH DO 'MUST' AND 'CANNOT' MEET? YET I MUST - BUT I CANNOT!" -RO-MAN

Elmer Bernstein, who composed the movie's soundtrack, also composed the music for "Michael Jackson's Thriller." *Three Dimensional Pictures/Heritage Auctions*

father of the family also happens to be some sort of genius scientist, so he has constructed an electric fence that keeps them invisible to radar.

So much of *Robot Monster* makes no sense. When Ro-Man first invades, part of the montage that is meant to illustrate the world being destroyed consists of scenes of dinosaurs fighting each other (apparently that just happens when the world comes to an end). Also, the young boy of the family, Johnny (Gregory Moffett), was asleep directly in the entryway of the cave that Ro-Man turned into his home *when* Ro-Man turned the cave into his home. Yet, somehow he was never spotted. And when Johnny wakes, he finds his family simply by wandering around for a minute, yet Ro-Man, the most powerful being ever to walk our planet, cannot find them at all.

Despite the horribly conceived plot, the special effects are the real stars of this junk heap. Ro-Man himself is the single most infamous part of the movie, as nothing more than an actor in a fat gorilla suit and scuba helmet with huge antennas. The monster's communication device emits little bubbles that do nothing (the "automatic billion bubble machine" is for some reason even listed in the opening credits). One of the aforementioned dinosaurs is a baby alligator with a fin strapped to its back. At one point a human hand can be seen holding a miniature aircraft. The list goes on.

Robot Monster is one of the funniest movies you will ever see, made infinitely funnier by the fact that

Roy (George Nader) tries to save Alice (Claudia Barrett) from the evil robot clutches of Ro-Man (John Brown). *Three Dimensional Pictures/Heritage Auctions*

it's not supposed to be funny at all. From its script to its special effects to the fact that it at no point succeeds in creating suspense or thrills, this movie fails completely. This is the rare treat you come across when wading through D-grade cinema.

Plan 9 from Outer Space

YEAR 1959

COUNTRY United States

RUNTIME 1 hr. 19 min.

RATED Not Rated; mild violence, but since scenes are poorly acted, it's more funny than disturbing

DIRECTED BY Edward D. Wood, Jr.

WRITTEN BY Edward D. Wood, Jr.

STARRING Duke Moore, Bela Lugosi, Gregory Walcott, Tom Keene

SIMILAR SCI-FI *Attack from Space*, *Bride of the Monster*, *The Day the Earth Stood Still* (1951), *Robot Monster*, *This Island Earth*

"We are all interested in the future, for that is where you and I are going to be spending the rest of our lives," states a Master of Ceremonies with eyes obviously reading from a board behind our field of view. From this opening, you already know the rest of the movie is going to be a disaster. Welcome to Edward D. Wood, Jr.'s *Plan 9 from Outer Space*, the film widely considered to be the worst of all time.

Something of a zombie-infused rip-off of *The Day the Earth Stood Still*, *Plan 9* tells the story of humanoid aliens who come to Earth to (brace yourself) keep us from literally blowing up the universe. The "*stupid, stupid*" human race, you see, is about to discover something called solarbonite, which apparently can do that. The aliens' plan to stop us? Resurrect three dead bodies as killer zombies. I'd like to know what the first eight plans were.

Everything about this production is a failure. UFOs dangle loosely from strings, some of the aliens' costumes look like they were taken from a low-budget *Lord of the Rings* adaptation, and at one point an "electrode gun" becomes jammed—and is later fixed by being dropped on the floor. The dialogue consists of lines like, "I don't like hearin' noises. Especially when there ain't supposed to be any." As for the actors in *Plan 9*, they are not only

Lt. John Harper (Duke Moore) confronts aliens Eros (Dudley Manlove) and Tanna (Joanna Lee).
Criswell/The Kobal Collection

UNSPEAKABLE HORRORS FROM OUTER SPACE PARALYZE THE LIVING AND RESURRECT THE DEAD!

PLAN 9 FROM OUTER SPACE

with BELA LUGOSI VAMPIRA LYLE TALBOT

A J. Edward Reynolds Production

Produced and Directed by Edward D. Wood, Jr.

Heritage Auctions

incapable of acting, they are only occasionally capable of looking like they *want* to act. You will find few films with less fervor from the performers.

The famous Bela Lugosi is sort of in this movie. In his later years, the sadly destitute Lugosi, in desperate need of a paycheck, occasionally acted in Wood's films. Lugosi died in 1956, but when Wood went to make *Plan 9* three years later, he couldn't resist posthumously including the actor in the movie. So, he threw in footage from an unmade vampire film in which Lugosi, naturally, played the vampire. However, since Wood's Lugosi-vampire footage was sparse, he hired another actor to fill in for the majority of the character's scenes, hiding his face by covering it with his cape. This is yet another example of how thoroughly absurd *Plan 9* is.

Is *Plan 9 from Outer Space* truly the worst film of all time? That is debatable. *Robot Monster* certainly gives it a run for its money, as does Wood's *Bride of the Monster* (under penalty of death, not to be confused with *Bride of Frankenstein*). There are even, if you look hard enough, some critics who will defend Ed Wood as an enthusiastic lover of cinema who didn't have the resources to make anything better than he did. While that is true, there is no denying that Wood also had zero filmmaking talent, no matter what his budget may have been. If there is a redeeming quality about this film, it is its unending ability to provide laughs.

Vampira and Tor Johnson as reanimated corpses lumber about in the movie. *Criswell*

Santa Claus Conquers the Martians

YEAR 1964
COUNTRY United States
RUNTIME 1 hr. 21 min.
RATED Not Rated; nothing objectionable
DIRECTED BY Nicholas Webster
WRITTEN BY Glenville Mareth, Paul L. Jacobson (source story)
STARRING John Call, Leonard Hicks, Vincent Beck, Victor Stiles
SIMILAR SCI-FI *Plan 9 from Outer Space*, *Robot Monster*, *The Star Wars Holiday Special*

All children love Santa, even Martian kids. *Embassy Pictures Corporation/Heritage Auctions*

There exist sci-fi movies that are worse than *Santa Claus Conquers the Martians*, but there are probably none cheesier. From its plot to its aesthetics, every element of this film seems desperate to please children, rather than confident that it will do so. The result is an irredeemable, overblown attempt to infuse childish amusement into a mindless story.

When the leader of Mars decides that Martian children need to scale back on their "electronic teaching machines" and learn how to have fun, he arranges for his people to kidnap Santa Claus from Earth. They know how to get to Earth just fine, but their Santa-tracking skills are lacking, so they are forced to kidnap two human children, Billy and Betty, to learn where Santa lives. Once old St. Nick is rounded up, they head back to Mars, but one defiant Martian thinks toys will make his people turn stupid, so along with getting back to Earth, Santa and the two human children have to avoid being outright killed by one of their captors.

Santa (John Call) and Martian Kimar (Leonard Hicks) put the kitsch in Christmas. *Embassy Pictures Corporation/Heritage Auctions*

Nothing about this movie on any level works. In a genre known for its lower-quality entries incorporating ridiculous costume designs, this film has some of the worst, with the Martians wearing green spandex suits complemented by helmets with giant antennas and metal hoses. As for the extent to which the writers seem desperate to please their target crowd, the final scene consists of five children using nothing but toys to assault and overcome a grown Martian man wielding a freeze ray-like weapon. Other scenes are simply confounding. At one point a Martian introduces Santa Claus to two Martian children. Santa walks in and, instead of talking, proceeds simply to giggle. After a moment the children begin giggling. This lasts for about sixty seconds.

In a movie like this, you don't bother to ask why the Martians speak English and even write using the English alphabet. Or why the names of Martian months are amalgamations of Gregorian months. Or why Martians look so much like humans. Or why humans can breathe perfectly well on Mars. Or why there is an enormous air duct in the Martians' ship's air*lock*. Or why Santa doesn't seem bothered by the fact that he's been kidnapped. Clearly, children's movies must be held to different standards from the rest. However, even children's movies are enjoyable (or at least tolerable) for adults if made properly. This one is a test of endurance.

The movie received newfound fame after being mocked on an episode of "Mystery Science Theater 3000." *Embassy Pictures Corporation/Heritage Auctions*

Gammera the Invincible

YEAR 1966
COUNTRY Japan, United States
RUNTIME 1 hr. 25 min.
RATED Not Rated; mild giant turtle violence
DIRECTED BY Noriaki Yuasa
WRITTEN BY Nisan Takahashi, Richard Kraft
STARRING Albert Dekker, Harumi Kiritachi, Yoshiro Uchida, Brian Donlevy
SIMILAR SCI-FI *The Deadly Mantis*, *Gamera: Guardian of the Universe*, *Godzilla* (1954), *War of the Monsters*, *Yongary: Monster from the Deep*

It's easy to see the logic behind *Gammera the Invincible*. *Godzilla*, a movie about nuclear weaponry knocking a giant monster loose into the world, was such a hit that it basically spawned Japan's fascination with giant monsters, so it might be surmised that a film with a similar premise would also be successful. There is one key difference, though. Despite having a relatively low budget, *Godzilla* was carefully made. *Gammera the Invincible* feels like it was created on the spot by someone who had never written a story for any medium.

The plot is as derivative as possible. A Russian aircraft carrying a nuclear missile is shot down, at which point the missile explodes and un-freezes a giant turtle with tusks. Said turtle, Gammera, then begins attacking the world, and Japan's military and scientists are left trying to devise a way to stop it. There is one original element: a young boy in a prominent role, playing a sympathetic angle toward the monster, at times insightfully explaining that Gammera may not actually be evil. Regardless of

Gammera takes time out from rampaging to scoop up a beauty. *Harris Associates/National Telefilm Associates*

the areas in which the film does or does not try to do something new, however, *Gammera the Invincible* remains simply stupid all the way through.

Some of this stupidity is contained in the script. We are told by a scientist that if Gammera isn't stopped, he could destroy the entire Earth within twenty-four hours—even though the giant turtle moves with a speed comparable to a normal one. We also have mindless bits of dialogue, such as one character's response to learning that the Army plans to use a "freezing bomb" against Gammera: "Do you mean the army has a bomb that will freeze things?" Yes. That is what that means.

Where the film's badness really shines, though, is in Gammera's attributes. To begin with, the turtle eats fire for sustenance. He also breathes fire on people, which basically means that he vomits on his victims as his primary mode of attack. The best part of all, though, is the turtle's ability to crawl into his shell and emit fire from the shell's openings … which then somehow causes him to spin at a high rate and fly around like a flying saucer. If there was any way to take the film seriously before we see these abilities, there is certainly no way to do so afterward.

Gammera the Invincible may be a horrible film, but it never gets old. It's like a giant monster story imagined and told by a child. It doesn't really make sense, and there are certain elements that seem to come out of nowhere, but in the end, you're glad it was dreamt up. Sometimes we need a break from the sensible.

This is the first movie in a series starring Gammera and the only one to be filmed in black and white. *Harris Associates/National Telefilm Associates*

Zaat

YEAR 1971
COUNTRY United States
RUNTIME 1 hr. 40 minutes
RATED PG; some violence
DIRECTED BY Don Barton, Arnold Stevens
WRITTEN BY Ron Kivett, Lee O. Larew, Don Barton, Arnold Stevens
STARRING Marshall Grauer, Wade Popwell, Paul Galloway, Gerald Cruse, Sanna Ringhaver
SIMILAR SCI-FI *The Creature Walks Among Us, Swamp Thing*

"NETS ARE NO LONGER FOR FISH. WE MAY USE THEM ON YOU HUMANS, IF ANY SURVIVE."
-DR. LEOPOLD

The world could use another good swamp monster-esque movie. Ever since *Creature from the Black Lagoon* in 1954 and to some extent its first sequel, there have not been any worth watching. So, maybe it's good that Don Barton and Arnold Stevens, who have only this film to their credit, at least tried (though this is more of a pond monster movie than a swamp monster one). Unfortunately, their attempt turned out to be one of the most dismal ever.

Zaat follows an ichthyologist who is bent on conquering the universe (yes, the whole universe), and his plan to do so consists of turning himself into a giant fish and starting a conquest from the sea. His thinking is that fish are particularly cunning creatures, so if he takes on fish-like qualities and can start a race of half-fish-half-humans, he'll be set to take over the entire world. To be fair, the absurdity of the scientist's thinking seems intended, as he's constantly depicted as being mentally unstable. Either way, though, it's a pretty terrible basis for a film that's trying to evoke horror.

This plot, along with the scientist's transformation into a man-fish, is established within the first couple of minutes of the movie, and things only get worse from there. The most prominently bad aspect of the film is the monster itself, which looks like Greedo from *Star Wars* mated with a tree. Other oddities abound. At one point, the plot comes to a halt so that we can listen to some guy sing a song for the townspeople who are hiding out from the monster. During the song's final verses the singer and his small crowd all get up, walk to the local police station, and put themselves in a jail cell. What?

As the plot progresses through mundane slayings, painfully slow pursuits of the creature, high school-quality acting, and editing that could have destroyed the film singlehandedly, *Zaat* solidifies itself as the worst movie ever to be made in or near the swamp monster subgenre. Even Wes Craven's insulting attempt at adapting *Swamp Thing* to film doesn't match the incompetence of this mess. *Zaat* is as much of an abomination as its monster.

Writer Ron Kivett has said he got the idea for the movie after reading an article about a species of "walking" catfish that could live both in water and on land.
Barton Films/Heritage Auctions

Night of the Lepus

YEAR 1972
COUNTRY United States
RUNTIME 1 hr. 28 min.
RATED PG; some fake blood and gore
DIRECTED BY William F. Claxton
WRITTEN BY Don Holliday, Gene R. Kearney, Russell Braddon (source novel)
STARRING Stuart Whitman, Janet Leigh, Rory Calhoun, DeForest Kelley
SIMILAR SCI-FI *The Killer Shrews*, *Kingdom of the Spiders*, *Tarantula*, *Them!*

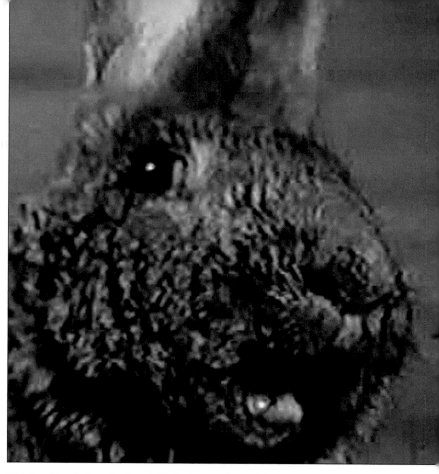

Despite attempts to make the rabbits look scary, they still just look like fuzzy bunnies.
Metro-Goldwyn-Mayer

If you aren't a linguist or a lagomorphic researcher, you might be wondering, *What is a lepus?* If so, the marketing team for this film did its job. You see, if the team had given the movie a more easily understood title, say, written in layman's terms, no one could possibly make it past the title without laughing themselves into disdain for the film. If "lepus" wasn't used and the studio opted for its more common synonym, the title would have had to be: *Night of the Rabbit*.

Yes, this film is about giant killer rabbits, made so by a botched experiment meant to rid the plains of the little furballs, which are digging holes everywhere and bothering ranchers. These are not hideously mutated monster rabbits, though. Nothing that cool. They're just normal old rabbits that have grown to human size, have an appetite for blood, and otherwise hop around on all fours in big furry groups just like they always have.

What more needs to be said? In this movie you watch rabbits covered in fake blood hop around miniature sets in slow motion while the camera occasionally cuts to big, vague, furry things jumping onto characters, knocking them down, and mauling them to death. Add in some frequently awful gore effects (the first torn-apart victim seems to have had a prosthetic for every limb), and you've got quite an entertaining way to spend an hour and a half. And as a bonus to fans of *Star Trek* and of classic cinema, DeForest Kelley and Janet Leigh have prominent roles in the film.

To be fair, *Night of the Lepus* as a whole isn't all that bad. It's a standard "Man tries to fix nature and ends up making things worse" movie with strong acting, impressive miniature sets, and unnerving growling rabbit sounds. In a final analysis, though, it all comes down to this: the movie is about killer bunnies. That's hard to overcome.

The Star Wars Holiday Special

YEAR 1978
COUNTRY United States
RUNTIME 1 hr. 37 min.
RATED Not Rated
DIRECTED BY Steve Binder
WRITTEN BY Pat Proft, Leonard Ripps, Bruce Vilanch, Rod Warren, Mitzie Welch
STARRING Peter Mayhew, Harrison Ford, Mark Hamill, Carrie Fisher
SIMILAR SCI-FI *Howard the Duck*, *Santa Claus Conquers the Martians*

Ackmena (Bea Arthur) and patrons of the cantina. *20th Century Fox Television*

Technically, it may not be a movie, but it's close enough and is so horrendous that it cannot be ignored in a discussion of bad sci-fi cinema. It is the ultimate embarrassment of all things *Star Wars*. It's the hour-and-a-half, made-for-television *Star Wars Holiday Special*, aired in the year following the original, 1977 theatrical release of *Star Wars*. This show treats the characters and the tone of the *Star Wars* mythology with such disrespect that it is maddening.

As if it isn't also simply bad, the *Holiday Special* starts off as a snooze fest, with a simplistic pastoral score accompanying an opening scene of Chewbacca's family, minus Chewbacca, sitting around getting ready for dinner. In the meantime, Han Solo is trying to avoid Imperial Star Destroyers so he can complete the daring task of … getting Chewbacca home in time to celebrate Life Day? *Deep exhale* Less than five minutes into the *Holiday Special*, we know we're in for a long ride. The plot goes like this: the Empire is out to get Chewie, so they've blockaded his home planet and have invaded his home, waiting for him to show up. There are so many lengthy, inconsequential interruptions, however, that the *Holiday Special* would have been better off titled *The Star Wars Variety Show*.

The problems with the special come in all shapes but in equally disastrous sizes. It's filled with sentimentalism all the way through, which leads the once rogue-ish Han to speak wildly uncharacteristic lines, such as when he returns an affectionate comment from Chewbacca with, "I feel the same way about you, too, pal, and your family." Luke Skywalker has a part in this mess, but he's wearing *way* too much makeup and has a strangely feminine haircut, both of which combine to make him look almost literally like a girl. Leia's singing of a Life Day song near the end of the show might have been the knockout blow if we had not already been subjected to something far worse: Bea Arthur singing a goodbye song to patrons while bartending at the Mos Eisley cantina—yes, that really happens.

The Star Wars Holiday Special has exactly one redeeming quality: it contains the first ever appearance (in animated form) of nearly every *Star Wars* fan's favorite bounty hunter, Boba Fett. Other than that, it is a failure of unimaginable proportions, made all the worse by the fact that it's inhabited by characters we love. Two years later, in *The Empire Strikes Back*, Han was subjected to torture at the hands of the Empire. After surviving this special, that was probably child's play.

> "I HOPE THAT THIS DAY WILL ALWAYS BE A DAY OF JOY, IN WHICH WE CAN RECONFIRM OUR DEDICATION, AND OUR COURAGE, AND MORE THAN ANYTHING ELSE, OUR LOVE FOR ONE ANOTHER. THIS IS THE PROMISE OF THE TREE OF LIFE."
>
> **-PRINCESS LEIA**

The whole *Star Wars* mythology gets boiled down to a typical 1970s' variety hour.
20th Century Fox Television

As he tries to find a way back to his home planet, Howard (voiced by Chip Zien) develops a relationship with Beverly (Lea Thompson) and also saves the world from an evil alien monster. *Lucasfilm/Universal/The Kobal Collection*

Howard the Duck

YEAR 1986
COUNTRY United States
RUNTIME 1 hr. 50 min.
RATED PG; some mild violence and language
DIRECTED BY Willard Huyck
WRITTEN BY Willard Huyck, Gloria Katz, Steve Gerber
STARRING Chip Zien, Lea Thompson, Tim Robbins, Jeffrey Jones
SIMILAR SCI-FI *Attack of the Killer Tomatoes, The Star Wars Holiday Special*

There is time for the ridiculous, and there is time for the humorous. It just has to be accompanied by creativity and wit. *Howard the Duck* aimed to fire on these cylinders, but the only functioning element is its ridiculousness. The result is a movie that is painful in its attempts to be funny, never delivering an enjoyable moment the entire time.

The plot is unbelievably stupid. In some far off galaxy there is a planet virtually identical to ours—similar brand names even adorn consumer products—but there is one key difference: the population consists of anthropomorphic ducks. One such duck, Howard (Chip Zien), comes home one

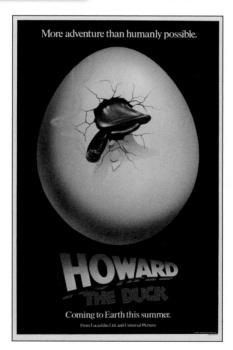

The movie won four Golden Raspberry Awards including Worst Picture. *Lucasfilm/Universal/ Heritage Auctions*

night, sits in his recliner, and is inexplicably ripped through space, landing in Cleveland, Ohio. Depending on what's convenient for the film's writers, some people are momentarily startled at the sight of Howard. Others don't seem to notice anything unusual about him. Either way, he soon befriends a punk rock girl name Beverly (Lea Thompson) and sets out to find a way home. Fate, however, has other plans.

For a movie based on such an off-the-wall concept, it has no imaginative elements. The insertion of duck-related words into everyday language quickly becomes obnoxious and rarely lets up. You get to hear terms and phrases as creative as "Bloomingduck's," "*Playduck*," "No more Mr. Nice Duck," and … "Quack-Fu." If you didn't just sigh after reading that sentence, maybe this movie's for you. The non-duck humor is equally uninspired. When one individual in a diner begins morphing into a "dark overlord of the universe" (I wonder how long it took them to come up with that title), a waiter remarks, "He must've ate the chili." You get the idea.

In roughly the final third of the film, *Howard the Duck* becomes something like a derivative *Ghostbusters* rip-off. Apparently it wasn't enough that we had to watch writers and actors try to make someone in a duck costume seem funny. For this latter portion of the film, we have to watch said duck save the Earth from the aforementioned dark overlord of the universe. Cop chases, scientific guns, and space monsters ensue. To paraphrase David Byrne, you may find yourself wondering, *How did I get here?*

George Lucas tends to catch the most flack for this film even though he didn't write or direct it (he was executive producer, and the film was made under Lucasfilm). It doesn't matter where you lay the blame, though. This movie is a special kind of bad regardless of who is most responsible. There are many horrible failures in the annals of sci-fi cinema, but only one of them has an actor in a duck costume playing the main character.

"PREPARE TO EAT BEAK." -HOWARD

Battlefield Earth

YEAR 2000
COUNTRY United States
RUNTIME 1 hr. 58 min.
RATED PG-13; intense sci-fi action
DIRECTED BY Roger Christian
WRITTEN BY Carey Mandell, J.D. Shapiro, L. Ron Hubbard (source novel)
STARRING Barry Pepper, John Travolta, Forest Whitaker, Kim Coates
SIMILAR SCI-FI *Plan 9 from Outer Space*, *Planet of the Apes*, *Robot Monster*

Giant humanoid Psychlos Terl (John Travolta) and Ker (Forrest Whitaker) rule Earth in the year 3000. *Morgan Creek/The Kobal Collection*

Ludicrous characters, uninspired visuals, and a frequently nonsensical story—*Battlefield Earth* has all of these things. A "repressed human race tries to take back the Earth" flick, this film doesn't even start off with high aims, yet it still manages to disappoint throughout its entire runtime. If you were to ask any sci-fi aficionado what the genre's worst film since, say, 1990 is, you're likely to get the same response nine out of— no, ninety-nine out of a hundred times: *Battlefield Earth*.

In this "saga of the year 3000," Earth has been invaded by aliens called Psychlos (please hold laughter until the end of the review), and humankind, with no civilization left, has been forced to recede to primitive ways of life. When one human named Jonnie Goodboy Tyler (I said "please") dares to go explore the world, he is captured by a particularly deceptive Psychlo who is bent on harvesting the planet's resources while giving as little back to his superiors as possible. Somehow this leads to Tyler (Barry Pepper) saving the world.

The tone of *Battlefield Earth* suggests an adult-oriented film, but it has the sophistication of a children's afternoon cartoon. The characters, particularly the Psychlos, are not only two-dimensional and clichéd, they are stupid. In the most unfortunate role of his career, John Travolta plays the lead Psychlo, Terl. Terl's evil is demonstrated through juvenile wordplay (like constantly falling back on the "I said *I* wouldn't [insert heinous act], but *he can!*" trick) and through continually referring to his enemies as—get this—"rat brains." This is the kind of movie where the hero and the villain refuse to kill each other even though they each have endless opportunities to do so. It's the kind of movie where, despite the fact that they are consistently as devious as they can be, the villains manage to maintain perfectly obsequious followers.

The plot frequently teeters into the asinine. At one point, Tyler begins teaching his fellow prisoners geometry, claiming that it will

Since *Battlefield Earth* only covers half of L. Ron Hubbard's 1,050-page book, a sequel was originally planned, but based on the reception of this movie, it was abandoned.
Morgan Creek

somehow free them. We never learn how. Later, these primitive humans teach *themselves* how to become ace fighter pilots by training for one week in an abandoned military simulator. And so on and so forth.

In 2010, the Razzies, an award show dedicated to shaming the worst in cinema, named *Battlefield Earth* the "Worst Movie of the Decade." Writer J.D. Shapiro accepted the award in person. In his speech he said, "I can't help but be strangely proud of it. Because out of all the sucky movies, mine is the suckiest." You gotta admit, that is an accomplishment.

"I AM GOING TO MAKE YOU AS HAPPY AS A BABY PSYCHLO ON A STRAIGHT DIET OF KERBANGO."
-CHERK

THE GOOD, THE BAD, AND THE BEAUTIFUL

In the following top ten lists, we will briefly cover the best that science fiction has to offer. We'll go over some of the basics (best movies and best directors), some of the genre's more fun elements (best robots and best villains), and some of its less-acknowledged treasures (best female characters). Any lists such as these are going to be subjective, based upon the opinion of the person compiling them (in this case, your dear author). Coming from the perspective of a science fiction enthusiast, though, these particular lists should at least partially reflect the general view of other aficionados.

We do this because in the end, no appreciation of science fiction – or of any genre – is complete without acknowledging its greatest creators and creations.

TOP 10 SCI-FI MOVIES

As this book itself attests, there are plenty of great entries in the world of science fiction cinema. Some, though, stand far beyond the rest. These are the films that demonstrate the aesthetic heights the genre is capable of reaching.

10. Bride of Frankenstein

For anyone unfamiliar with *Bride of Frankenstein*, the title may create expectations of mid-level camp. Make no mistake, though. This is a great sequel, remaining true to its predecessor, *Frankenstein*, in tone, story, and style. In this installment, Dr. Frankenstein has renounced the science of creating life but gets pulled back into the game by another scientist, Dr. Pretorius, who is not only mad but evil. Right around this time, the monster rises from the rubble that ensued in the finale of *Frankenstein* and begins roaming the countryside. After wandering through the woods, however, the creature finds something that he has never known: companionship.

These events lead to some of the most moving moments in *Frankenstein* history, culminating in the creation of a bride for the monster (not, as the title would make it seem, for Dr. Frankenstein). But will she give herself to the creature for which she has been fated? Or will she deem him an abomination as the rest of the world has done?

This movie is a worthy successor to *Frankenstein. Universal Pictures*

Godzilla evokes the horror of the nuclear age. *Toho Film (Eiga) Co. Ltd/Heritage Auctions*

9. Godzilla (1954)

Godzilla, because of its dumbed-down American cut and because of the campiness of nearly all of its twenty-seven follow-ups (not even counting the poorly executed 1998 American remake), has experienced a mediocre reputation throughout the years. All it takes is one viewing of the original Japanese version of this film, though, to understand just how great the movie is.

Godzilla is a diatribe of the horrors of the nuclear age. Its aim was not to provide thrills of watching a monster wreck cities; rather, it was to evoke terror by depicting the utterly destructive nature of atomic weaponry, represented by the title monster, which is itself the product of such weaponry. After all, for Japanese viewers just under a decade after the bombings of Hiroshima and Nagasaki, such images of destruction could hardly be enjoyed for thrills. Accompanying its plot with an oppressive visual and emotional atmosphere, this sci-fi/horror film rarely lets you catch your breath. And whenever you do get a break, it's just so that you can begin building apprehension for the monster's next attack. This film opts to be a meaningful experience rather than a fun one.

8. Metropolis (1927)

Metropolis director Fritz Lang has said that he doesn't care for this film of his. This is actually half-understandable. The plot is filled with holes, the story frequently delves into sentimentalism, and the theme is, if not forced, at least trite. However, despite the movie's shortcomings, it succeeds so phenomenally well in delivering great visuals that it cannot be held back from achieving masterpiece status. Just try to erase this film's imagery from your mind; it won't happen.

Among the most prominent images are low-level factory workers pulling levers in perfect unison with one another, main character Freder envisioning a factory turning into Moloch and devouring those who work within it, a cityscape that seems to consist solely of obscenely large skyscrapers, and, of course, the robot that might be science fiction's first: the "Machine-Man" (which probably should have been called a "Machine-Woman").

Through both the plot and the visuals, Lang presents a profound fear of classism. It is exclusively in the visuals, though, that this fear is not only conveyed but evoked in viewers. This is science fiction's first great visionary achievement, and it remains one of the best.

Metropolis is a visionary wonder. *Universum Film (UFA)/Heritage Auctions*

7. Star Wars: Episode V - The Empire Strikes Back

Master Yoda teaches Luke (Mark Hamill) the way of the Jedi. *Lucasfilm/20th Century Fox*

How do you follow up the greatest sci-fi action/adventure film ever made? Watch *Star Wars: Episode V – The Empire Strikes Back*, and the answer is clear: you take the main characters, put them through constant trials of strength and will, and watch how they develop. By doing this, *Empire* becomes a dramatic work rarely matched in the realm of science fiction. This is a story about overambitious heroes learning patience and humility through hardship. *Empire* also introduces one of science fiction's most memorable characters (Yoda), delivers one of the genre's coolest lines ("I know"), and contains one of the most famous twists in all of cinema ("I am [spoiler redacted]").

Empire would almost certainly have failed if George Lucas and director Irvin Kershner had tried to make it another upbeat space romp. Instead, they took the more measured route and created a dramatic masterpiece. This is not only one of the best science fiction films ever made, it may be the second best sequel in all of cinema, topped only by *The Godfather: Part II*.

6. Frankenstein (1931)

Monster (Boris Karloff) and creator (Colin Clive). *Universal Pictures/Heritage Auctions*

Despite being made at the dawn of cinema as we know it today, *Frankenstein* exhibits a deep understanding of the art of film and all of its facets. From its scenery to its cinematography to its story to its makeup and acting, *Frankenstein* succeeds in virtually every way. The decadent gray sky in the film's opening scene seems to portend some impending abominable act. The angles used during the creation scene are both disorienting and intensifying. The effect on viewers could hardly be fuller.

Boris Karloff and Colin Clive's acting put the finishing touches on the film. Karloff manages to make the monster both pitiable and fearful, and Clive brings such fervor to the character of Dr. Frankenstein that outbursts such as "Now I know what it feels like to be God!" are as believable as they are startling. With all of these elements infused into a plot focused on the classic theme of man overstepping his bounds, *Frankenstein* achieves a greatness that is rarely approached.

Solaris is a meditative drama. *Mosfilm Studios/Heritage Auctions*

5. Solaris (1972)

Solaris could have cut its near-three-hour runtime in half and not missed a beat of the plot. That, however, is part of its genius. This film is concerned with far more than plot. It aims not only to present an existential dilemma but to appreciate the beauty of its characters and their world while it does so. Its opening shot establishes this aim: slowly panning across swaying reeds before finding its main character, Kris Kelvin, standing nearby and gazing in silence. From there the film progresses through a slow-paced journey in which we are forced to question the very definition of humanity, and it does so with one of the most nuanced love relationships ever to hit the screen. Few directors have the confidence to allow their films to halt plot progression in favor of meditation. *Solaris* director Andrei Tarkovsky is one of those few.

4. Alien

Just like the creature the characters encounter in this movie, *Alien* was like nothing film fans had seen when it was released in 1979. It is based on an inherently unsettling premise: a small crew aboard a deep space freight hauler is ordered to investigate a distress beacon on a nearby planet. When they do, an alien life form attaches itself to the face of one of the crew members and eventually paves the way for a bloodthirsty creature to board the ship.

Crew members investigate the source of a distress signal. *Brandywine Productions/20th Century Fox/Heritage Auctions*

The pacing and the atmosphere feel as if they were measured according to some esoteric formula for perfection, evoking in viewers the same feelings of seclusion and trepidation that the characters must feel. Within this atmosphere, the images of the alien species in its various stages of life are as viscerally dynamic and horrifying as the environment is haunting. The result is an exercise in pure terror as these space truckers find themselves being hunted by the creature that has come on board. Take into consideration the things the alien wants to do with the humans it is hunting, and you have a film that never loses its edge.

3. Blade Runner

Upon a first viewing, *Blade Runner* can seem to be little more than commendable, as a detective story punctuated by beautiful images. It's about a Humphrey Bogart-like character hunting down robots that look exactly like humans. Upon subsequent viewings, however, numerous details become apparent and affect our understanding of the film and its themes. In full bloom, *Blade Runner* is a sprawling examination of humanity, technology, and the inextricable nature of creation and destruction. It questions our understanding of life at the same time that it examines the effects technological advancement has on society.

In the end, however, *Blade Runner* is about the beauty of the world, found everywhere from the streets of Los Angeles, to the death of an android, to a close-up of an eye gazing at the city. Indeed, the leader of the androids being hunted reveals his personal apprehensions to

Deckard (Harrison Ford) falls in love with replicant Rachel (Sean Young). *Ladd Company/Warner Bros./ Heritage Auctions*

be aimed not at the idea of death itself but at the fact that, upon death, his memories of beautiful images will no longer exist. In a film able to find beauty even in the reflection of light in a wet road tunnel, this is a poignant loss.

If science fiction has a *Citizen Kane*, this might be it. The further main character Rick Deckard progresses in his investigation, the more questions he finds himself facing. In the end, even if he completes his mission, there is no way for him to solidify a sense of self. All that he can be sure of are his feelings.

2. Star Wars

Luke Skywalker (Mark Hamill) and Han Solo (Harrison Ford), stuck inside the Death Star's trash compactor. *Lucasfilm/20th Century Fox/Heritage Auctions*

Star Wars may be the most exciting and fun sci-fi film ever made. With this movie, George Lucas used stylistic techniques that had never been used in the genre and special effects techniques that had never been used in cinema, period. The result was an unprecedented level of realism for a space-bound adventure film and one of the biggest blockbusters of all time. One of the movie's greatest merits is the degree to which it was realized by Lucas. This far away galaxy is populated by life forms of all types, and even throwaway background characters are frequently as dynamic as those at the forefront of the plot.

It's the characters that complete *Star Wars*, though. There's the young and secluded but aspiring main character, Luke; the mythologically powerful old hermit, Obi-Wan; the companions that help Luke along the way, R2-D2 and C-3PO; the rogue that turns out to be not quite as cold as he thinks he is, Han; the princess in distress, Leia; and the malevolent force bent on conquering the world, Darth Vader. The dynamics between these characters and the chemistry between the actors could hardly have been more engaging.

Plus, *Star Wars* is basically a combination of all the most exciting movie types there are: sci-fi, fantasy, western, samurai, and adventure. It sounds so simple: Create a movie that utilizes the best elements of everything everybody likes. It took the vision of someone like George Lucas, though, to combine those elements in a cohesive way.

1. 2001: A Space Odyssey

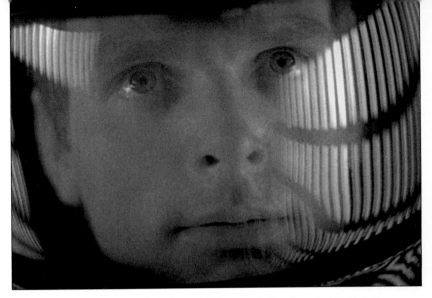

Dr. Dave Bowman (Keir Dullea), the hero of _2001_. _Metro-Goldwyn-Mayer/The Kobal Collection_

Of all the great movies science fiction has to offer, none achieve the scope and imagination of _2001: A Space Odyssey_. Beginning before the dawn of man, spending most of its plot in the stage of exploration of our solar system, and ending with something akin to our race's next major stage of evolution, _2001_ covers all points of our existence. The effect created by this vast span is one of awe at what we are capable of accomplishing. When a group of our apelike ancestors wakes to see a monolith inexplicably placed in their midst, we are shown a bottom-up view of the object, pointing directly toward the moon, as if to tell these creatures that they will one day go there. To imagine such a race of beings one day achieving such a feat is mind-blowing. This sense of amazement is matched only by the scenario the film offers as man's ascension beyond beings walking the Earth.

It's not just the ideas that make _2001_ the genre's best film; it's the way the movie presents those ideas. This film's events and visuals are accompanied by classical pieces by Johann Strauss, Richard Strauss, and others. This music, combined with visuals of planets floating in orbit, shuttles flying through space, and astronauts attempting to emulate their usual ways of life in the environment of a spacecraft, emphasizes the delicate and nearly immaculate ability of our own creations to allow us to travel beyond our planet. These elements, too, are portrayed with an unmistakable sense of awe.

The film's final moments, imagining a future for our race, are both enigmatic and sublime. Even if we can't fully comprehend the events contained in the finale, we can feel their magnitude. With _2001_, director Stanley Kubrick and writer Arthur C. Clarke present a film more audacious than any other. This audacity, combined with Kubrick's cinematic vision, Clarke's ability to craft an engaging plot, and both individuals' ability to think far beyond the bounds of conventional understandings of the world, resulted in science fiction's single best film and one of the greatest films of all time in any genre. This, truly, is a work unlike any other.

AFI'S TOP 10 SCI-FI MOVIES

In 2008, the American Film Institute honored America's 10 greatest films in 10 classic film genres, including science fiction. These were chosen from a ballot of 500 nominated films, by a jury of more than 1,500 leaders in the film industry. The ballot included films from 1915 to 2006. Here are AFI's picks:

10. **Back to the Future**
 9. **Invasion of the Body Snatchers** (1956)
 8. **Terminator 2: Judgment Day**
 7. **Alien**
 6. **Blade Runner**
 5. **The Day the Earth Stood Still**
 4. **A Clockwork Orange**
 3. **ET: The Extra Terrestrial**
 2. **Star Wars, Episode IV – A New Hope**
 1. **2001: A Space Odyssey**

TOP 10 DIRECTORS

Many hands go into the making of a feature-length film. It is the director, though, who establishes the vision for the movie and who coordinates all efforts to achieve that vision. Here, we pay tribute to the genre's ten greatest directors ever. These are the men who have led sci-fi cinema throughout its short history, and who inspire our efforts to advance it further.

10. Ishirô Honda

Ishirô Honda on the set of *Godzilla*. Toho

Though he occasionally faltered with works such as the confused mess of *The Mysterians* and the pure ugliness that is *King Kong vs. Godzilla*, Ishirô Honda's contribution to science fiction is one that cannot be ignored. Not only did he make one of the all-time greats, *Godzilla*, but in doing so he effectually gave birth to the long-lived giant monster craze of Japanese sci-fi, and he reinforced it regularly. Though *Godzilla* was his first, Honda also gave us such great monsters as King Ghidorah, Rodan, and Mothra. That alone makes him one of the genre's greatest assets.

9. David Cronenberg

David Cronenberg and a grotesque friend from *The Fly*.
20th Century Fox/The Kobal Collection

You'll have to step outside of science fiction if you want to find a twisted genius comparable to David Cronenberg, and even then it's going to be a tough search. This is the director responsible for such grotesque masterpieces as *Videodrome* and the 1986 remake of *The Fly*, as well as lesser but still imaginatively disturbing works like *The Brood, Scanners, They Came from Within*, and *eXistenZ*. Apparently fascinated by the concept of technology's interaction with the flesh, Cronenberg is uninhibited in his willingness manipulate and mangle characters' bodies in order to examine the ways in which technology affects our lives. It's a rare director who has the guts to depict something like a character inserting handguns and VHS tapes into a giant slit in his abdomen. It's an even rarer one who can use such things in a way that actually adds meaning to the film.

8. Andrei Tarkovsky

Tarkovsky may be one of the most unapproachable directors of science fiction, but for those with the patience to sit through long, meditative works, he is also one of the most rewarding. This is a director so interested in his main characters that he is happy to watch them even when they are doing nothing in particular, as if the still, silent moments reveal just as much as any dialogue or action. Though he has only a small number of science fiction films to his name, *Solaris* and *Stalker* are both astonishing in their devotion to the issues at hand. For Tarkovsky, science fiction is but a way of examining the human experience, and he is willing to take such examinations to the extremes in which there might not exist any answers to be found.

7. Steven Spielberg

Known for being simply a great director in general, Steven Spielberg has had more than his fair share of successes in the sci-fi genre. With *Close Encounters of the Third Kind* and *E.T.: The Extra-Terrestrial*, Spielberg made his mark by imagining humanity coming in contact with aliens who want not to conquer us but to become our friends. In *Jurassic Park*, he tackled the classic theme of man attempting to control nature and eventually paying dire consequences. Later, in *Minority Report*, he examined how the subjective, fluid nature of the world allows for the redemption of even those who are seemingly predestined for evil. The common theme among all of these films is one of treating the world with an optimistic but careful and respectful approach. Above all, though, Spielberg's sci-fi films evoke a sense of awe at the world and the possibilities it contains. For that, not only is he one of the best, but he may be the genre's most refreshing director.

Andrei Tarkovsky uses science fiction to examine the human experience. *The Kobal Collection*

Steven Spielberg directing Henry Thomas, who plays Elliot, in *E.T. Universal Pictures/Amblin Entertainment/The Kobal Collection*

James Cameron with actor Sam Worthington on the set of *Avatar*. *20th Century Fox Film Corporation/ The Kobal Collection*

6. James Cameron

Matched perhaps only by George Lucas in his tendency to expand the limits of filmmaking technology, James Cameron has yet to make a sci-fi film that hasn't been notable in some regard (we're going to ignore his freshman effort, *Piranha Part Two: The Spawning*, okay?). In *The Terminator*, he gave us a killer android like the world had never seen. In *Aliens*, he succeeded in the impossible task of following up Ridley Scott's masterpiece, *Alien*, by providing a relentless onslaught of bloodthirsty xenomorph action. In *The Abyss*, he did what was then unthinkable by creating a believable-looking entity made entirely out of water. *In Terminator 2: Judgment Day* he solidified himself as a master of sequel-making by upping the ante of visual effects in sci-fi/action cinema. Finally, in *Avatar*, he changed the landscape not only of motion-capture cinematography but of 3D filmmaking. We may at times criticize Cameron's writing style, but as far as the visual aspects of movies are concerned, there are few directors who have achieved so much.

5. Jack Arnold

During the heyday of science-fiction cinema in the 1950s, Jack Arnold surpassed all other directors in the enthusiasm with which he approached the genre. Just look at the guy's résumé: *It Came from Outer Space, Creature from the Black Lagoon, Tarantula*, and *The Incredible Shrinking Man* are but his better films. When this director made a sci-fi movie, chances were it was going to become a classic. In an era in which we were exploring the kinds of stories sci-fi films could deliver, Arnold was responsible for many of the genre's best entries.

Jack Arnold, right, with actors on the set of *Creature from the Black Lagoon*. *Universal Pictures*

4. George Lucas

Say what you will about the *Star Wars* prequels, but with the first *Star Wars*, George Lucas changed the way people viewed science fiction. He did this by incorporating one deceptively simple concept into his directorial approach: realism. No longer did lasers emit lazy, recoilless beams of light at their targets. No longer did spacecraft battle each other with the maneuverability of nuclear submarines. No longer were objects and environments as pristinely polished as if they had never been used. Lucas's film had dynamics, energy, and grit. Some of the elements he wanted to include were not possible with the technology available. Whenever that was the case, his production team invented new technology. The result of this dedication to verisimilitude was the most energetic and exciting sci-fi film that had ever been made.

Though Lucas didn't actually direct *The Empire Strikes Back* and *Return of the Jedi*, those movies would never have been possible without his input and without the film that started the saga. His focus has turned more to the production- and business-oriented areas of filmmaking in recent years (with the prequels as an exception), but it's almost scary to imagine the things of which Lucas is capable, should he ever undertake a new project as director (see *THX 1138* for proof of his versatility in the genre). Then again, he's already done much more than anyone could dream of accomplishing in a lifetime.

George Lucas and Jake Lloyd as the young Anakin Skywalker pal around with R2-D2 during the filming of *Star Wars: Episode I - The Phantom Menace*. *Lucasfilm/20th Century Fox/The Kobal Collection*

3. James Whale

If Jack Arnold is the king of 1950s sci-fi cinema, then James Whale takes the throne for the 1930s. Preceding the popularity that science fiction would attain later in the century, Whale directed three science fiction films in his time, and they all turned out to be undisputed classics: *Frankenstein*, *Bride of Frankenstein*, and *The Invisible Man*.

Whale tackles a common theme in all of these films: that man's thirst for greatness will be his undoing. It's the flair with which he depicts these tragedies, however, that makes the movies great. In *Frankenstein*, we got such a striking depiction of the famous monster that it practically became the creature's standard appearance. In *Bride of Frankenstein*, we got the monster's bride, which is so memorable that it is instantly recognizable despite being on screen for only the final few minutes of film. In *The Invisible Man*, Whale's team accomplished invisibility effects so amazingly competent that they stand up even against modern day standards. Whale didn't always make science fiction, but when he did, he did it right.

James Whale with a model of Frankenstein's monster on the set of *Bride of Frankenstein*. *Universal Pictures/The Kobal Collection*

Stanley Kubrick and actor Gary Lockwood on the set of *2001*. *Metro-Goldwyn-Mayer/The Kobal Collection*

2. Stanley Kubrick

One of the most daring, most imaginative, and flat-out best directors ever, Stanley Kubrick's two efforts in the science fiction genre are not only as good as his other works—they are two of his best. Kubrick's uncanny sense of precision, both narratively and visually, guides *2001: A Space Odyssey* and *A Clockwork Orange* into the upper realms of greatness. In these movies, Kubrick forgoes any sense of convention in order to tell stories that are unique, engaging, and at times mind-blowing. Coupled with this originality, every person, every object, and every color in virtually every frame of these films seems as if it was meticulously measured and placed so as to evoke a certain effect. And perhaps most importantly, Kubrick has a knack for combining his visual and narrative elements with what must be the most perfectly complementary classical soundtracks possible. Even for those whose tastes don't comply with the peculiar genius of Kubrick, there is no denying the beauty of these films.

1. Ridley Scott

Ridley Scott has made two sci-fi films, and they have both turned out to be masterpieces. Interestingly, despite the two films' nearly equal aesthetic success, they are almost nothing alike. *Alien* managed to be one of the most horrifying films ever made when it was released, using striking visuals to fuel a methodically paced plot that progresses through a suffocating atmosphere. *Blade Runner*, on the other hand, combines recurring imagistic themes, brilliant color use, provocative religious symbolism, unexpected existential crises, and a futuristic film noir feel into a cerebral experience that examines the nature of humanity and the way technological progress affects our world on a fundamental level. Both of them belong in any top ten list of the greatest science fiction films.

If there is a commonality between these films' aesthetic success, it is their longevity. *Alien* is so fundamentally effective that it is equally enjoyable upon repeated viewings. *Blade Runner* is packed with so many poignant details that it seems to offer something new each time. Neither shows any signs of age. A good director can make a summer blockbuster or even an Academy Award-winning film. It takes a master, though, to create something as perpetually relevant as these two films.

Ridley Scott and actress Sigourney Weaver on a break during the filming of *Alien*.
20th Century Fox/The Kobal Collection/Robert Penn

TOP 10 FEMALE CHARACTERS

There are many great characters in sci-fi cinema, be they inspiring, intriguing, or just plain entertaining. Most of them are also male. However, for the relatively few great female characters that exist within the genre, there is some special, unquantifiable quality that no male character can possess. Here we take a look at the best characters of that oft-neglected sex.

Dr. Frankenstein (Colin Clive) and the Bride (Elsa Lanchester).
Universal Pictures/Heritage Auctions

10. The Frankenstein Monster's Bride

Appearing for but a few minutes in the end of the film titled after her, this woman built to be a monster's bride is as memorable as any other aspect of *Bride of Frankenstein*. Maybe it's the iconic hair, maybe it's the confused hissing, or maybe it's the quick, birdlike movements of her head, but, as portrayed by Elsa Lanchester, something about this female monster is inherently intriguing even though (or especially because?) we learn very little about her. We are left only to imagine what she could have been.

9. Barbarella

She may not be any sort of feminist role model, but there's no denying the allure of Jane Fonda's Barbarella, "Queen of the Galaxy." The woman's beauty is topped only by her naïveté, as she travels the galaxy in search of the world's only existent weapon, changing outfits the entire time for no good reason. Add in her ability to somehow take herself unflinchingly seriously, and you have a character that is simply fun to watch.

Jane Fonda as the alluring space vixen Barbarella. *Paramount/Heritage Auctions*

8. Alice

In the early 1900s, Luigi Pirandello wrote a play called *Six Characters in Search of an Author*. Alice, main character of the *Resident Evil* films, is a character in search of a better movie. Because none of the *Resident Evil* films are good (albeit they do offer a select few entertaining scenes), it's easy to overlook both the awesomeness of the Alice character and the talent of Milla Jovovich, the actress playing her. Alice is a highly trained, genetically enhanced, psychokinetically enabled former agent of the megacorporation responsible for a pseudo-zombie apocalypse, and she wants to bring the organization down. We've seen similar highly formidable women attempted before with less success, but the dedication, fluidity, and intensity that Jovovich brings to the role provides Alice with just enough nuance to make us care. The *Resident Evil* movies may not be generally fun to watch, but Alice herself definitely is.

The formidable Alice. *Davis Films/ Impact Pictures/The Kobal Collection/ Ralph Konow*

7. Padmé

One of the best elements George Lucas brought over from the original *Star Wars* trilogy into the prequels is the idea of a female character who, though holding a position of royalty, is also surprisingly tough. Played by Natalie Portman, Padmé Amidala, starting off as a queen and eventually making the move to senator, is one of the *Star Wars* films' most formidable female characters, understanding both the nuance of politics and the practicality of gunfights. She may not be a particularly layered character, but she is so strong-willed that she is appealing on a fundamental level. Plus, look at what her children accomplished.

Padmé knows how to handle politics, as well as guns. *Lucasfilm/The Kobal Collection/Keith Hampshere*

The complex and perplexing Hari.
Mosfilm Studios

6. Hari

In a sense, Hari (Natalya Bondarchuk) does not even exist. That is what makes her so fascinating. This is a deceased woman materialized from her husband's memory by the sentient planet Solaris, and as such her mere presence confronts *Solaris*'s main character, Kris Kelvin, with the ultimate existential crisis. She looks and acts exactly like the "real" Hari and indeed seems to feel emotion, but this Hari consists completely of neutrinos and would dematerialize upon leaving Solaris's orbit. Can she be considered a living being, or is she merely a simulacrum of life? We are left to ponder.

5. Lois Lane

Pick whichever version you want—Margot Kidder from the original *Superman* film franchise, Kate Bosworth in the 2006 attempt at revitalizing the series, or even Christina Hendricks as the character's voice in the 2011 animated adaptation of *All-Star Superman*—there's no denying that Lois Lane is a vital component to the most iconic superhero of them all. Lane isn't just Superman's girlfriend; she is his connection to the human race. By extension, this makes her one of the most powerful people on Earth. It's one thing to have superpowers, but it's another to have the inspiration to put them to use. Lane is that inspiration.

Intrepid reporter Lois Lane (Margot Kidder) keeps Superman grounded. *Warner Bros./DC Comics/The Kobal Collection*

4. River Tam

Any fan of Joss Whedon's astounding but ill-fated TV series *Firefly* is a fan of Summer Glau's mysterious character, River Tam. It wasn't until *Serenity*, Whedon's feature-length follow-up to *Firefly*, however, that we learned the full extent (or is it?) of what River is capable. As it turns out, this awkward young woman is not just brilliant and indecipherable; she is also … an unparalleled master of hand-to-hand combat? Yep, this latent skill shows up in *Serenity* just in time to be put to great use. We always knew there was something special about her. Until *Serenity*, we just didn't know precisely what that was.

River Tam is a master of hand-to-hand combat. *Universal Studios/The Kobal Collection/Sidney Baldwin*

3. Sarah Connor

Who knew an average diner waitress would turn out to be instrumental in (potentially) saving the human race from extinction at the hands of killer robots? This unexpected burden is placed on Sarah Connor (Linda Hamilton) in *The Terminator*, but she responds with an equally unexpected display of level-headedness and becomes one of the strongest female characters in science fiction cinema. In *Terminator 2: Judgment Day*, she returns, going somewhat rogue in order to nullify the chance of the robot apocalypse once and for all with a merciless "ends justify the means" mindset. You can fault her for what are arguably temporary lapses in morality, but you can't say this woman isn't as tough as she is determined.

From minimum-wage everywoman to gun-slinging heroine, Sarah Connor saves the human race in *The Terminator* and *Terminator 2*. *Carolco/The Kobal Collection*

2. Princess Leia

She's smart, she's strong, and she's not afraid to get her hands dirty. Princess Leia (Carrie Fisher), starlet of the original *Star Wars* trilogy, could likely have chosen for herself a life of leisure. Instead, she put herself in the midst of a Rebellion's seemingly futile battle against the evil Galactic Empire. Able to devise strategies, carry out covert missions, and do battle with ground forces, there's no task Leia isn't ready to take on. And she also looks pretty good in a metal bikini.

One of the main protagonists in the original *Star Wars* trilogy, Princess Leia is equally at home in a combat operation or metal bikini. *Lucasfilm/20th Century Fox/Heritage Auctions*

1. Ellen Ripley

She may be the hardest-edged woman in all of sci-fi cinema. Ellen Ripley is like Sarah Connor in that she is essentially an everyday woman confronted with extreme and dire circumstances yet tackles those obstacles unflinchingly. The ongoing pains that this character endures throughout the *Alien* franchise, though, catapult her past all others in the ranks of the genre's greatest female characters. Ripley faces one of the most vicious creatures the human race has ever encountered, defeats it, comes back for more after being cryogenically frozen, defeats legions of its buddies, crashlands on a prison planet, defeats it again, and then … well … to go on would be to reveal a mountain of spoilers. While the writers are mostly responsible for Ripley's greatness, it would be criminal to ignore actress Sigourney Weaver's role in portraying Ripley as the epitome of a fearless, resolute hero. Needless to say, Ripley isn't just tough for a woman; she's one of the genre's toughest characters regardless of sex.

When maternal instinct kicks in, Ellen Ripley becomes a fierce warrior who will do anything to save her surrogate daughter, Newt, in *Aliens*. *20th Century Fox/The Kobal Collection*

TOP 10 ROBOTS

Science fiction is known for a number of unique types of beings, including aliens, monsters, and robots. Whereas other genres (namely horror) also use aliens and monsters for their own purposes, though, robots are largely exclusive to this genre. These metal characters can range from being resourceful champions to machines of destruction to possibly sentient beings in their own right. The following are the most memorable and, in some cases, the most loved.

10. The Machine-Man

Created by Professor Rotwang in Fritz Lang's *Metropolis*, the "Machine-Man" is, as far as anyone can tell, cinema's first robot. That alone makes it a shoo-in. It also has a pretty cool design, with its slender figure, halo-like headpiece, and fair facial structure. In fact, its design has been so influential that George Lucas, fifty years later, would use it as a template for designing a robot of his own—C-3PO. The Machine-Man was one of the first movie robots, and it remains one of the most memorable.

9. Gort

Gort doesn't do a whole lot in *The Day the Earth Stood Still*, but that is part of what gives the robot such a commanding presence. It simply stands silently and immovably for much of the film, always ready to take action but never being utilized just for the sake of producing a thrilling scene. And when Gort does make use of himself—namely, by deactivating

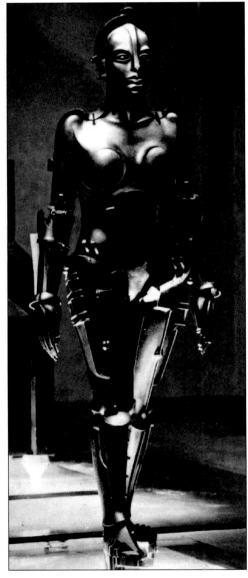

The Machine-Man is one of science fiction's first, and most memorable, robots. *UFA/The Kobal Collection*

The 8-foot Gort's weapon of choice is a beam he projects from underneath his visor to vaporize other weapons and obstacles. *20th Century Fox/Heritage Auctions*

the electricity of an entire city—his suspected power is only confirmed. Main character Klaatu tells us that Gort's power has no bounds. After watching the robot throughout *The Day the Earth Stood Still*, that's not difficult to believe.

8. Robby the Robot

Robots still hadn't fully come into style by the 1950s, but that didn't stop Robby the Robot from becoming what might be the first robot celebrity. This creation of *Forbidden Planet*'s Dr. Morbius is not only practically invincible; it is also capable of carrying tons upon tons of material without the slightest sign of strain, creating diamonds on a whim, and duplicating the molecular structure of whiskey in order to replenish space chefs' supply on an exponential basis. It's probably the physical design and friendly attitude of the robot that make him so enjoyable, though. He's always accommodating and polite, and Robby also has a design that just screams 1950s. You also gotta love his obviously analog inner workings. Robby, you have something that's rare among men and robots alike: charm.

Robby the Robot's distinct personality helped him become an icon in the decades that followed his debut in *Forbidden Planet*. *Metro-Goldwyn-Mayer*

7. Optimus Prime

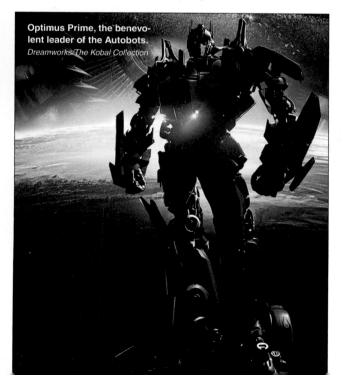

Optimus Prime, the benevolent leader of the Autobots. *Dreamworks/The Kobal Collection*

For straight-up heroic, awesome robots, you can't do much better than Optimus Prime, leader of the Autobots, a naturally evolved race of robots from another planet. This is a giant robot that can take on virtually any other in a clash of big, metal, sentient machines and then after doing so can transform into a huge truck. But it's the actual character of Optimus that makes him so easy to love. This is one of the most virtuous characters you will find of any type. Optimus uses his immense power only when necessary to protect his comrades and the human race. Otherwise, he's perfectly complacent with the often ridiculous sentiments our government holds for him. It is as if we are an infantile race compared to his, and for him to use force against us would be more abusive than it could ever be helpful. For that, science fiction fans will not only hold him in esteem, we'll even forgive him for being in *Revenge of the Fallen*.

6. The Iron Giant

We don't know where he came from, and we don't really know if he has any goals, but we do know this: rarely has sci-fi cinema given us a robot more deserving of our sympathy. Though he's generally as kind as can be, he is immediately hunted down by the government simply for being a giant robot. Throughout the plot of *The Iron Giant*, we come to love the machine as he befriends a young boy named Hogarth, who takes him in and hides him much in the style of *E.T.: The Extra-Terrestrial*—quite a feat when you're dealing with a robot taller than any building in the town. It's a machine that simply wants not to be bothered, but our society won't even afford him that leisure.

The 50-foot metal-eating Iron Giant. *Warner Bros.*

5. T-1000

Upon the release of *Terminator 2: Judgment Day*, the T-1000 must have been the most unique robot ever to hit the screen. In the first *Terminator*, we saw a man fight an incredibly powerful android. The sequel ups the ante by pitting that android against a new one, made of something called liquid metal. The T-1000 is extremely strong, but it also has the ability to take the form of any human with which it comes in contact, can freely morph its arms into weapons, and upon being blown to pieces can simply melt back into liquid and reform. But there is one more characteristic that makes this robot stand out: its sinister persona. Actor Robert Patrick imbued this liquid metal monster with a frighteningly calm and focused evil. This is the robot you find in your nightmares.

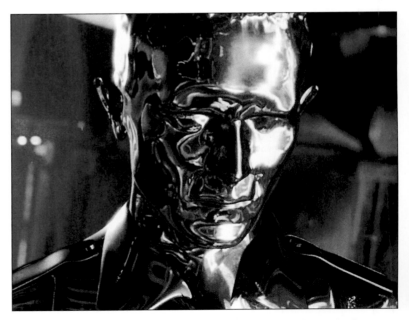

The shape-shifting liquid-metal T-1000 is all frightening calm and focused evil. *Carolco/The Kobal Collection*

4. Mechagodzilla

Technically speaking, Mechagodzilla isn't actually a robot. It's a vessel controlled (sometimes remotely, sometimes by a pilot) by human hand. Still, it's pretty close to being a robot, and since it's just so cool, we're going to grant it "robot" status for this list.

Mechagodzilla is a giant metal lizard built for combatting giant monsters. If you need more to convince you that this is an awesome machine, take a look at a few of its abilities: missile fingers, rainbow eye lasers, and tornado force fields. It's definitely one of the sillier monsters of the *Godzilla* franchise, but it sure can fight in style.

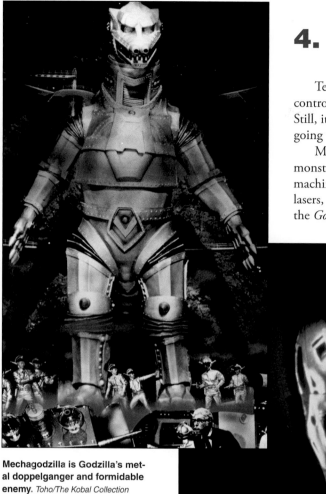

Mechagodzilla is Godzilla's metal doppelganger and formidable enemy. *Toho/The Kobal Collection*

3. T-800

He may not be as technologically advanced as the T-1000, but the T-800 will remain the favorite Terminator among fans of the franchise. When we saw him in the first film, this robot dressed in muscular human flesh was one of the more frightening and menacing androids we had ever witnessed. The glowing eye and metal bone beneath torn flesh was (and is) simply unsettling. The T-800, as played by Arnold Schwarzenegger, was also the perfectly formidable antagonist, a force that couldn't be stopped even by bullets, inexorably marching toward its prey, Sarah Connor.

In Terminator 2: Judgment Day, the T-800 returned,

Pure unstoppable evil in *The Terminator*, the T-800 is reprogrammed to be a force of good in *Terminator 2*. *Carolco/The Kobal Collection*

but this time it was reprogrammed by the good guys with a new mission: to protect Sarah Connor's son, John, from another Terminator. One particular scene encapsulates the essence of this machine: The Terminator, naked after traveling through time to present day (1990s) Los Angeles, steps into a biker bar and demands a patron's clothes. After effortlessly thwarting an attack by said patron's buddies, the Terminator walks out of the bar with the camera gazing up at him wearing jeans, boots, and a leather jacket while "Bad to the Bone" plays on the soundtrack. When a bartender steps out to confront him with a shotgun, the Terminator walks up to the man, swipes the shotgun, and, just for effect, steals the man's sunglasses (which he leaves on for most of the rest of the film). Then he rides off on a stolen motorcycle to save John Connor (and, hopefully, the world).

What more needs be said?

2. Roy Batty

Roy Batty (Rutger Hauer) in *Blade Runner* is yet another tremendously powerful android, but this one is significantly more layered than most. This robot isn't simply programmed to protect or kill someone. This one is fully self-aware, has developed emotions, and, distraught over the four-year lifespan with which he has been created, is seeking out his maker in order to find a way to extend his life—or gain revenge for his short existence. Interestingly, one of the things that makes Batty's knowledge of his quickly approaching death so torturous, is that, having spent his time in the off-world combat for which he was built, he has seen so many amazing things. It's the beauty of those memories, not necessarily his life itself, that Batty fears losing. The character's concerns are so existential at times that we cease to view him as a machine. For all practical purposes, Batty is a human. It's just that he's had an especially unique life experience.

Blade Runner's lead antagonist Roy Batty is the most advanced machine ever built. *Ladd Company/Warner Bros./The Kobal Collection*

1. R2-D2

R2-D2 may not be as strong as a Terminator, and he may not be as cool looking as Optimus Prime, but he has three qualities that combine to make him the best robot of them all: his bravery, his gadgets, and his personality. You will be hard-pressed to find more courage crammed into such a small package, as this little droid, roughly the size of a large trash can, seems never to have been programmed with an understanding of fear. Unimpeded by his perpetually apprehensive counterpart, C-3PO, R2 will un-hesitantly put himself in the midst of blaster fire, confront intergalactic gangsters, or wander alone in the deserts of Tatooine if his doing so can help the cause at hand.

R2's gadgets prove to be invaluable in virtually any task he is given, as the droid is armed with everything from electric pikes to biological sensors to (as we see in one mildly controversial revelation of endowment) thruster jets. The droid's courage combined with these gadgets make him possibly the most resourceful little robot ever to appear in a film.

Above all, though, what makes R2 so great is that, despite resembling a large can, he has a ton of personality. This is thanks mostly to *Star Wars* sound designer Ben Burtt. In creating the noises for the robot, Burtt came up with sounds that so clearly convey emotion that even though R2 communicates solely through blips, beeps, and whirs, we can always extract the essence of what he is saying. It's the combination of bravery, helpfulness, and relatability that make the droid not only fun and capable but endearing.

The spunky and resourceful astromech droid R2-D2 is a beloved character in the *Star Wars* universe. Along with his counterpart, protocol droid C-3PO, R2 has been involved in some pivotal moments in saving the galaxy. *Lucasfilm/20th Century Fox/Heritage Auctions*

TOP 10 VILLAINS

As John Milton demonstrated with *Paradise Lost*, there's something about even the most reprehensible villains that, though we despise them, we seem to find fascinating. Science fiction also frequently demonstrates this. Sometimes these characters are just so powerful and dynamic that they inspire a certain type of awe. Other times, various nuances of their characterization create a level of intrigue that cannot be ignored. Here we look at some of sci-fi cinema's most memorable antagonists.

The demented Dr. Heiter surgically joins three people in a hugely grotesque way. *Six Entertainment*

10. Dr. Heiter

It might seem a stretch to call *The Human Centipede* a science fiction film, but with antagonist Dr. Heiter's twisted surgical experiment upon three unwilling test subjects, the application of science is all-too-unfortunately present. In this vomit-worthy film of unspeakable horrors, actor Laser Deiter devotes himself so fully to the role of the demented Dr. Heiter that the movie would have been tense enough if he had simply talked with his unwitting visitors for the whole film. Alas, he does much worse than just talk with them, though, and the sort of concentrated sadism and hatred he demonstrates himself to harbor throughout his attempt to play god is so unsettling it almost rivals his actions themselves.

… Almost.

9. Admiral Helena Cain

Even though she was primarily a TV series character she did appear in a made-for-TV feature-length film, so because of that and the fact that she's just so bad, we'll let the technicality suffice for this list. Admiral Helena Cain (Michelle Forbes) of the reimagined *Battlestar Galactica* series and prominent character of the movie *Battlestar Galactica: Razor* is on the side of the good guys, but her aggressively utilitarian way of getting things

Admiral Helena Cain is not afraid to make difficult decisions and remains unflinching in her will to do what she sees as right.
The Sci-Fi Channel

done makes her one of the meanest women in the universe. Never even flinching at the ethical implications of torturing for information or of killing crewmembers for acts of moderate insubordination, Cain may have helped a lot of people stay alive following the annihilation of their home world, but even then it's hard to say her actions are redeemable.

8. Darth Maul

There's not a lot of depth to Darth Maul, but this red-and-black-skinned Dark Jedi with horns is simply awesome. Along with his vibrantly evil appearance, Maul (Ray Park) was the first character in the *Star Wars* movies to wield a lightsaber other than the traditional single-blade type. When we see Maul confront Obi-Wan and Qui-Gon in *Star Wars: Episode I - The Phantom Menace* and pull out a lightsaber that ignites blades off both ends of the handle, we know we're in for a special fight. Maul delivers as the most acrobatic Dark Jedi of the whole film series, in a lightsaber battle that is also the franchise's best-choreographed. We never got to see quite as much of him as we would have liked, but such is the way of the candle that burns at both ends.

Wielding a double-bladed lightsaber, Darth Maul engages Obi-Wan and Qui-Gon in a deadly ballet. *Lucasfilm/The Kobal Collection*

Magneto makes it his mission to conquer the human race to prevent the oppression of mutants. *20th Century Fox/The Kobal Collection*

7. Magneto

In the early 2000s, the famous villain of the *X-Men* comics found his way to the big screen in the *X-Men* film trilogy. Magneto (Ian McKellen) is particularly memorable because of the combination of his wielding massive power and his being the friend of Professor Xavier, leader of the X-Men who find themselves fighting Magneto at every turn. With his ability to control and manipulate metal through mere will, Magneto is one of the most formidable opponents anyone could face, but the fact that he commits his villainy for what he believes is the betterment of the world adds a touch of depth that generic "conquer the world" villains lack. Plus, how many other villains are there who would sit down with an arch rival for an amicable game of chess?

6. Lex Luthor

It takes an extremely resourceful villain to be able to present Superman with a noteworthy threat. Lex Luthor is this villain, able to cause Superman more trouble than any other human. Endlessly irritated by the Man of Steel's ability to be a paragon of humanity despite his not being human and not having to work to develop his strength, Luthor is the perfect arch rival for the most archetypal hero ever created. He may not have been all that well portrayed in *Superman: The Movie*, but his roles in *Superman Returns* and some of DC Comics' animated features, like "All-Star Superman" and "Superman/Batman: Public Enemies," are thoroughly antithetical to the ideals of Earth's greatest hero. This isn't the kind of villain you would fear meeting in a dark alley. This is the kind you fear because he's actually smart enough to potentially conquer the world.

In 2006's *Superman Returns*, Kevin Spacey's Lex Luthor is darker and more serious than the villain is in *Superman: The Movie*.
Warner Bros./DC Comics

Fredric March as the evil incarnate Mr. Hyde in 1931's *Dr. Jekyll and Mr. Hyde*.
Paramount Pictures/Heritage Auctions

5. Mr. Hyde

There are villains whose actions have led to their own deformity, but Mr. Hyde, the evil half of Dr. Jekyll, is so bad that his very malevolence causes his body to transform into a contorted version of its usual appearance. It is as if he is literally infected by sin. This character is depraved in the purest way: not with the intent to strong-arm the world into order or to carry out acts in a demonstration of supposed superiority over humanity, but simply to have fun by giving in to his basest desires. He is the very embodiment of evil.

4. Roy Batty

Roy Batty (Rutger Hauer) may be a villain in the context of the story surrounding him, but this *Blade Runner* android is arguably not all that bad. He's just a robot who has become self-aware to the extent of developing emotion and is thus compelled to seek revenge against those who designed him with such a short (four-year) lifespan. He may be super-strong and have heightened intelligence, but those are negligible qualities in an appreciation of this character. Batty causes us to question our definition of life and humanity as his character, often through violent means, forces those around him to acknowledge his existence as a sentient being. This villain has something to complement his antagonism: complexity.

Roy Batty may be a violent android, but his only goal for himself and fellow replicants is life. *Ladd Company/Warner Bros./The Kobal Collection*

Ultraviolent Alex is irredeemable, yet manages to be occasionally likeable. *Warner Bros./Heritage Auctions*

3. Alex DeLarge

There are times when Alex DeLarge (Malcolm McDowell), the "ultraviolent" main character of *A Clockwork Orange*, exhibits some sort of allure. In those moments, the film becomes temporally horrifying. This character doesn't just commit heinous acts because he finds them fun; he commits such acts because they're the *only* way he knows how to have fun. However, the calm and collected demeanor which Alex perpetually upholds, even while engaging in morally reprehensible behavior, makes him feel occasionally likeable. In a way, he forces upon viewers their own crises of conscious and identity. What does it say about us when we have to remind ourselves that we're not supposed to like someone so evil?

2. Khan Noonien Singh

Khan Noonien Singh (Ricardo Montalban) made his first appearance in the original *Star Trek* series episode "Space Seed" and was the greatest villain the show had yet seen. At the episode's end, Khan's fate was left somewhat open, so when the writers needed an antagonist fifteen years later for their second *Star Trek* movie, they turned back to this icon of villainy.

The thing about this character is that he believes himself to be superior to all other humans, but, as opposed to other similar villains, when you judge Khan by his physical strength, mental capacity, and genetic makeup, he actually is superior to all other humans. Of course, this doesn't mean that he is above morality and the law as he believes he is, but it does mean that he's one of the few humans who could best Captain James T. Kirk in almost any type of engagement.

Perhaps the best thing about this character, though, is that the danger he poses to Kirk and the *Enterprise* crew is so immense that it forces the protagonists to return to the Starfleet roles for which they were fated. Regardless of the ranks to which they have ascended in the years since their famous voyages aboard the starship *Enterprise*, these characters know that the only way they can defeat Khan is to do the things they do best. In this process, the main characters' identities are basically affirmed by the wrath of Khan.

Khan Noonien Singh remains a favorite villain with *Star Trek* fans. *Paramount Pictures/ The Kobal Collection*

Cutting a huge, imposing figure in an outfit that hides any sign of humanity, Darth Vader remains the supreme villain of the galaxy. *Lucasfilm/20th Century Fox/The Kobal Collection*

1. Darth Vader

As the *Star Wars* franchise progresses, we learn more and more about Darth Vader (David Prowse/ James Earl Jones), but even in the original *Star Wars*, where we are afforded only a barebones look at what motivates this character, his appearance and powers alone make him a great villain.

The black cape, mask, and life-support suit encasing Darth Vader and hiding any sign of humanity create an ominous presence that few characters can match. Furthermore, his adeptness with the Force and his skill in lightsaber combat make him one of the most dangerous foes the characters of *Star Wars* could ever face. It is in *Star Wars: Episode V – The Empire Strikes Back*, though, that we learn of a crucial, surprising relation that connects Vader to one of the heroes of the *Star Wars* universe, and it is then that we learn more about Vader himself. From that point on through *Star Wars: Episode VI – Return of the Jedi* (and then further in the prequels), Vader is revealed to be a tortured soul, hiding an abundance of pain and sadness beneath his strong and seemingly impenetrable outer layer. But that never detracted from Vader's menacing nature. It was because of Darth Vader that a Sith Lord was able to conquer an entire galaxy. How can you beat that?

INDEX

ANOTHER GREAT MOVIE FREAK BOOK!

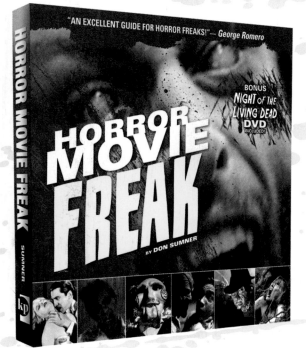

You'll scream with delight as you take in this gloriously gruesome book about frightful flicks. This engaging book discusses the flicks all horror fans need to see to ascend to the true level of a Horror Freak. From heart-clutching classics like *Dracula* and *Psycho*, and modern masters of mayhem including *Drag Me to Hell*, to lesser known gems such as *Dog Soldiers*, the more than 130 movies included in this book are represented in an awesome collection of photos from movie stills and posters. Plus, you'll find the clear organization of categories is a real help in locating your favorite types of horror films—be it homicidal slashers, supernatural thrillers, or zombie invasions.

On top of all this, you'll also discover a *Night of the Living Dead* DVD in the back…making this book a must-have for your own library, and a great gift for any horror movie fan!

> "THIS IS AN EXCELLENT GUIDE FOR HORROR FREAKS AND ASPIRING HORROR MOVIE MAKERS. IF YOU'RE NOT ALREADY A FREAK, HORROR MOVIE FREAK WILL TURN YOU INTO ONE, SO BE CAREFUL…AND STAY SCARED."
>
> ~ HORROR FILM LEGEND GEORGE ROMERO, DIRECTOR OF NIGHT OF THE LIVING DEAD

BY DON SUMNER · ITEM# Z6494 · $19.99
PAPERBACK · 8 x 8 · 256 PGS · 400 COLOR PHOTOS